WRONG CABIN, RIGHT TIME

WRONG CABIN, RIGHT TIME

C. HALLMAN

Published by Montlake, Seattle

www.apub.com

Amazon, the Amazon logo, and Montlake are trademarks of Amazon.com, Inc., or its affiliates.

EU product safety contact:
Amazon Media EU S. à r.l.
38, avenue John F. Kennedy, L-1855 Luxembourg
amazonpublishing-gpsr@amazon.com

ISBN-13: 9781662540141 (paperback)
ISBN-13: 9781662540134 (digital)

Cover design by Caroline Teagle Johnson
Cover typography © Casey Moses
Cover image: © PJ_nice, © Far700, © Anton Porkin, © checha, © ondacaracola photography, © Elena Filitova / Getty Images; © Anton Chernov / Shutterstock

Printed in the United States of America

*To everyone who chokes on their own spit, trips over
nothing, and accidentally wears pants inside out*

Chapter One

The sound metal makes when it's being dragged across stone has always been therapeutic to me. The familiar rhythm and precise angle of the blade as I'm carefully shaving off just a thousandth of an inch from its edge. Even if the knife isn't dull, the repetition of the process soothes a part of me. Do you know what else soothes me? Killing people.

But I can't go around killing people on a daily basis. That would be impossible without getting caught, and I don't have any intentions of getting caught, ever. *I'm way too smart, anyway.* So, when I need to occupy my hands, this seems to be the efficient way. I hold the blade at a twenty-degree angle to ensure a sturdy edge, one that can take a lot of damage, being careful to grind both sides evenly. If not done correctly, a burr will form, ruining the edge completely.

I want the blade perfect for when I kill Kevin on Thursday.

Before me lie the stones I have collected throughout the years. Each one is diamond-plated with varying degrees of grit, ranging from 80 to 10,000. The best of the best.

I angle the blade just right and admire how the mirror finish of the edge is really starting to come through. I'm so enthralled by the blade that when a bird flies past the window, it slightly startles me. My finger slips mid-sharpening, and I nick my thumb.

Dammit.

My eyes zero in on the single drop of blood pooling over the tiny cut. It's approximately half a millimeter deep and won't need care besides a little cleaning, but I make a mental note to adjust my wrist torque, regardless.

Pulling a hair from my head, I lay it against the blade. The follicle splits in two with little to no pressure, signaling the waste of metal if I go any further.

Satisfied with my work, I start to clean up, carefully arranging and placing each stone in its storage box, the exact way I always do. Just when I'm about to place the last one where it belongs, a knock at the door interrupts the task at hand.

A knocking . . . at my door . . .

My heart rate picks up, and nervous energy spreads from my gut to my chest. Without moving a muscle, I glance at the clock on my kitchen wall: 3:30 p.m. It's too late for the mail, and that's the only time someone would knock.

There's a reason why I live on the side of a mountain for most of the year. This has always been the favorite property I own. I don't like people in my space. Someone knocking at my door means someone is in my space.

The knocking intensifies, sounding like nails on a chalkboard. *Who the hell is at my door?*

I should just ignore it until it goes away, but my curiosity gets the best of me. Reaching for my phone on the glass table, I pull up the front door camera, and the screen loads instantly.

The first thing I see is a messy bun of pink hair stacked on top of a head. A bun attached to the girl who is furiously knocking on my door for the third time. There's no car, so she must have come on foot.

There's a large backpack slung over her slender shoulder. It's so enormous compared to her small frame that I'm surprised she's able to stand upright instead of being pulled back by the sheer weight of it.

She drops the obnoxiously big bag on my front step before sitting down next to it.

Ugh. What the fuck is she doing?

Why is she even here, and more importantly, why isn't she leaving?

Too bad dogs don't like me. A guard dog to chase her off would be great right about now.

Frustrated beyond belief, I toss the phone down on my kitchen table. I stand up, and the sound of my chair scooting back against the teak floors fills the otherwise quiet space. Stomping through the kitchen, I make my way through the foyer to the front door.

I turn both dead bolts before unlocking the handle to pull the door open.

Fresh mountain air fills my lungs, reminding me that I haven't been outside in a few days.

"Oh, hey!" The girl jumps up from where she was sitting. As soon as she turns toward me, a wide smile spreads across her face. Usually I'm not great at reading people, but even I know smiling means someone is happy.

What the fuck she could be happy about right now is beyond me.

"Heeeeeeey," she repeats, but this time, for some reason, she draws out the word. Licking her lips as she looks up and down my body.

I glance down at my white button-down shirt and gray slacks to see what she's looking at. When I don't find anything out of the ordinary, I lift my gaze to where the annoying woman is standing in front of me. Realizing I was wrong to call her a "girl" before.

She may be a foot shorter than my six feet, two inches, but now that I've seen her up close, I'm guessing she is in her late twenties. Same age as me, and that's the extent of things we have in common. I can say that after one look at her.

She's wearing a washed-out purple, oversize shirt that hangs off her right shoulder, paired with black leggings and flip-flops. Yes, flip-flops. What kind of lunatic wears flip-flops like they're some kind of actual footwear? *Yeah, we're not the same.*

Propping one hand on her hip, she waves at me with the other. "I love your whole vibe."

I have no idea what that's supposed to mean, so instead of entertaining her weird use of the English language, I ask the only thing that comes to mind. "What are you doing here?"

"Oh, it's me, Sage!" She points both of her thumbs at her face.

Sage?

"What an odd name," I think out loud.

"Well, it's better than the rest of my name." She giggles. "Juniper Sage Featherstone, but I go by Sage."

I don't care what her name is—though it is quite a ridiculous name, I take note. It still doesn't tell me why she's here. I open my mouth to ask just that when she steps toward me . . . into my personal space.

Immediately, I take a step back, not wanting her to get too close. Who knows what kind of diseases she carries. Especially someone who goes outside dressed like that.

"Did you know that the safest social distance, without disrupting someone's personal space, is between eighteen inches and four feet? Personally I prefer the four feet. But intuitively, for me, when it comes to instances of this nature, no less than eighteen inches is mandatory," I inform her, leaning back and away.

She swats her hand at me while letting out a hearty laugh. "You're so funny! Well, aren't you going to invite me in?" She takes another step toward me, causing me to lean back and away once more.

I shake my head. "No." But instead of complying, she pushes right past me and into the house, *my house*. The audacity of this woman is nothing short of infuriating. Frustrated, I stomp my foot on the floor. My chest is tight, and my pulse is racing. She's invading my privacy in the most basic way.

"Wow! Your cabin is just as beautiful on the inside too. Everything is so modern and clean," she exclaims, completely ignoring my refusal to let her into my house. "You must spend a lot of time cleaning. Do you have a cleaning service that comes out here?" she asks, but doesn't give me time to respond. "I bet you have a hard time getting someone to come this far. But I guess that's the price you pay to live out here in such a beautiful place. Man, your view must be killer! I can't wait to see the upstairs."

I feel my eyes go wide with terror as she keeps walking farther into my space. Her flip-flops make the most annoying slapping sound as she scurries across the pristine wooden floor.

Slap, slap, slap . . . My eye twitches at the sound, and I think about googling "how to install silent floors fast."

I want to clasp my hands over my ears so I don't have to hear that awful sound or her voice. I want my quiet house back, and I want it now.

"Hey! Stop!" I call after her, but she's already in the kitchen.

My anger threatens to boil over as I follow her through my house.

"Oh my god! I was right. The view *is* amazeballs!" she exclaims, dashing to the window.

"That's not a word," I inform her, nervously crossing my arms over my chest. I'm overwhelmed by her presence, and when I glance at the table where my knives are still laid out, I briefly think about using one to slit her throat. That would surely shut her up . . . but also leave a huge mess in my kitchen.

No, I don't kill randomly or messily. I kill smartly. It takes me weeks to prepare for a kill. Meticulous planning is a must.

"Well, as you know, I've stayed in a lot of cabins, but this one will definitely be one of my favorites. I mean, look how spacious this is! And your kitchen is a dream! Did you pick all of this out yourself or have someone design it?" She pauses and looks at me with a big smile on her face.

Finally I have a moment to get a word in. "Who the hell are you, and why are you in my house?"

"I told you, I'm Sage. We spoke on the app," she explains.

"I've never talked to anyone on some app." I lift my hand to pinch the bridge of my nose as the pressure builds behind my eyes. Great, a headache is coming. This infuriating woman is giving me a migraine.

"Wait, are you not Ryan?"

"No, I'm Travis," I say, my voice strained with anger. "Ryan lives half a mile from here, on the other side of the mountain."

They don't know me, but I know all my neighbors within a five-mile radius. I had my private investigator dig up everything on them, and that's how I know Ryan Mitchell rents out his cabin when he goes to visit his second home in Florida.

I state the obvious: "You are at the wrong place."

Her mouth pops open as her eyes go wide. I think she is about to apologize, but instead she throws her head back and laughs. Her hands come to her chest as her whole body shakes with laughter. "OMG!" she says between laughs. "I can't believe this happened."

I just stand there, waiting for her to calm herself to explain more.

She finally stops laughing and clears her throat. "I'm so sorry about all of this, and I'm sorry for barging in on you. This is all just a huge misunderstanding. See, I'm an Airbnb reviewer. It's kind of my job. I travel around to different scenic locations and post about my stay. Since it's easy to get turned around even with GPS, Ryan gave me directions to his place. I guess I'm not great at reading maps."

Clearly not.

"Anyway, sorry again. I'll try and give Ryan a call, see if he can help me find his house." She spins around and heads toward my front door.

Finally.

I follow her. I need to make sure she actually leaves. I'm only a few steps behind when she suddenly stops and spins around, causing me to almost run into her.

Once again, she's in my personal space, and all I can do is look into her light-blue eyes, tainted by a brown freckle on her right iris.

"Hey, at least I crashed the house of a nice guy and not some serial killer."

The corner of my lip lifts up. "Yeah, lucky," I say with a grin.

Chapter Two

SAGE

"Yeah, lucky." His gravelly voice echoes in my head as I stand there, staring at him like a lovestruck teenager. I'm pretty sure my mouth is still hanging open. *Wait, am I drooling?*

He's smiling now, which makes him look even sexier than before—hard to top when he already looks like someone who just stepped out of *GQ* magazine.

His brown hair is neatly styled, and his chocolate-brown eyes glare at me as if he's about to eat me alive. His jawline is so sharp it could cut glass. He's wearing a white shirt that stretches over his muscular shoulders and chest, but my favorite features are his strong arms and large hands. I can already imagine being wrapped up in them, cuddling closer . . .

"Can I help you with something else, Miss Featherstone?"

Miss Featherstone? Not for long. If I have a say in it, I'll be Mrs. Travis whatever-his-last-name-is.

I wonder what kind of color palette would work well for a wedding at the lake. I'm mentally building a mood board for us when my mind jumps to kids.

Without thinking, I blurt out, "I wonder what our kids will call you. Dad, Daddy, or sir?"

Only when Travis looks at me in confusion does it sink in that I just said this out loud. Panicked, I backpedal. "I mean . . . kids in general, not *our* kids in the sense of me and you. I meant more like the world's children. Our kids, like the people's kids."

I press my lips together to stop my rambling.

Even with my word vomit, this feels like the happiest fucking mistake of my life. At first, I really thought this was Ryan's cabin. There were only a few pictures on the listing, and I may have been a little high yesterday when I booked the place. So I wasn't surprised when I pulled up and nothing looked familiar.

"So did you need something else?" Travis finally asks.

"Nope, that's it, Mr. . . . ?" I wait for my future husband to give me his last name so I can google him later.

"Just Travis is fine." *No such luck.*

Swallowing down my slight frustration, I give him a megawatt smile before begrudgingly turning away from him to walk out the door. As soon as my feet are planted on the front step, the door slams shut behind me.

Well, that was rude. But it's okay, I've already forgiven him. Maybe he's in a hurry to get back to the awesome knife collection I spotted on the kitchen table. I wonder what he does with them. Does he like to cook? Or hunt? Maybe wood carving. *Mmm, wood.* I wonder what his looks like. If the rest of his body is any indication, his cock must be magnificent.

Jesus, calm your tits, Sage.

I shake my head, trying to rattle some sense back into my brain, but my lady bits are on fire thinking about Travis that way. *God, why does he have to be so hot?*

Okay, get a grip.

I still need to find my actual cabin. Pulling my phone from my pocket, I unlock it. "Shit," I say to myself when I see there's zero signal out here. Calling Ryan is definitely out of the question now. How the heck am I supposed to find the correct Airbnb?

There's only one option.

Spinning back around, I lift my arm and rap my knuckles over the wood. Not even a second later, the door is yanked open, and I shriek in surprise, shocked by Travis's quick response. Hold on, was he waiting by the door? Did he want me to knock again?

A smile spreads across my face at the thought.

"Why are you still here?" Travis asks, his voice even but laced with annoyance.

Okay, maybe he didn't want me to knock again. Regardless, I force my smile to remain intact. "I have no signal here," I explain, holding up my phone to show him.

He doesn't look at the screen. His icy gaze remains locked on mine. I swallow, awfully aware that no spit is left in my mouth. Why is his stare so intense? All he's doing is looking at me, but all my senses are going haywire.

"We're in the mountains, Miss Featherstone. No one has a signal up here," he explains, like I should have already known that. He's right. I've traveled enough to know that not everyone has a signal in rural areas like this.

"Could you tell me how to get to Ryan's cabin?" I ask, giving him my sweetest smile as I attempt to bat my lashes.

I must suck at flirting, because he completely ignores my advances.

"Go back the way you came in, take the first road on the left, and keep going until you see the cabin on the right. It's a half-a-mile walk."

"Oh, that's okay. I walk a lot anyway, when I'm hitchhiking—"

"You hitchhike?" he asks, shocked. "Do you know how dangerous that is? What the statistics are for the likelihood of a female falling victim to a crime while hitchhiking?" His voice is raised now, and he's shaking his head like he's disappointed in my life choices.

Oh my god, he's totally worrying about me.

I can't hold in my giddiness toward his reaction. I really think he likes me but is too shy to flirt back.

"Thank you for the directions." I grin at him. "I'll see you around."

"We'll see," he says ominously before closing the door again.

We'll see, indeed.

I can't help but giggle as I turn, pick up my backpack, and walk away from his door. There's an extra pep in my step as I make my way down his driveway. I just can't stop thinking about Travis. I don't know what it is about him: his good looks or that he just doesn't try. He doesn't care about pleasantries when around people; he's honest and says what he thinks. I like his bluntness.

I notice his mailbox at the end of his driveway and immediately get excited. Maybe his name is displayed on there. I speed walk to the black box on the other side of the driveway. Excitement fills my veins with each step. Only to go to hell when I get close enough to see that only numbers are displayed.

Still, there's a little hope left in me. I walk up to the box, open the hatch, and look inside.

Bingo.

I grin widely at the piece of junk mail lying inside. I snatch it up quickly and flip it over: *Travis Blacksburg.*

"Mr. and Mrs. Blacksburg," I say out loud, loving how fancy it sounds. Okay, I know I'm getting a bit ahead of myself. But damn, we would make a cute couple.

I briefly clasp the junk mail to my chest, holding it close to my heart like it's a freaking love letter to me. I give it a little kiss, then come to my senses and frantically wipe off the lip gloss with my possible DNA on it. Snooping through someone's mail is a crime, no matter if it's your future husband.

Nope nope nope, I am not ready for prison. Especially not in leggings.

Only when I'm sure it's clean do I stuff the thin paper back into the mailbox.

I look around as I close the hatch to see whether someone could have seen me. I should have done that before I committed a crime. Luckily, I see nothing but an empty road surrounded by a million trees.

Satisfied with myself, I follow Travis's directions and make my way to Ryan's cabin. It takes me less than thirty minutes to finally spot the large cabin to my right, just like Travis said.

This cabin is just as magnificent as Travis's—built on the side of the mountain, surrounded by trees, and overlooking the lake.

I walk up the driveway and knock on the door. A few moments later it opens, and a middle-aged man appears on the other side.

"Hey, you must be Sage. I'm Ryan," he says, pointing at his chest. Then he holds out his hand.

I lift my arm to shake it. He wraps his warm fingers around mine, squeezing lightly. He holds my hand a few seconds too long for comfort, but I keep a friendly smile plastered on my face.

He finally lets go, but not before I see his gaze lower to my tits, then he quickly glances away.

Not interested, my dude.

"Let me show you the cabin," he offers. Stepping back, he waves his arm around to usher me in.

"Oh, you don't have to. I'm sure I can find my way around," I say, hoping he doesn't push it. But of course he does.

"No, please, I insist. I want to make sure you know where everything is," he quips, his muddy brown eyes watching me.

It gets harder and harder to force a smile. When all I want to do is throat-punch this weirdo so he'll get out of here and leave me alone.

"This is the kitchen," he tells me as we walk into the room that's obviously the kitchen. *Damn, I'm glad you are here to show me around.*

"It's beautiful," I murmur, my smile finally faltering.

"Not as beautiful as something else I'm looking at right now."

Gag. Double gag.

Desperate to change the subject, I quickly interject, "So I met your neighbor Travis Blacksburg on the way to the cabin."

"Travis who?" Ryan asks.

"Blacksburg, he lives about half a mile from here," I explain.

"Hmm . . . that name doesn't sound familiar. But I still don't know all my neighbors." He shrugs.

Interesting. Travis seems to know who Ryan is, but he has no clue who Travis is. *That's odd . . . and a shame. Since I was hoping to get some more info on my future husband.*

"Oh, well, he was nice enough to give me directions to your cabin."

Ryan just nods, his beady eyes now blatantly staring at my tits. *Wow. What a loser.*

"So, Ryan, I don't want to rush you out or anything." *Even though that's exactly what I want. I'm just too damn polite to actually do it.* "I've had a really long day and just want to lie down."

"Of course, let me show you the bedroom, and then I'll be out of your way." He turns around and walks toward the staircase.

As soon as his back is turned, I reach into the outside pocket of my backpack, where I keep my pepper spray. Quickly fishing it out, I grip it tightly in my palm as I slip my bag off my shoulder to set it on the floor.

Ryan is already halfway up the stairs when I decide to follow him, reluctantly. I keep the hand with the pepper spray behind me, hiding it from him. After all, I'm relying on the element of surprise here.

He leads me down the hall and into the primary bedroom. An icky feeling of danger instantly spreads through me, sending a trail of goose bumps across my skin. With a knot in my stomach and my hand clutching the pepper spray for dear life, I step into the bedroom.

My heart beats against my chest as he turns around, his gaze pinning me once more. "So, Sage . . ." He licks his lips, taking a step closer to me. "Are you sure you want to stay here all by yourself? I could stay here with you, keep you company and maybe—"

"Don't finish that sentence," I warn, quickly shooting my arm out in front of me. I point the pepper spray right at his face. "If I didn't make myself clear before, I'm not interested. So unless you want your eyeballs burned all the way out of their sockets with high-potency Mace, I suggest you back the fuck off."

Shocked, his eyes go wide and his mouth pops open as he immediately jumps a step back. His hands come up in front of him to protect his face. "Whoa, whoa, calm down!" he yells at me. "I was just being flirty."

Flirty, my ass. Future sex offender is more like it.

"How about I just leave, and we can forget this whole incident ever happened," he offers with a forced smile, his gaze darting to the door. "I actually have a flight to catch. Like I told you before, I'm leaving the country for a month."

"Yeah, I remember." Which is now the only reason I'm still staying here. "Just go already." I tilt my head toward the door.

He nods, keeping his hands up. He walks past me with hurried steps and out the door. I keep pointing the pepper spray at him until he's out of my sight. The sounds of his footsteps retreating and the front door slamming fill the cabin.

When I'm sure he's gone, I suck in a deep breath and sigh in relief. Knowing what kind of person he is now, I do a quick sweep for hidden cameras. I'm probably overreacting, but Ryan creeped me out. I'm seriously considering not staying here anymore . . . but that would mean saying goodbye to Travis too.

After going downstairs, I lock and dead bolt the front door before making my way back into the kitchen, where I left my backpack.

Unzipping it, I pull out my laptop. Luckily, Ryan already sent me the internet password through the app. Logging in, I pull up Google, searching for *Travis Blacksburg*.

And just like that, I've become a stalker.

Chapter Three

Watching Kevin through the city cams is almost as fun as the killing itself. His patterns are immaculate. Six a.m., he wakes up, sorts through the copious amounts of booze bottles he's collected the night before.

A good morning is when he finds one that still contains alcohol. In which case he'll down the rest of the liquid and sleep for a few more hours. If not, he climbs out of bed angrily, setting off for the day's booze money.

In order for me to know and see his precise habits, I have to constantly watch and track his every move through the cameras. However, I already know his preferred location for another beer: the corner store.

Luckily for Kevin, today is one of those days when he finds the source of his happiness right away. He downs what I assume is whiskey until it's gone. Then, for some reason, he throws the bottle against the wall.

Filthy.

One of the many things that bothers me about him. I finish wrapping up the kit I take to every kill, mostly necessities. A change of clothes, toothbrush, and the specific tool I've selected for this. Just as planned, everything is perfect and in order.

The genius in me makes me smile sometimes.

I like to consider myself an equal opportunity killer, but I have to admit, Lake Lure has always been my favorite hunting ground. I think I'm doing my best kills here. Who am I kidding? All my kills are pretty spectacular.

The alarm on my computer interrupts my self-adulation. Leaning over to look at the screen, I see a mess of pink hair as it darts across. The breath rushes from my nose, and I squint. *What the . . . Is she . . . crab-walking?*

Watching her trying to sneak around the perimeter of my house is like watching a child who's invested a lot of time in watching bad ninja movies. I exhale sharply and walk over to my desk.

Sitting down, I open my laptop. *Juniper Sage Featherstone. How could I forget?* She idiotically gave me her government-issue name yesterday. *Didn't her parents teach her not to offer personal information to strangers?*

Typing out her name in the search bar, I shake my head. *What a stupid fucking name. What parent names their child that? The same parents who didn't teach their kid about basic safety.*

I press enter, and her Instagram pops up, confirming the story she told me yesterday. She does reviews on Airbnbs. Which basically equates to her being homeless.

It's fairly easy to get lost in these mountains. Given her proclivities to hitchhike and walk, I'd say she is a fairly good target.

My gaze returns to my screen. Her futile attempts to peep through my windows annoy me. I don't make it a habit to kill this close together, but this woman needs to go away.

I watch as she seemingly gives in and starts walking back up the driveway. Not even trying to disguise that she was just snooping around my house.

I'm killing Kevin on Thursday, I remind myself. *Then I could kill her next. Yes!* It's decided. I will start planning her demise today, during my scheduled free time.

I get back to running through Kevin's murder before I eat my lunch as scheduled. Pleased that the rest of my afternoon has gone as planned,

I decide to take a little nap when it gets dark outside, setting my alarm for midnight.

When my phone goes off at twelve a.m., I'm more than ready to go on my little recon mission. I jump up and dress in a pair of black pants, a dark-gray long-sleeved shirt, and boots before grabbing my leather gloves and lock-picking kit.

Making my way to my attached garage, I think of how satisfying it will be to find out more about Miss Featherstone. I love the process of collecting data when needing intel on my kills.

Deciding a walk will probably do me good, I forgo taking the car. Plus, I'll be less noticeable on foot. As I make my way to Ryan's cabin, I can't help but think, *How in the world did she make this hike in those ridiculous flip-flops?*

When I finally walk up to the cabin, I'm pleased to see that all the lights are off. *Good. She's asleep.*

I make my way around the house and pick the lock on the back door. It takes only a few minutes to get it unlocked. Satisfied with my quick work, I shove the kit back into my pocket.

Opening the door softly, I sneak inside, making sure to close it quietly behind me. My eyes have already adjusted to the darkness. The night sky is the only thing illuminating the inside of the cabin right now, and since I'm standing in front of a huge bay window, it's enough.

On light feet, I make my way through the house, seeing her recording equipment set up in the living room against the large window overlooking the lake. There aren't many personal belongings down here, so I decide to head up the stairs to the bedrooms. All the doors are open, making it easy for me to look into each room.

When I see the empty bed in the first one, I move on to the next. Empty. The third room at the end of the hall must be the main bedroom. It's much bigger than the others.

Stepping inside, my eyes immediately land on the figure lying in the center of the king-size bed. My feet move on their own, as if an invisible string is pulling me into the room until I'm standing at the foot of the bed.

She isn't wearing a shirt. But the blanket covers everything besides her shoulders and head. I notice how, in the moonlight, her skin seems porcelain, making her look like a doll. Her hair falls in a light-pink halo around her head. Black lashes fan over her cheeks, and her plump lips are slightly parted. She looks so peaceful sleeping—the opposite of what her personality is, I have to remind myself.

I'm unaware of how long I stand there, just gazing at her sleeping form. But for some reason it calms the storm inside me. Maybe it's the realization that she's not a real threat. At this moment she's at her most vulnerable, and she doesn't even know what kind of danger she's in. If I wanted to, I could kill her tonight. But I can't, because it's not on the schedule yet.

I force myself to step away, taking in the rest of the room instead. Her clothes have been pulled out of her backpack and are scattered around the room. *Of course she would be messy.*

Making my way to the attached bathroom. I take note of everything on the counter. Toothbrush and paste. *At least she brushes her teeth.* Lotion, hairbrush, razor, shaving cream . . . nothing out of the ordinary for a woman her age.

Unimpressed with what I find, I walk back into the bedroom, where I stop and look at her one last time. She's still sleeping, completely unaware of my presence.

I grin, knowing how much more superior I am to her.

Moving quickly but stealthily, I make my way back out into the hallway. I suddenly hear the rustling of sheets, making me jump to the side and into the shadow in the corner. I freeze, holding my breath, before slowly looking over my shoulder to see Sage turning onto her side.

My shoulders relax, and I sigh in relief as I turn back around and start walking again. Unfortunately, I don't realize how close to the wall I've gotten until my arm brushes against a piece of art.

Watching as the picture falls in slow motion, I reach my hand out to catch it, but I'm not fast enough. The frame falls to the ground, causing me to dash into the closest bedroom. I am frantically looking around to find somewhere to hide when my gaze lands on the closet doors. I quickly slide inside and close them, but not all the way, leaving an inch open so I can still see what's going on.

"Hello?" Sage calls out. "I swear to God, Ryan, if that's you . . . I will pepper spray your ass for real this time!"

This time? I can't analyze that tidbit now, but I store the info away for later.

The light in the hallway flickers on, and a moment later Sage appears . . . completely naked. She holds a small can—of what I assume is the pepper spray—out in front of her. Like it's a lifesaving weapon.

"Ugh!" she groans, noticing the picture on the ground. "He better not charge me for that."

She's standing with her back to me, and my eyes are glued to her firm ass as she leans down to pick up the fallen art piece. When she bends over, her pink pussy comes into view, and all the blood drains down to my dick.

Down, boy! Not now.

This isn't on the schedule and definitely not the place for my cock to be getting hard. Yet here I am, staring at Sage's shaved private parts while my dick strains against my zipper.

She picks up the picture, placing it back up on the nail. When she turns around, my eyes wander down to her chest, where a set of perky tits greets me.

Dammit, I hate having these urges. They're so inconvenient.

I squeeze my eyes shut and think of things that will get my erection to go down. *Worn socks, wrinkled grandmas—and flip-flops.*

When I hear movement coming from the hallway, I open my eyes and see Sage walking toward the staircase instead of going back to bed.

Fuck. That's my way out.

The sound of her footsteps descending the stairs has me slowly opening the closet door. I slide out and head toward the window, quickly unlocking it and pushing the window panel up. Just enough for me to slip through.

I climb out until I'm hanging on the windowsill by my fingertips. I'm only on the second floor, and there are shrubs beneath me. I'm not too worried, as they will soften my fall. I finally let go, dropping down.

I hit the ground with a quiet thud. My legs give out, and I roll face-first into what I assume is high grass. It's only when I sit up and look around that I realize I'm not sitting in grass at all, but in poison ivy. *Poison fucking ivy. Great.*

I get up in a hurry, glad that my body is covered with clothes and that I'm wearing gloves. The only place I have to worry about it touching is my face.

Frustrated with myself, I make my way around the house, staying close to the walls—just in case Sage looks out the windows. I walk back to my cabin, cursing myself for being so clumsy today. That's what I get for not sticking to the original plan. That woman is causing me to lose my mind. She's a distraction I don't need. I have to get rid of her sooner rather than later.

Maybe I could come up with a plan for dealing with her if I didn't have to spend the walk reminding myself not to scratch my face.

Something tells me that dealing with Sage is not going to be as easy as I want it to be. She seems to have a habit of creating chaos around her, and that's something I can't let happen.

Chapter Four

SAGE

I stare at one of the pictures of Travis I have pulled up on my computer. He is so handsome in a suit. Everything about him is so neat and perfect. Especially his face, which I would like to sit on one day.

Since my fortunate encounter with the man of my dreams two days ago, I have been obsessed with researching him online . . . and maybe a little in real life. Okay, I went back to his house to check it out. And maybe to be close or possibly run into him. I don't even know if he was home or not. I couldn't see through the windows, and there was nothing useful in his trash either. Yes, I went through his trash. Bite me. It was mostly just protein-bar wrappers and dental floss. Disappointing. Like, not even a mysterious vial?

I'm so consumed with Travis that I haven't thought much about last night. The picture falling in the hallway was odd, but after I found the window open in the second bedroom, I figured it was just the wind blowing it from the nail. Plus, if there was really someone in the house, why would they just leave without taking anything?

Shaking the thought away, I go back through the last article on my screen.

Travis Blacksburg, 23-year-old tech genius, sells his startup for $750 million.

That article was posted five years ago, which means Travis should be twenty-eight now. Just two years older than me. *We are basically made for each other.*

I click back to a new article with an up-to-date picture. In this one, he is dressed in a tux, looking like a fine hunk of meat.

CEO comes to Blacksburg Tech's yearly fundraiser without a date, reads the caption of the image. *Don't worry, you'll have a date for the next one.*

I ogle Travis on the screen for a few more minutes when the peeping from the oven reminds me to take out the cookies I'm baking.

After closing my laptop, I rush toward the kitchen. I grab the mittens before opening the oven. A wave of hot air hits my face, the smell of sugary goodness invading my senses.

Grabbing the pan with the mittens, I pull the cookies out of the oven and set them on the counter to cool off. While I wait, I take a few cute selfies showing off my baking skills in the background and post them on my social media with the caption Baking for someone special!

Just like always, a bunch of my regulars comment right away. I reply to and like a few before putting my phone to the side and getting back to the cookies. I find a plastic container with a lid and carefully stack the still-warm sweets into it.

Excitement fills my veins when I think about bringing these to him. I catch myself smiling simply because I'm so eager to see him again.

I slip into my sneakers and put my hair in a high ponytail before grabbing the cookies under my arm. On my way out, I snatch my purse from the hook and sling it over my shoulder.

The walk goes by fast, and before I know it, Travis's lavish cabin comes into view. My heartbeat quickens with every step toward his house. By the time I walk up to his door, my heart threatens to beat out of my chest.

I raise my hand to ring his doorbell, and butterflies take flight in my gut. I'm not a patient person, so when he doesn't appear right away, I ring the bell one more time. A few more moments pass, and I grow increasingly anxious. The thought of him not being here enters my mind and sours my mood immediately.

I'm about to turn away when the door is suddenly ripped open. My eyes go wide, and I suck in a quick breath before holding it in. My mouth goes dry, and my tongue feels heavy as I look Travis up and down.

He is wearing a thin white T-shirt, a pair of black workout shorts, and sneakers. But his outfit is not what has my ovaries throbbing. It's the fact that he is sweaty, and his clothes are clinging to his muscular body so deliciously I want to lick his abs like a lollipop.

"What are you doing here? You are interrupting my scheduled workout time," he informs me in a stern voice.

I tear my eyes away from his intoxicating physique so I can take in his handsome face. His forehead is currently set in an angry frown, his lips are in a thin line, and his eyes are squinting against the sun, shining directly at him. Then I notice a weird-looking rash on the side of his face. I wonder how he got that.

He clears his throat, dragging me from my thoughts.

Plastering a megawatt smile on my face, I make my desert mouth work and say, "I came to apologize for barging in the other day, and I baked you some cookies to show you how much I mean it." I hold out the container of chocolate chip cookies and wait for him to grab it. He stares at it for a moment before shaking his head at me.

"So you are interrupting me to apologize for interrupting me?" he asks, his frown deepening.

A giggle bursts from me, and I slap my hand over my lips to hide it. I cover up my laugh with a cough, but I don't think Travis is fooled much. He crosses his arms over his broad chest and scowls at me, making him look sexy as hell. Like a disapproving professor who is about to put me over his knee.

Okay, get your mind out of the gutter.

I shake my indecent thought of Travis spanking me away and concentrate on him standing in front of me now. "I'm sorry I'm interrupting you again. Maybe I can join your workout?" I wiggle my eyebrows suggestively.

"You are not wearing workout clothes," he points out flatly, totally ignoring my advances. He is playing hard to get, and I like the challenge.

"I could go naked." I wink and shrug my shoulders.

"That would not be very functional," he replies, making me laugh again. *He is so funny.*

"I guess it wouldn't be, but I would still enjoy it."

"I doubt that," he quips before finally snatching the box from my hand. "Thank you for these. You can go now."

He takes a step back, ready to close the door in my face. I take a step toward him in return, ready to dash past him and into the house.

"I guess you would be eager to get back to your workout. I read about your disciplined nature in a newspaper article," I admit unashamedly.

His eyebrow arches. "You looked me up?"

"I did. I wanted to know who my new neighbor is," I explain without missing a beat.

"Well, you are right. I'm very disciplined, especially when it comes to my schedule, and answering the door isn't on it. So why don't you go back to your cabin now so I can continue my workout?"

"Is that poison ivy on your face?" I ask, desperately trying to change the subject. "You know, I fell into poison ivy once while trying to go pee. I squatted right into it without realizing what it was. Had a rash just like that, but on my butt." I giggle. Now, thinking back on it, the story is kind of funny. "Anyways . . . why don't I help you with a cold compress?"

Before he has a chance to answer, I swoop past him and dash into the house.

"Ugh, not again," Travis murmurs under his breath as I make my way toward the kitchen triumphantly. He follows with a grunt.

"Have you tried an oatmeal paste for your rash?" I ask as I walk around his counters. "Do you have any oatmeal? I can make you some." I open what I assume is the pantry door and have a peek inside.

"I don't have any oatmeal," Travis tells me, annoyance dripping from his voice. He places the box of cookies on the counter.

"Okay, I'll just make you a cold compress," I announce before grabbing a kitchen towel hanging over the oven handle.

"That's not necessary," Travis assures me, but I ignore him and step in front of the sink to run cold water over the towel. After it's soaked, I wring it out and fold it into a thick square.

When I turn around, Travis is standing a few feet away from me, his arms folded in front of his chest again while his eyes stare daggers at me. I close the distance between us and bring the damp towel to his cheek. He pulls away at first, but once I press the compress against his skin, he stills.

His face relaxes, his frown evening out, and a hint of a smile plays on his lips . . . lips that I am very aware of, standing so close to him. God, I want to kiss those lips so badly. I wonder how they would feel pressed to mine. What would he taste like?

"This actually feels nice. It helps with the itching," Travis admits, his voice even and smooth.

I smile at him, enjoying the moment. We just stand there, looking at each other for a few seconds. I could stay like this forever, gazing into his dark-brown eyes while my hand is pressed against his cheek, his body heat seeping through the towel.

"How long are you staying in the area?" he suddenly asks.

"Longer than I had planned," I answer vaguely, on purpose. "I might stay indefinitely if someone plays their cards right." I drop my voice an octave to sound seductive.

His gaze intensifies, like he is trying to figure out what I'm saying. So I'm making it very clear to him. Raising my free arm, I gently place my hand on his biceps. Travis's posture goes rigid, as if he is surprised by me touching him like this.

I let my palm rest against his warm skin, feeling an electric current running between us. His eyes lower to where I am touching him, and he looks as if he is trying to figure out if he likes this or not.

Another moment passes before his gaze snaps back up to mine. "You should go now. I'm very busy, and I need to get back on schedule."

Disappointment and rejection hit me all at once. I pull my hand from his arm, immediately missing the connection.

I pull the towel away from his face, too, inspecting the rash again. "It didn't get you too bad, but it still sucks. I hope the itching isn't too terrible. You can put this in the freezer, too, get it super cold," I suggest, holding out the towel to him.

He uncrosses his arms and takes the towel from my hand. "That's some good advice. You should share it with your twenty-eight thousand followers," he suggests.

His comment makes me perk up in a jiffy. Because the only reason he would know my follower count is that he also looked me up. *Oh my god, he researched me!* Hope blooms in my chest, washing away all my earlier self-doubt.

"You know what? You're right. I will share this on my page," I say cheerfully. "I better head out and let you get back to your schedule." I grin.

"That would be greatly appreciated." Travis nods.

"I hope you like the cookies," I say as I turn away from him to walk out of the kitchen. Part of me wishes he would stop me. He follows me through the foyer and toward the front door, where my eyes are drawn to three large bottles of bleach. *Wow, that's a lot of bleach.*

"Doing some spring-cleaning?" I point toward the bottles.

"Something like that," he answers just as we get to the door.

I reach for the knob and twist, pulling the door open. I don't really want to leave, but I step outside anyway.

"See you around, neighbor," I chirp over my shoulder as I walk down the front steps.

"We'll see," he challenges, making me giggle.

I hear the door closing behind me as I make my way down his driveway with a smile on my face. He doesn't know it yet, but we will see each other again soon . . . very soon.

Chapter Five

Travis

Today is the day. After studiously watching every move Kevin has made over the past week, I'm confident I know his schedule almost as well as my own. Well, that might be hyperbole, but I'm feeling particularly jubilant knowing what's to come tonight.

The high before a kill is almost as intoxicating as the act itself. It's what I love about this. The planning, the prep work, meticulously making sure every step I take is perfectly executed. The routine of it is titillating.

Even so, my nerves are on edge. I *need* this. All I can think about is the look that will be on Kevin's face as my knife slices into his flesh. I can hardly wait another minute. I don't know how I'm supposed to wait until nightfall.

I guess I could make myself some herbal tea to calm down a little. I walk into my kitchen and boil some water. While I wait, I get the cup ready with my favorite overpriced tea. When the water boils, I pour it into my cup and look at the time above the oven. It reads 03:15:35, which means the tea will be done at 03:18:35.

I keep my eyes trained on the timer, but my mind keeps going back to killing Kevin. I'm so excited about tonight I can barely contain myself. Too excited, because it's not long before I realize I've zoned out, and now the timer reads 3:18:46, which means it's steeped eleven seconds too long.

"Unacceptable," I murmur to myself before pouring the still-steaming cup down the drain. I look as the hot liquid disappears, and somehow I feel like it betrayed me personally.

With a huff, I walk back to my office. Just as I sit down, my phone chimes. If I don't answer it, nothing will stand in my way of finishing my plan tonight. I don't want anything stopping me.

It chimes again, the vibration rattling against the reclaimed wood of my desk. *For fuck's sake. What the hell is it now?*

I suck my teeth as I grab my phone and look at the text message ringing through. Peter Dawson?

I got an alert for an uptick in your name being searched, the text reads. Attached is a screenshot of the alert, with a timeline of how frequently my name has been searched. Being the public figure I am, there is a reluctant amount of notoriety that comes with the territory.

Even considering that, it doesn't take long for me to put the pieces together. *Juniper Sage Featherstone.*

Ever since forcing her way into my life, she's been interrupting me in ways she can't even comprehend. I'm certain it's her. More of an annoyance than a threat, but I can't risk something slipping through the cracks. I pay too close attention to everything I do to let her ruin my plans. I pick up the phone and press the call button by Peter's name and wait for him to answer.

"Is this anything I should be concerned about?" I ask, not sparing a moment for useless pleasantries. Peter has been working with me as my PI long enough that he knows what to expect.

"Depends on how nervous you're feeling," Peter replies, his North Carolina drawl hanging on each word as it slowly leaves his mouth. I can already feel myself getting impatient. "They're searching for information about you and an Amelia Banks."

My blood runs cold at the mention of her name. There's a long moment of silence between Peter and me as my brain works furiously to figure out what's going on.

How does Sage know about Amelia? She couldn't possibly have the resources to find out anything about her.

"Travis?" Peter says on the other end, waiting for my reaction.

"Can you tell where the search is coming from?" I purposely keep my voice as level as I can, but my fist is balled tight at my side, fingernails digging into my palm.

"Lake Lure," Peter promptly answers.

How can this be? I'm so meticulous, so careful. Nobody can possibly connect me to Amelia. Can they?

I hang up on Peter and drop the phone onto my desk. He must realize I'm upset, because he doesn't bother contacting me again. I jump to my feet and pace back and forth in my office. Pacing helps me think. It calms me down, and right now I am on edge.

I've been busy lately. Amelia might have been my first kill, but she is far from my last.

All my victims have been disposed of properly. I bought a crematorium in every town where I own property for that specific purpose. To the few people who knew my victims, it seems like they vanish off the face of the earth. They leave no belongings behind, no letters, and no trace of where they go. I even have someone who scrubs their digital trail for me. All that remains of them are small vials filled with their ashes hidden in my room.

Could I have made some kind of mistake? The idea is preposterous. I don't make mistakes. I don't leave room for error in anything I do. That's why I take precautions before I act. That's why my routine is so strict and why I study each kill so meticulously.

No, nothing I've done here in Lake Lure or anywhere else has given me away. I'm confident about that. I especially wouldn't consider someone like Juniper Sage Featherstone to be the one to finally catch me. But who is searching for Amelia?

The doorbell rings, jolting me out of my retrospective analysis. Without even looking, I know it's her. She can't leave me the fuck alone to save her life. I know what she's thinking too. She sees me out here, alone, and thinks she might be able to seduce me and win my heart like this is some sort of romantic comedy. The more she shows up and pesters me, the weaker my resolve, and eventually I'll just realize she's exactly what I'm looking for.

Well, she is exactly what I'm looking for. It just isn't what she is hoping for. If she's looking into Amelia, the sooner I can wrap my hands around her pretty little throat, the better.

I yank the door open, ready to reprimand her for bothering me yet again, only to find the mail carrier standing there.

"Signature, please," he says with a strained smile. I grab the pen he's holding and sign the clipboard before he hands me the package.

I've been so preoccupied with planning the kill that I completely forgot about the extra security cameras I ordered. After the crab-walking incident, I realized there are some blind spots on my property.

I close the door and lean against it, taking a nervous breath. I can feel the paranoia and stress creeping in around my vision. I know the stress I'm feeling is just because my schedule has been off, thanks to Sage. I'm frayed, and mentally exhausted. But I also know the kill will help with that. I know that I'll feel so much better after. I'll finally feel calm again.

The alarm on my watch beeps, and I look down. Even with my nerves on edge, my schedule persists. It's time for my daily walk.

I slip on a pair of athletic shoes and make my way outside. During the walk, my mind wanders without restraint. I've always found walking to be therapeutic in a way. I don't care for nature or the sound of birds chirping happily in the trees, but I enjoy the repetition. One foot in front of the other, over and over and over again. There's rarely any room for error. I know the path I take like the back of my hand.

As I walk, my mind drifts back to her. *Amelia Banks.*

I would be lying if I said I haven't thought about her. In the same way you never forget your first kiss, you don't forget your first kill. It's been years since Amelia went missing, and the two of us weren't linked together in any official capacity. Why are we being searched together now?

My thoughts come to an abrupt stop when I see a vibrant pink mess of hair moving at the end of my path. I clench my fists at my sides. Yet another thing Sage has trespassed on.

She's standing at the edge of the path, the overlook there staring down at the lake itself. She has her phone set up on a tripod, with a ring light behind her, completely ignoring the natural daylight that is illuminating the entire area. I stand motionless as I watch her sway back and forth, clearly trying to master some kind of trendy internet dance.

Her cheeks are pink from a mixture of the heat and what I can imagine is exhaustion from her repeated attempts. My eyes lower to her round ass, swaying to a rhythm I can't hear. Her dancing has me mesmerized, her moves draw me in, and for a long time I just stand there staring at her.

She stumbles and stomps her feet on the ground, running her fingers through her hair as frustration takes over. *Now she knows how I feel every time she knocks on my door.*

Sage doesn't notice me as I watch her. My mind moves seamlessly from Amelia and the searches to Sage and all the things I want to do to her. I don't usually kill with my bare hands, but I can clearly imagine it with her.

Even now she's practically teetering on the edge of the mountain. It would be easy to push her off. Once authorities watched the videos of her dancing so close to the cliff, it would be ruled an accident. It could be my easiest kill yet. I wouldn't even have to deal with any cleanup.

But that's not part of the plan, I remind myself. I haven't watched her and studied her as I know I should. Besides, when it's her time, I want to enjoy it.

Chapter Six

SAGE

If Ryan weren't such a perverted creep, I might consider staying in this house a little longer. Well, if I have it my way, I'll be moving in next door any day now. After all, *Mrs. Blacksburg* should be living with her husband.

I wonder if Travis would mind if I hyphenated my name. My followers already know me as Sage Featherstone, so I wouldn't want to risk confusing them . . .

Lying on the floor in the living room with my laptop spread out in front of me and a newly dropped podcast from *Pretty Grim* playing, I feel calm. I could never afford a place like this on my own full-time, but for now I can pretend. Once my career takes off, and when Travis and I are Instagram official, this can be my every day. I can hardly wait.

"Lake Lure, North Carolina, may seem like a small, idyllic town nestled in the heart of the Appalachian Mountains," Beth, my favorite *Pretty Grim* host, says in her introduction for the episode. "But even small towns have mysteries. With stories of mythical creatures roaming the woods at night, missing people, and even suspected killers roaming the streets, it begs the question: If you aren't safe in the nicest of places, then where are you safe?"

Beth and her sister Caroline both go back and forth talking about their podcast tour and the sold-out shows they have all across the country before they get into the good stuff. I can tune that out with ease as I open Instagram on my phone and look at the analytics for the video I posted.

Trust me, I'm no dancer. I have the coordination of a bumblebee missing a wing, but that doesn't stop me from getting in on the trends. After all, I am relatively new in the content creator space, and the best way to get followers is by being relevant and trendy. I'm living proof of this because it's only been two hours since I've posted the video, and I've already amassed a thousand new followers.

My heart skips a beat. This is what I've waited for. I could go *viral*.

I look at the comments, and, of course, DarkHours99 left one for me. Why is this video five hours long?

In real life, I roll my eyes and take a deep breath while I think of a response. However, to the man behind the username, my blushing and laughing emojis will make him feel like I value his comment.

I go through about twenty other comments, liking them and leaving cheeky responses just to make my followers feel like I know them. Sure, sociologists are saying parasocial relationships are dangerous, but if I have loyal fans who will share my content all over the internet, it's pretty beneficial.

After I'm done, I set my phone down and get back to work. While I was out there filming the dance video, I shot a few more to post at later dates. I figure, if I can get a lot of content done in one day, I can spend the rest of my time here relaxing and focusing on what's important: Travis Blacksburg.

"In recent years, there have been several missing person reports coming from Lake Lure," Beth says when they finally start discussing the actual crimes they're reporting on. "A majority of the missing persons have been transient types: unhoused individuals, travelers, and runaways. Local police have been informed of the disappearances, but there's little evidence for them to go on. Friends of the missing have urged them to look into the disappearances, to no avail."

"Some people just make it too easy to be murdered." I sigh, shaking my head at the podcast.

I'm traveling as a single woman across the country. I don't drive a car, and I often rely on the kindness of strangers to take me where I need to go. But even considering that, I'm savvy. I can spot danger from a mile away. I know that nobody thinks these things will ever happen to them, but this wouldn't ever happen to me.

I rest my chin on my hands as I stare at the computer screen and wait for the rest of my footage to upload. I have a few videos of me lip-synching to a popular song at golden hour, as well as a few stitches with some other popular creators. My phone chimes, and I look at it, not surprised to see a message from DarkHours99.

He's sent me a lot of messages in the past, and I rarely respond to them. I like his comments, and I reply when I see them, and he clearly takes that as an invitation to slide into my DMs. Even though I don't respond to him privately, he doesn't seem to take the hint.

He's replied to almost all my stories, telling me that I look beautiful and wishing that he was at certain places with me poolside while I'm in a bikini. I try not to think about what I know he does to those images, which is a large part of why I don't respond to his messages. It might potentially lead him to send me explicit content I don't want.

The message reads, Don't forget us small people when you get famous lol, your last video is popping off! You got an Amazon wishlist yet? I'm sure there are a lot of guys willing to buy you anything you want.

It sounds ungrateful to say this, but I feel bad for him. I know he's just a lonely person finding connection in our internet relationship. It's not real. He knows nothing about who I really am, and I don't even know his name. He clearly thinks it goes deeper than content creator and follower.

I ignore it and put the phone back down to focus on editing. The more I think about DarkHours99 and his almost constant snooping on my page, the more I think about Travis doing the same. Did he see pictures of me in my tiny bikini sitting by the pool at the last Airbnb I reviewed? Did he like those pictures enough to touch himself?

Even the idea of it is a turn-on, and I squeeze my legs together a little tighter to release some of the pressure building between them at the thought.

My footage finally loads into iMovie, and I take a deep breath as I get to work scrubbing through it. At first everything appears normal. Then I notice something in the background, just out of focus enough for me not to have noticed it right away—Travis.

"Oh, Mr. Blacksburg," I say as I sit up and stare closely at the computer screen. "Why didn't you come say hi?"

I zoom in on him as much as I can to try to get a look at his face. My entire body feels featherlight as I see the intense look in his eyes as he watches me. I was right about him. He feels the same connection to me that I feel to him. After all, you don't watch someone as intensely as he did without being a little interested in them.

"Travis, I'm going to make your dreams come true tonight," I say as I jump to my feet and rush to the bedroom.

I strip out of the denim shorts and tank top I'm currently wearing and kneel in front of my suitcase, completely naked. The first thing I do is find the sexiest bra and panties I own. A nice lacy red pair that would seduce anyone. I check myself out in the mirror and admire how perky my boobs look and how the underwear gives my ass the perfect shape.

"Try to resist me in this," I say, laughing to myself.

I find a sage green—obviously my favorite color—mini slip dress that hangs delicately on my body and put it on. It exposes just enough of my thighs to keep anyone wondering, and my cleavage is on full display. I can already imagine Travis drooling when he sees me on his doorstep in this.

I slip on a pair of wedge sandals and make my way over to his house. Travis is clearly interested in me, and I don't want the two of us to waste another moment apart. On the walk there, all I can think about is wrapping my arms around his broad shoulders and feeling him press himself against me.

Tonight, I'm going to show him what I can offer. I'm going to make him mine. I'll do whatever it takes.

It's dark by the time I reach his driveway. His front door is in my sights, and I take a deep breath as I make my way over.

As if out of nowhere, two bright headlights meet my eyes, and a black SUV comes barreling out of the garage. I barely manage to jump out of the way, crashing into the concrete driveway.

The car comes to a screeching halt as I'm trying to wrap my brain around what just happened. The car door slams shut, and I turn around to see Travis standing there, all dressed in black. My mind immediately goes to how good he looks. Black is a great color on anyone, but he pulls it off particularly well.

The long-sleeve black shirt clings to his muscles, and his pants are perfectly tailored for his long limbs. As I study him, my eyes catch on the black leather gloves he's wearing.

"What the fuck are you doing here?" Travis shouts, glaring down at me on the ground.

"Why are you dressed like that?" I retort. "With the gloves and everything?" My mind tries to paint a picture of him that I can't quite finish. Even googling everything I have about him, he's a mystery. You would think a public figure like him would be a little more transparent.

"You're injured," Travis says, shaking his head at me as he points to my knees. Obviously, I felt that something was wrong when I fell. I guess I didn't realize the severity of the scrape until he points it out. "You need to go back to your cabin and clean the wound immediately. A severe bacterial contamination can lead to an infection that spreads to your entire body, possibly resulting in limb loss, sepsis, or even death."

He's really worried.

I stand up, with no help from Travis. If we're going to be together, he's seriously going to have to work on his chivalry. I wipe the dirt from my hands and look down at my knee, poking the wound gently.

"Don't touch it," Travis scolds me, rolling his eyes.

"Thank you for caring about my well-being," I say, flashing him a soft smile.

He shakes his head and exhales a long breath before running his fingers through his hair. He takes the gloves off and clenches his fists tightly together and glares at me with his lips in a thin line.

"What are you doing here?" He folds his arms in front of him, clearly annoyed at my presence. I'm a little confused because I definitely thought he wanted me here. After all, *he* was watching *me.*

"Well, I thought you might be getting lonely up here all by yourself," I delicately say, bringing my hands to my hair to twirl a wavy coil around my finger. "Besides, it's pretty lonely at Ryan's place. I was thinking we could keep each other company."

Travis stares at me, and I feel the hope blossoming in my chest. He's going to invite me in and pour each of us a glass of wine, and I'm going to jump his bones until neither of us can see straight. By the end of the night, he's going to be on his hands and knees, begging me to stay with him.

Instead, he turns around and climbs back into the car. The headlights turn on as he slams the door shut and puts it back in drive.

"Where are you going?"

He rolls down the window but doesn't look at me as he drives toward the garage. "You've completely thrown off my schedule. I'll have to do this another day."

The garage door closes behind his car, and I'm left standing in his driveway, blood trickling down my leg from the open wound on my knee. I'm confused, and frankly, my feelings are a little hurt as well.

I head back to the cabin, giving Travis some time to cool down. He'll come around eventually.

Chapter Seven

TRAVIS

All that planning for nothing. Today was supposed to be the day. But then *Juniper. Sage. Featherstone* came into my life and ruined it. I was looking forward to finally being able to calm down and relax after the kill.

I suppose Kevin can count his blessings that he has another day to beg on the streets for money and booze.

I *had* two hours scheduled for the kill that are now free. I hardly know what to do with myself. The rush from the kill is exhilarating, and I usually schedule self-pleasure time afterward. I look at my calendar and see it penciled in for the time I anticipated being home.

Frustrated and angry, I sit down on my couch and spend the next sixty-eight minutes thinking about killing Sage. That's when I start to get bored with imagining all the ways she could die.

I decide to try something different and just relax for a bit—*chill*, as people would say. Grabbing my phone, I pull up my music app and scroll down the most popular playlists.

Romantic Acoustic Favorites? No, thank you.

'90s Urban Hits. Who listens to this nonsense?

I finally settle on classic rock, the least annoying option. I click on the playlist, and to my disdain, a rock ballad starts to play. The singer's raspy voice comes through the speaker: "I miss you so hard . . ."

With a frustrated growl, I stop the song so fast my phone slips from my grasp and smashes against the floor. *Ugh.*

I pick up my phone and stuff it in my pocket. I spend the next few minutes sitting there seething about nothing going right.

When it's finally time for the next event on my schedule, I stand up and walk to my bathroom. I undress and turn on the water, making sure it's the precise temperature I like before stepping in. Water cascades down my back, and the absence of blood rinsing off my skin is palpable. There's nothing like seeing that after a kill.

I force those thoughts away as I wrap my hand around my cock. It's soft, but it doesn't take long for me to feel it stiffening in my palm. I have a few fantasies I run through regularly. When it comes to these things, I prefer the tried and true. I don't want to make things up with new women or scenarios.

I'm normally very picky regarding women, and there are a select few I find sexually arousing. One I think of often is my former assistant, Penny. Before I sold my company, I noticed how beautiful she was. She was petite, with natural black hair, green eyes, and a curvy figure that caught my attention several times.

When I think of Penny, I think of a late night in the office. I'm slaving away behind the desk, coding a new feature for the user interface on our website. Sure, it's something I can pass down to an underling, but I like to have control. Penny usually waits for me to leave so she can lock everything properly. Today, it's late and almost everyone else is gone.

She knocks on the door, and I reluctantly look away from the code to see her standing with her arms behind her back, pressing her chest forward.

"Mr. Blacksburg, you seem stressed." Penny strolls across the office and sits on my desk, her legs stretched out right next to me as she slowly hikes up her skirt. "It's my job to make sure you're not stressing out."

She grabs my hands and places them on her thighs. I instinctively spread them apart, splaying her out on the desk before me. Only this time, when I look up to see her face, expecting her red lips to part mischievously as she unleashes her black hair from its bun, I see Sage.

Her pink hair hangs around her shoulders as she sits naked on the desk. The very same pink pussy I saw nights ago is on full display.

My eyes open in the shower, and I move my hand from my raging hard-on and shake off the thought. I can't think about her like that. *Not right now.* She shouldn't be a part of these fantasies.

I close my eyes to try to think of Penny again, but all I can think about is Sage hopping out of bed, completely naked, and inspecting the house.

I groan as I squeeze myself hard in frustration. I force the image of Penny back into my head. I try to concentrate on her black hair as I pump my hand harder on my cock. I blink, and the black turns to pink.

I forget the hair and think of Penny's lips wrapped around me, her head bobbing up and down while she sucks me eagerly. I can feel myself climbing closer and closer to the edge, but I'm just not getting there.

I shift the fantasy to send me over, imagining us taking it to the bed, Penny completely splayed out while I shove my cock inside her. I close my eyes, and all I see is Sage in her bed, her pussy bare and ready for the taking.

No. No. No. I'm not thinking about her like this . . . Can I?

Nothing's working.

Whatever I do, I can't force the thought of her aside, so maybe I should just go with it?

I close my eyes again, this time imagining her on purpose. The thought is weird at first, almost taboo, but when I stroke my cock, it feels right. She is lying in bed, her legs spread, her pussy glistening, but then she opens her mouth and lectures me on drinking cow's milk instead of oat. Ugh, that would be just like her. She would go on and on about essential oils or some nonsense.

"Fuck!" I shout, opening my eyes and slamming my fist against the tile wall.

My frustration is clouding my vision as I step out of the shower. It's like there's something on my shoulder nagging me about everything I can't do today. Things I can't do because of *her*.

I can't kill because of Sage, and I can't even fucking jack off because of her. Everything is messed up, and it's all her fault.

I'm done. This is it. *Today she dies.*

My stomach churns as I decide to forgo my routine. Anxiety fills my chest, thinking about how I am deviating from my schedule, but what other choice do I have? I can't get her out of my head. She has to go.

This might be the quickest I've ever decided to end someone's life, but what can I say? Sage has a very negative impact on me.

I put on a pair of pants and my black shirt and storm out of the house. Halfway there, I realize I was in such a rush I didn't bring my gloves or any of the tools I would usually use.

Fuck it. I'll make this a quick-and-easy strangulation. Not my preferred method by any means, but it'll get the job done. That's all I need right now.

I laugh out loud on the way there, running my fingers through my hair as I anticipate the calm I will feel when this is finally over. It's not Kevin, but it'll do. Maybe I can finally relax.

My frustration is clouding my judgment as I get to the cabin, popping open a window she's so foolishly left unlocked and climbing in. I'm in the living room and looking around for any sign of her. It hasn't been that long since our last encounter, and there's a chance she'll be defensive seeing me, but I doubt it. Common sense doesn't seem to be her friend. At least I can take advantage of that.

I move toward the couch as quietly as I can, peeking inside the hallway where the bedrooms are. Just as I manage to look through it, Sage walks out of a room and stares at me. Her eyes widen from the surprise, and my entire body goes stiff.

She's in the same dress she was wearing when I almost hit her with my car, but her knee is now bandaged. I try to ignore the part of my brain telling me she looks good. I'm immediately reminded of the fantasy I had in the bathroom that I couldn't finish.

Sage doesn't say anything as she closes the distance between us, and neither do I. This entire excursion is unplanned, and I need it to go my way. I can't very well tell her I'm here to strangle her.

Before I know what's happening, she's running at me, and her hands are on my face, pulling me down toward her. Her lips fall on mine, and confusion overwhelms me. I shouldn't feel this way. I can easily wrap my hands around her neck and squeeze. That's what I came here for. What is stopping me?

The kiss is sloppy and frenzied, like she has been waiting for this for years. I can't help myself as I open my mouth and taste her on my tongue. She wraps her arms around my neck and practically climbs up on me. Sage moans loudly as she kisses me, almost like she's putting on a show.

I came here to kill her. That's still my plan. But I could kill two birds with one stone and check off my pleasure time right now. I'm horny, and I didn't finish in the shower, and this has already been allotted for in my schedule. Efficiency is always appreciated.

I feel the blood rush to my cock as I allow myself to give in to this. Sage is on me, pressing her body hard against mine as her hands wander all over. If this is going to happen, I just need to be the one in control.

I back away from her, unbuckling my pants as I stare her down.

"Take your dress off," I say, leaving no room for debate. Sage smiles and does exactly as I say, lifting the dress off her shoulders to reveal a delicate matching pair of lace underwear. She looks so fucking sexy. "I want it all off."

She doesn't waste a moment before slipping out of her panties and unclasping the bra. She stands in front of me, her firm, perky breasts standing up all on their own.

I lower my pants to the ground, revealing my hard cock to her for the first time. She stares at it and licks her lips as if she's hungry to taste it. It's a damn shame I won't feel those lips around my cock before I strangle her.

I walk over and grab her to pull her toward the couch. She moves exactly as I do, not hesitating for a moment. She has no idea what's coming, and the anticipation is almost as exciting as the prospect of fucking her.

"Bend over," I say as I force her over the arm of the couch. She laughs as her face crashes into the cushion, and she sways her hips readily in front of me. I can see her folds already glistening as I hover outside.

"I knew you wanted me," Sage says, looking over her shoulder with a satisfied smile. "I've been waiting for this."

"Don't talk," I say, grabbing her hips and grinding myself against her for a moment, allowing my cock to soak itself in her juices.

"Ooh, you're a little rough, then?" Sage asks with a slight giggle at the end. "I'll play along. Why don't you fuck me hard?"

She looks at me with an eager grin, and I can't help but let out a small laugh. She really has no idea what is about to happen, and the irony is priceless.

"Ask and you shall receive." I grip her waist firm in my hands and hold her steady as I shove the full length of my cock inside her.

Her body stiffens as she feels me from within. It takes a moment for her to adjust, and she moans on the couch below. "Oh my god, Travis," she squeals, trying to stand up a bit.

I force her back down with my hand as I start slowly pumping my cock into her. She moans and shakes as I thrust into her. Her back is perfectly arched, and I squeeze her ass cheeks with my hands as I watch my cock moving in and out of her tight hole.

The block I felt in the shower is gone, and I know I can finish this time. There won't be anything holding me back from the absolute pleasure that this is going to bring me.

"Fuck me harder!" Sage shouts, looking over her shoulder with a wink. Her hair is tousled around her face as she cries out and moans.

I can feel her getting wetter with each movement, and I do exactly as she suggests.

"Careful what you wish for," I say as my grip tightens on her waist. I pull away from her, leaving nothing but the tip of my cock in her pussy. All of a sudden I slam myself against her while pulling her close, my skin slapping against hers.

She stares at me with her eyes practically rolling back in her head as I continue doing that, the force of my thrusts moving the couch forward.

"Yes, Travis!" Sage shouts as I fuck her senseless. Her pussy clenches around me as she cries out and spasms below me when her orgasm crashes over her. I can't take it anymore, and I feel myself teetering on the edge. I pull out, ready to come on her ass. "No, no, no! Please, don't stop."

A few dribbles of my cum land on her skin, but hearing her beg for release does something to me. Without thinking, I ram my cock into her again and thrust more and more, filling her with ropes of my cum. She trembles below me as the pleasure recedes, and I completely drain myself inside her.

When I'm finished, I pull out and stand motionless behind her for a moment as her body goes limp on the couch.

What the fuck have I done?

How could I be so careless to come inside her? Not even considering the fact she could get pregnant with my child, I just left my DNA. That's a rookie mistake.

Calm the fuck down. Everything is going to be fine. All evidence can be burned in the crematorium.

Sighing, I compose myself just as Sage moves to lie on the couch and stares at me with a satisfied smile. Her lips curl up softly, her button nose wrinkles as her hand lazily reaches for me.

"Come here." Sage beckons me to lie with her, and for a crazy split second I think about curling up beside her.

Where the fuck did that come from?

I shake my head. I've got to get out of here before this woman drives me completely insane.

Sage reaches for my hand, but I shrug her off. Something flashes across her eyes, though I can't read exactly what it is. All I know is that I don't like her looking at me this way. I turn away from her and pull my pants back on.

"Wait," Sage calls after me as I make my way out of the cabin. My body and mind are at odds. My brain tells me to leave, but my body wants to stay. I'm so confused by it that I pick up my pace.

I walk back to my house, reprimanding myself for being such a fool.

My feet slam against my driveway when I come to a sudden halt. Closing my eyes, I tilt my head up to the sky and groan in frustration.

Dammit, I forgot to strangle her.

Chapter Eight

SAGE

Juniper Sage Blacksburg. Juniper Sage Featherstone-Blacksburg.

I can't decide what sounds best. I write it down a few times in my journal just to look at it. I write it in print, cursive, and I type it out on my phone. No matter how I look at it or spell it, it simply doesn't get old.

I can't lie. After Travis sent me away in my sexiest dress, post–almost killing me with his car, I thought we were done. Maybe I'd been a little delusional and thought he was more into me than he was. But then he came to the cabin to fuck me, and now I know the truth. Travis is as in love with me as I am with him.

He just shows it a little differently.

I have to admit, he is kind of an oddball, but in a cute and special way. Travis plays to the beat of his own drum, and that's one of the things I love about him. He is different, an enigma of sorts. He is guarded, and a bit of a recluse, I think, but I even like that about him. He is like an onion I plan on peeling back layer by layer.

Seriously, it feels like magic. Like something in the air is thick with opportunity. Anything feels possible. I could fly right now if I wanted to. All because of *Travis Blacksburg.*

He left before we could talk about what happened, and I know I need to go see him. I just don't know how yet. I thought about making him more cookies. Or maybe I could make him a nice home-cooked meal. They say the fastest way to a man's heart is through his stomach, but that's not entirely true. The fastest way is through their cock, and Travis and I already have simmering sexual chemistry, so I have that base covered. I just have to lock down the stomach now, and I'll have a ring in no time.

While I may be lacking ingredients in Ryan's bachelor pad of a cabin, I'm sure Travis has plenty at home. So, after a little primping in the mirror, I make my way over.

It's a beautiful day, so I consider a picnic. Maybe Travis and I can go to the cliff overlooking the lake with a blanket, a bottle of wine, and some toasted Brie on a fancy baguette, and fall in love with each other. He seems like a man who would appreciate a nice wine-and-cheese pairing.

Note to self: Learn about wine and cheese.

I knock on his door, expecting him to answer all grumpy like he always does. Now I know it's nothing but a facade, and I'm slowly cracking that hard shell around him. I wait for a minute, and when he doesn't answer, I knock again. Once more, I get no answer. I stand on my tiptoes to peek through the garage windows and notice his car is gone.

You know what? This is even better. Now I can surprise him when he gets home, the same way he surprised me.

Obviously the door is locked. Which means I need to sneak around the perimeter of his house and look for another entrance. I walk around, and all his windows are covered with blinds, so I have a hard time seeing through them. They're all locked on top of that.

As I'm walking, I spot a privacy fence in his backyard, and I jump so I can see what's over it. That's when I spot the hot tub. *How romantic!*

Imagine Travis coming home after a long day out, wherever the fuck he is, walking through his house, all alone, just to spot me in his hot tub, completely naked. What a surprise.

I look around for something to help me climb when I spot a log that seems sturdy enough. I drag it toward the fence and carefully scale it, reaching for the top.

As I pull myself up, I feel the log fall from under my foot and roll away. I fight to get on top of the fence, thankful it's at least a few inches wide to give me some stability.

I must look ridiculous, huffing and puffing while I struggle to swing my leg over. "And here we have the rarely graceful *Love-Sickus influencera*, awkwardly trying to navigate suburban terrain while deeply, stupidly in love," I say, narrating my life as if it were a nature documentary.

When I'm finally straddling it, ready to hop over to the other side, I realize my mistake. The other side is way too far down to just hop off without hurting my ankle. After the fall yesterday, my legs are already a little sore.

The only option would be to turn back. Well, at least it would have been if the log hadn't up and rolled away. I'm stuck.

I consider just jumping down the way I came since it's a shorter fall, but I'm afraid. What if I break my ankle out here? Sure, that would mean Travis might be inclined to take care of me, but I'd be sitting out here on my own, for God only knows how long, waiting for him.

Thankfully, I don't have to consider my options much longer, because I hear his car pulling up the driveway. I can't see him yet, but I'm hoping I will soon enough. It doesn't take long before he is opening the back door to his house and walking directly toward me.

"Funny story," I call to him, hoping it will break some of the immediate tension.

"Why are you doing this to me?" Travis asks, standing below me with his arms crossed in front of him. "I have things to do. I had to leave what I was doing because I got a security alert about you snooping around my house."

I can see the annoyance in his eyes, and I feel bad for a moment. "I just wanted to surprise you. After how you surprised me last night, I thought it was the least I could do."

He shakes his head and lets out a reluctant sigh, dropping his arms to his sides. "I don't want you to get the wrong idea about that. That's not what I was there for."

"Oh yeah? Then what were you there for?"

"I was there to strangle you," Travis replies without a moment of hesitation.

"Kinky." I laugh it off before realizing what I just said out loud. I don't want him to think I think strangulation is sexy. *Do I?* "I meant k-kettle chips!" I blurt out the first thing that comes to mind.

Smooth move, Sage.

He gives me a confused look, and I recover with a nervous giggle.

"I'm a very busy man, and I can't have you constantly interrupting me. I need you to stop showing up like this and leave me alone."

"You didn't really seem to want to be alone last night." I laugh as I wiggle on the fence, looking at the ground in front of him. "I could use a hand getting down, by the way."

He huffs once again and looks over his shoulder at a shed with a tall metal ladder lying on the ground next to it. "Fine, I'll get you the ladder if you promise to stop showing up out of nowhere and interrupting my life."

I squint at him to try to see how serious he is. He might appear like he means what he's saying, but the way he fucked me last night told me something else entirely. He doesn't want to be left alone.

"Fine, I promise," I say, knowing I have no intention of keeping my word.

Travis turns around, and I watch him as he walks away, admiring how good he looks in jeans. He grabs the ladder without any struggle, which is impressive because that means he's strong. He presses it against the wall, and I grab the top of it to steady myself before swinging my leg over to the other side.

I feel my center of gravity being pulled as I swing my leg over and lose control. I fall off the fence and cry out.

Instead of collapsing to the ground, two strong arms wrap around me. My breath catches in my throat as I open my eyes to see Travis holding me in his arms, having caught me before I landed on the ground.

It feels like one of those romantic moments in every superhero movie where the hero catches the damsel in distress. What comes after those moments? A passionate kiss.

Logically, I grab Travis's face and pull it toward mine, letting my lips swish against his. He holds me close to him for a moment, kissing me back as I hold on to him for dear life. My fingers cling to his shirt collar as if I could pull him into me.

Remnants of the pleasure I felt last night warm my core, and I want nothing more than for him to take me to his bed and make love to me. By the way he's kissing me back, I think he wants the same thing.

His mouth envelops mine as if he can't get enough, and it only stirs the desire growing in my chest. If I have it my way, every day for the rest of my life will be just like this.

But then Travis pulls away. I'm still in his arms, and he looks down, realizing that, and sets me on the ground. I move toward him again, hoping to kiss him once more, but he backs away.

"This isn't on the schedule for today," Travis says, shaking his head at me. His eye twitches as he takes a deep breath and wipes any trace of me from his lips.

He turns around to walk back into his house, and I instinctively follow. Now it's my chance to cook the dinner I wanted and woo him properly. But instead of sitting down on the couch and taking a chance to get to know me better, he leads me directly to the front door.

"Every time you show up here, you keep getting hurt," Travis says as I linger in the doorway, trying to think of any excuse to stay behind. "You should be careful. Next time you come around, you might get seriously injured—or worse."

He nudges me over the threshold and closes the door, promptly locking it afterward. His words linger in my mind, and I wonder what he means. Travis is mysterious, and it's clear to me he has nearly impenetrable walls up around him. If he thinks he's going to hurt me, he's wrong. I'm going to make sure I break down those walls and make a nest in his heart.

It's only a matter of time before Travis Blacksburg is mine and I am his.

Chapter Nine

TRAVIS

And just like that, all my planning has been for nothing. I spent two whole weeks of my goddamn life planning for Kevin's kill, and now it's all over.

I watched with a stone in my chest as Kevin's brother from Massachusetts came into town to search for him. Most people would have looked at that as a heartwarming reunion, but I was ready to break every window in my house from the fury I felt.

Kevin is going to get back on his feet. His brother's going to take him to rehab, and when he's out, he's going to get him a job at his construction company.

Yippee.

Now that Kevin is gone, I need a new target. I haven't gone this long without a kill in years, and every moment that passes is torture. I'm not thinking clearly. There is a thick fog in my brain I can't get rid of. I'm on edge, and this is destroying me.

Sage managed to destroy a perfectly good target. Kevin was a nobody. He had no friends in Lake Lure, and the family that he did have were done with him. He'd stolen from them and used them long enough and they cut him off. After all, how can you help someone if they're not willing to help themselves?

Now, with Kevin completely off the table, I can soon make another attempt with Sage. I don't know how long she's going to be my neighbor, but I can't let her upend my life like this anymore. I'm going to teach her that actions have consequences.

Stalking her has been incredibly easy. Since she constantly posts pictures and videos of herself, I know exactly where she is and what she is doing. This morning she climbed up the stairs to the Chimney Rock American flag, and now she is checking out some of the souvenir shops in front of the state park.

In town, I find an empty seat at one of the picnic tables outside Scoops Ice Cream. It's swarming with children and parents who aren't paying nearly enough attention to them. Their shrieks and high-pitched laughter only make my nerves more frail.

Oh no. I cringe when I see a little boy walking up to me. He is still a toddler, waddling while holding an ice cream cone in his little hand. I shake my head at him, hoping he will get the message and not come any closer. *He doesn't get it.*

His tiny feet carry him to where I sit until he stops mere inches from me. I lean back, hoping this germ-infested child won't touch me. It's nothing personal. All children are carriers of sickness. He smiles at me, and I desperately look around for this boy's mother.

When I can't find her, I huff. "What do you want?"

The little kid doesn't say anything, but holds out his ice cream cone to me, urging me to either take it or, worse, lick the melting chocolate ice cream currently dripping down his sticky hand.

Barf. I gag internally before saying, "This is not the blood sacrifice I require."

The boy's eyes go wide before tears form in them.

Oh, fuck no.

I plug my index fingers into my ears a split second before the boy opens his mouth and starts crying with the most annoying high-pitched sound. Finally, the mom comes running toward us. She grabs the boy and lifts him up into her arms, rubbing his back while he keeps crying.

They walk away, and I do my best to tune it all out as I train my eyes on the crowd around me. I'm not here to let myself be annoyed by these dreadful children. I'm here to potentially get eyes on my target. Even though I can easily follow her online and get visuals through various security cameras around town, sometimes I like to get a real look. Feels more personal that way.

In the distance I see an unmistakable mop of fading pink hair tied in a bun, and I grin at how easy it is to find her. If I believed in fate, I would say this is it. My smile fades when I realize she is turning my way and walking toward me.

Shit, I wanted to see her from afar, not up close. I quickly stand up and turn away, but it's too late. I thought I could evade her, but I have no such luck when it comes to Juniper Sage Featherstone.

She catches up with me a few seconds later. "I never took you for much of an ice cream guy," Sage says, playfully patting me on the shoulder.

"And I thought we had a deal," I reply, staring at her with a blank expression in the hope that she can finally take the hint and leave me alone.

"Listen, you told me to stop showing up out of nowhere, and I was just in town," Sage says, holding her hands up as if to proclaim innocence. "This is nothing more than an innocent chance encounter. I swear."

I stare at her blankly.

She flashes me a smile. "How about some apology ice cream?" Sage says, gesturing to the shop behind us. "Consider this me waving a white flag. I've caused you a lot of inconvenience, and I really am sorry."

Something tells me she's not being entirely truthful, but I do appreciate the gesture. Besides, it doesn't look like she's about to take no for an answer.

"Fine," I say, walking inside with her.

It's a hot summer day, and Scoops Ice Cream is a hot spot in town, so the line is long. Sage and I stare up at the chalkboard menu in silence while we try to figure out what we want. All the ice creams have funny names, so it's hard for me to decipher exactly what each flavor is.

"What's your favorite?" Sage asks, looking up at me with fluttering eyelashes. "I'm a Rocky Road girl."

"So you're a heathen?" I say.

"And you're dramatic." Sage laughs. "Clearly, you've never had Rocky Road. Otherwise you wouldn't be saying that."

"It's inconsistent. The very premise of the flavor is to add variety to something that should be uniform." I shake my head at her. "Ice cream was invented to be a creamy, smooth dessert. The textural differences in each bite of Rocky Road are a disgrace to the concept of ice cream."

Sage laughs and nudges my shoulder as she rolls her eyes. "Okay, so if you're such an ice cream expert, what are the best flavors?"

"There's a very particular order for these things," I say, scouring my mind for my ice cream list to share with her. "The top of the list is vanilla. It's a classic for a reason, and everything about it is perfect, considering what ice cream is supposed to be. It's smooth, creamy, and the flavor is palatable to nearly everyone. They don't sell 425 million gallons in a year without reason."

"That's rich, because knowing what I know about you, I would not expect anything vanilla." Sage cocks an eyebrow at me with a devious smirk.

"Funny," I say. "The next flavor is chocolate. After that, not ice cream per se, but rainbow sherbet—"

"Well, is that some variety I see?"

"Well, with an anticipated variety like that, it's acceptable. Besides, the flavors are all meant to meld together in sherbet." Sage laughs again, clearly not taking my ranking seriously. I feel a flicker of annoyance at that. "I suppose you just have whatever is interesting to you at the moment?"

"Yeah, that's what cravings are," Sage says, shrugging.

We get to the counter, and she asks for three different flavor samples, and I feel my annoyance level spiking. The lack of organization and order in this woman's life drives me insane. What is she, some kind of psycho? Just living life by the seat of her pants?

"I'll have one scoop of Rocky Road and one scoop of cotton candy in a waffle cone, please," Sage says as she finally puts in her order. The idea of the textural-and-flavor nightmare of her order sends shivers down my spine.

"I'll have one scoop of vanilla and one of chocolate in a bowl." That's how you order ice cream. Simple, easy.

Sage pulls out her wallet and pays for both of us, and a moment later we're both handed our ice cream. Beside the cash register is a toppings bar that a bunch of kids are swarming around, holding small spoons and dropping them over their ice cream cones to cover everything in sprinkles and M&M'S.

Of course, living life with absolutely no boundaries or order, Sage goes to the toppings bar and starts covering her cone. "Do you want any nuts or anything?"

I shake my head and stare at her, aghast.

"Do you know how disgusting these toppings bars are?" I ask, already knowing she either knows and chooses ignorance or has no interest in knowing at all. "These toppings are left to sit out all day long, with many hands reaching for spoons that don't get washed. The nuts and other toppings that you are covering your ice cream with are filled with bacteria from countless different people. That's how viruses spread. That's how pandemics happen."

She finishes coating her ice cream with candied pralines and turns with an amused smile on her face. "You're a pretty quirky person. I didn't expect that from you."

She turns around and walks outside toward a picnic table to take a seat before I can say anything back. I have to bite my tongue to keep from lashing out at the comment.

How can someone go through the world so recklessly like this? Honestly, I should have strangled her the other night. I would have done her a favor with a quick death.

I join her at the table. I guess I can do some one-on-one research with her, for recon purposes only. It's still in my revised schedule for the day, and I don't want Sage to continuously disrupt my life. She needs to die sooner rather than later.

Sage talks incessantly. She hardly stops, and she doesn't have a filter. She's excited about life. She's young and she has nothing tying her down. She goes from town to town reviewing Airbnbs, getting to live in places like this for free.

She's the perfect victim.

"I don't see my parents that much anymore," Sage says, licking a drip of ice cream off hands I know she didn't wash before eating. However, her statement catches my attention.

"Why is that?"

"It's kind of a silly story," Sage says, laughing and shaking her head as she leans forward. "My parents were major hippies—exhibit A being named Juniper Sage Featherstone. I grew up super sheltered in a commune with them, and because of that, there were so many experiences I didn't get to have. I don't know. I guess I resent them a little for that."

"And now that you're an adult, you're experiencing life on your own without letting them guide you." It's a story I've heard before. Sage may think she is some original, trailblazing free spirit, but she is nothing if not an amalgamation of all the people who have come before her.

"Exactly!" Sage replies, seemingly excited that I can see a part of her she thinks most people don't.

Ice cream is dripping down her arm, and it's all I can focus on. She doesn't seem shy about licking it off her hands, but she at least has the decency to get up and get a napkin when it's practically at her elbow.

I sit at the table and watch her for a moment as she holds her cone in her hand, still licking the atrocity, and grabs a handful of napkins in the other. Then she snaps a few ridiculous selfies. Turning away from her and looking out at the town, my eyes lock on someone's car.

Sitting in a silver sedan is a man looking in my direction. He is wearing a baseball cap, pulled down enough for the shadow to hide his face. A chill runs up my spine, and I'm immediately reminded of the search Peter told me about. He already sent me information eliminating Sage as the suspect. Apparently two IPs were searching for me, and the activity linked to Sage didn't raise any flags.

Without thinking, I start approaching the sedan. He lingers for a moment as he watches me step closer, but when I'm about ten feet away, and my ice cream is dropped on the ground beside me, he puts the car in drive and speeds off.

I run to the road, where I just catch the license plate number, repeating it over and over again in my head as I pull out my phone and text it to Peter so he can run it immediately.

"What's going on?" Sage asks behind me. I turn around, ready to give her an excuse about seeing an old friend but being mistaken. The lie is on the tip of my tongue, but something tells me she won't believe me anyway.

My phone buzzes in my hand before I can say anything. Peter has responded already. Looks like a rental car registered to a John Doe. What's going on?

Without a shadow of a doubt, I know that's who was searching for me. Now I just have to figure out why.

Chapter Ten

It's Sunday morning, which means it's time for my weekly scheduled check-in with my parents. Regardless of what either of us has going on, they always call me at noon. Other than that, I don't talk to them that often. I live on my own now, and I don't need their approval to do what I do.

The commune doesn't have internet, for the most part. The only place with access is the community office that they order supplies from. I've always found it to be majorly hypocritical that they constantly preach environmental activism and socialism while simultaneously handing their money directly to Jeff Bezos when they need a re-up on toilet paper and rolling papers.

Don't even get me started on the overpriced moon-charged crystal nipple clamps my mom sells online. *We don't talk about the nipple clamps anymore.*

I fall back on the couch in the living room and look at my Instagram while I wait for their call. I have a few posts scheduled to go up, but the analytics for my last post are already impressive. At a place like Scoops Ice Cream, I *had* to take some cutesy photos with spots of ice cream on my nose. Travis was glaring at me the entire time, but this is how I make my living.

I wish I was that cone!!! DarkHours99 comments with a string of drooling faces and fire emojis.

This time, he's not the only one making comments like that. There are about a dozen other guys under that parent comment making various suggestive comments about other things they'd like to see me lick. Normally I would laugh it off, but they rub me the wrong way now. Maybe it's because I'm in love with someone else that I'm offended by it.

I'm interrupted from my work when the FaceTime from my parents rings through. I sit up on the couch and move my hair out of my face before answering the call. Both of them are smiling in the frame, squeezed in together to wave at me.

"Juniper, hello!" my mom chimes through the video. She has a soft, gentle singsong voice that most people feel calmed by. Maybe it's the fact that I'm their daughter and have issues with the way they raised me, but it doesn't do that for me.

"Hey, guys, how are you doing?" I force myself to sound excited, not wanting to make them think something is wrong. I'm going to tell them about Travis, but I don't know how they'll react.

"Doing great!" my dad cheers. "Before I tell you the big news, I have to tell you a joke Steve just told me."

Mom rolls her eyes and slaps my dad playfully on the arm. "He's been telling everyone who will listen."

"Here it goes," my father starts, his voice filled with the excitement of a toddler on Christmas morning. "What do you call an alligator in a vest?" His smile widens, his eyes staring at me expectantly.

"I don't know, Dad. Tell me."

"An investigator!" He bursts out laughing, throwing his head back like he just heard this joke for the first time. My mom shakes her head, but her face lights up. She pretends she is annoyed by my dad, but in reality she loves his little quirks and dad jokes.

"Okay, I admit, that one is pretty funny." I don't laugh as hard as my dad, but I do find myself grinning widely.

My parents look at each other, smiling from ear to ear as my dad wraps his arm around her shoulders. Despite my own problems with them, they have a relationship that would be nearly impossible to live up to. They've known each other since they were in diapers, and ever since they could walk and talk, they knew they were soulmates.

Both of them grew up in military families, which I think is the biggest reason they became the mega-hippie flower children they are now. I never got to have a relationship with my grandparents because of it.

"We've been elected as the chairs for the commune's annual solstice festival," my dad excitedly says, pushing up his wire-frame glasses as he speaks.

I know it's impossible, but they both look older than they did last week. My memory of them is as a youthful, sun-kissed couple, though I'm sure nostalgia plays a big role in that. But now they look small—frail, even. My mom's usual auburn hair is speckled with gray, and the lines on her forehead are deep. Both my parents have smile lines around their mouths and eyes from decades of finding the inner harmony most people can't even dream of.

"What's going on with you?" my mom asks after they go into excruciating detail about the solstice festival. "Are you still at the cabin in Lake Lure?"

I sit up straighter as I prepare myself for the life-changing information I'm about to give my parents. I've dated people in the past, mostly other young people from the commune I went to school with. My parents believe in free love, and they've always been accepting of everyone I've introduced them to. Even though they've never given me a reason to doubt them, I have a feeling Travis is going to be different.

"I'm still in Lake Lure, and I have some news," I begin, watching the excitement grow on both of their faces. "I've met someone, and I think he's the one."

Both of them cheer at this information, excitement radiating through the screen. My mom claps her hands together in joy. "Tell us everything about him!"

Where to begin . . .

I tell them how we met and about our date at the ice cream shop—Travis might not think it was a date, but it had all the characteristics of one, so I'm counting it. For the most part, the story sounds like the plot of some cheesy rom-com movie, where you just *know* the characters will end up together.

"Okay, but how is he in the sack?" my mom asks out of the blue.

"Mom!" I roll my eyes at her bluntness.

"What? Sex is an important part of any relationship," she explains.

"Your mom is right," my father agrees. "Tim and Linda stopped having sex, and see what happened to them."

I'm somewhat curious to know what happened to Tim and Linda, but not enough to actually ask. I'd much rather keep talking about Travis.

"I'm not discussing mine or someone else's sex life with you," I say sternly, hoping they get the hint.

My parents look at me disapprovingly but don't push the subject further.

Thank fuck.

"So needless to say, I'm probably staying in Lake Lure for a while."

"But your travel channel? How are you going to keep that up? Doesn't that pay your bills?" My father raises a valid point.

"Well, I do have some money saved up, but also I don't really have to worry about money if things work out with Travis."

"Why is that?" my mom asks curiously.

"Travis is kind of a billionaire," I say, watching my parents' faces fall immediately.

This is why I didn't want to tell them.

"He is very smart. Founded a tech company when he was younger and sold it for millions."

"That's a lot of money for only one person," my dad says, shaking his head, unimpressed.

I don't want to entertain this conversation. I won't listen to them speak badly about Travis—my future husband. If they love me, they'll support him too. So I make up some excuse about having plans I need to rush to and hang up the phone, falling back on the couch with a huff.

I close my eyes, and I think about Travis, which immediately brings a smile to my lips. My parents may not know him, and doubt his sincerity because of their preconceived notions of what a man like him should be. But that doesn't stop me from feeling the buzz in my heart.

I grab my phone and walk toward the balcony, situating myself in a perfect ray of sunshine and snapping a few pictures. When I'm done, I post it to my story with the caption Never thought love could feel this good. I pick a trending song to put in the story with the picture and post it.

After only a minute of being on the internet for everyone to see, DarkHours99 replies to my story. I thought I was your one and only?

I ignore the comment and put my phone down, shaking it off as him just being flirty, as he always is. Then I get a notification on Instagram alerting me to our direct-message channel. What do you mean you're in love? Do I need to come out there so you and I can have a talk?

"Out *there*?" I say, sitting upright and furrowing my brows as I stare at our chat exchange. "He can't know where I am. Right?"

I look at my profile to see if there is any indication of where I currently am. I post travel content, so my followers know where I've been, but I stagger the content about the Airbnbs themselves so they never know where I am currently posting from. It's one of the many internet safety protocols nearly everyone in this industry has in place. Unfortunately, the picture I posted of myself at the ice cream shop very clearly has the name of the shop in the background.

Would someone actually try to find me? I've always thought the relationship DarkHours99 has with me is a little strange, but I never thought he would be a problem like this. Was I wrong all along?

I jump to my feet and slip on some flip-flops before I can think about it anymore. Luckily for me, I just so happen to be in a relationship with a tech genius who might be able to help me out.

I make my way over to his house, where I knock on his door and wait a few moments before I hear his feet pattering across the hardwood floors of his cabin.

"I thought we had an agreement?" Travis says, standing in the doorway, a hand firmly on the knob as he's prepared to close it in my face.

"Do you have a way to trace someone's messages or where they're coming from?" I ignore his first comment. We can play this cat-and-mouse game later. The worry must be clear on my face, because his entire demeanor changes.

"What's going on?" He opens the door wider so he can stand in front of me, but I slip through and invite myself inside. I hear a slight huff as the door closes, and he walks to the kitchen with me. The savory smell of what I'm guessing is lasagna fills my nose and makes my mouth water.

My stomach growls as I explain the whole situation, letting him know DarkHours99 has been a follower for a long time, and I never thought anything bad of it until now. He listens intently, as if he's hanging on every word I say. When I tell him about the most recent message I received, I see a flicker of anger in his eyes.

In a weird way, I feel as though I should thank DarkHours99 for this. This is proving to me that Travis *does* care. He might pretend he is this hard-ass who doesn't want to get close to people, but I've wormed my way into his heart, and I'm going to stay there. I'm a burrower.

"I'm just really scared right now," I say, shrinking myself down to look as meek and helpless as possible. If Travis is worried, I might be able to take advantage of the situation and get even closer. "I'm staying at Ryan's place all alone, and if this guy wants to do something, how am I going to stop it? Can I stay here with you? At least until—"

"Yes," Travis says, cutting me off before I finish.

And just like that, my heart swells, and I feel like I'm soaring through the air once again. Now *this* is a step in the right direction. With Travis and me sleeping under the same roof, our relationship is bound to develop.

"You're a lifesaver!" I run toward him, wrapping my arms around him for a hug. His entire body stiffens, and I stand on my tiptoes to give him a small peck on the cheek. "Thank you so much."

Turning and walking to the living room, I see him in a mirror, wiping his cheek with the back of his hand. That stings, but by the end of my stay here, he's going to be begging for more. I take a seat on the couch, making myself at home.

Chapter Eleven

TRAVIS

Who the hell does this man think he is? If anyone is going to hurt Sage, it's going to be me. He doesn't know what he's getting himself into.

I find myself mentally comparing myself to him. I'm above average in height, with a perfect BMI and athletic-fat percentage. My IQ is in the genius range, and my net worth is around two billion. I'm clearly superior to this guy in every way and the better option.

Sage takes a seat in the living room and starts talking about something I don't care to listen to. Her feet are on the couch, which is infuriating. She just walked over here in those godforsaken flip-flops, of course, and now she's putting her bacteria-ridden feet all over my couch.

I wonder what the pathogen-transfer rate is for this.

I'll google it later, right after I search for "how to get hippie foot stank out of microfiber."

I immediately get the disinfectant spray from the kitchen and spray a healthy amount on the spot where her feet have been. I regret having her stay here already, but it will be easier to learn everything about her if I have her close by.

I could do it now. Yeah. It could be swift and easy. She's already foolish enough to put her trust in a stranger. I can walk over to her and wrap my hands around her little neck and squeeze until her eyes are bulging out of her head.

"The commune has the solstice festival every year, and it's not like they do anything different," Sage continues, sitting upright. She crosses her legs underneath her so she almost looks like a pretzel sitting in the corner of my couch.

I feel a ringing in my head as her voice drones on and on about something senseless. Seeing her here now, all I can think about is Kevin and what she cost me. She owes me this. Her life. She doesn't understand just how much her mere presence has destroyed me since I've met her. Taking her life will be an easy solution.

I sit down on the couch beside her, looking at her without saying a word. Does she think I'm listening? Does she really think I care about whatever inane bullshit she's spewing off?

I could use a knife. I could stab her slowly in the side, watching as her eyes widen from the shock. Her entire body would tense, and her breath would quicken as she tried to rationalize what was happening to her. I could see the trust she so foolishly put into me vanish from her eyes as I tasted her distress.

Strangling feels more intimate, which I know someone like Sage might prefer. The proximity of our bodies while I hold her in my hands, feeling the life draining from her flesh, would be intoxicating.

I could poison her, but that's no fun. Plus, getting the right toxin on the black market is tricky and not worth the danger.

"But the post at the ice cream shop has really been taking off. It's mostly good, with the exception of the potential stalker here and there," Sage continues, droning on with a slight laugh.

Her stalker . . .

As much as I have loathed being around her, she might have just gifted me something I couldn't have dreamed of. A new victim.

A stalker isn't my usual target, but something about this one makes me want to kill him. I'll find a way to figure out who he is, kill him—then, when I'm done with that, I'll kill Sage. Just when she thinks she's going to be safe, I will obliterate those fantasies.

"I just don't know what I would do without you here," Sage says, scooching closer to me on the couch. Her hand is draped over the back, and her fingers are slowly moving closer to me.

The timer in my kitchen rings, and I jump to my feet. *Perfect timing.*

Without saying a word to excuse myself, I go to the kitchen and open the oven, seeing how the low-fat cheese on top of my veggie lasagna is golden brown and bubbling perfectly. I grab an oven mitt and pull it out, setting it on the counter to cool for two minutes.

"That smells heavenly," Sage says as she walks into the kitchen and looks at the glass pan filled with my dinner. I pull a knife from the kitchen block and hold it in my hand for a moment, wondering what it would be like to sink it into her flesh. "Can I have some?"

I'm pulled from my thoughts, and I shake my head, looking down at the steaming-hot lasagna. "This has been perfectly portioned for my dinner tonight and lunch tomorrow."

I know I told her she can stay, but she's already intruded upon my routines and schedule too much. This is how I operate. I make two portions of dinner, carefully assembled for my exact caloric needs. If I sacrifice part of my meal now, tomorrow for lunch I'll have to make something new. It's inefficient and wasteful—but someone like Sage doesn't care about that.

Maybe the knife is a better option. I grip it tighter in my hand as I look at her. She's moderately disappointed she can't have lasagna as well, but I don't care. I'm sure she has food at Ryan's cabin she can grab when she brings the rest of her belongings over.

"Is there any way I can repay you for letting me stay here?" she asks, turning around and pressing her back against the counter while staring at me with a half smile on her lips.

Trust me, you already have.

"It's fine," I say, taking the knife to the lasagna to cut a portion of it free.

She walks around the counter, slowly tracing her hand along the pristinely clean marble countertop. "There has to be some way."

Before I can say anything else, she drops to her knees in front of me, and I stop what I'm doing. The knife is still in my hand as I look down at her while her fingers cling to my belt. It takes her only a moment to undo the buckle and start unbuttoning my pants to free my cock.

She wraps her hands around me, and within an instant, my blood rushes from my head to my groin. I want to stop her, to tell her it's dinnertime. I don't have any scheduled pleasure time right now. I should push her away. I need to end this, but something stops me.

Her eyes shift from my swollen cock to my hand, where the knife is still firmly gripped. "I bet you're really into knife play, aren't you?" She laughs as she pulls her hand away from my cock to lift her shirt and bra up, exposing her breasts for me to see. "Maybe we should try that sometime?"

I can't help but smile. "Why wait?"

She opens her mouth and traces her tongue along my shaft, smiling as she watches it twitch in front of her. She lets go completely, admiring how hard she made me in such a short amount of time. My cock is already throbbing and begging for release, and I don't know if I can deny it.

I bring the knife to her throat, holding it there while she continues licking my cock eagerly. The sharp edge dances over her skin, but she doesn't seem fazed by it. If anything, she looks more turned on.

Right now Sage is vulnerable. She's on the ground in front of me, and I'm standing above her with a knife in my hand. It would be so easy to slam it into her, stabbing it through her ear. She wouldn't know what happened. There might be a few brief moments of confusion before her brain dies, but that would be it. She wouldn't even feel any pain, which is a better death than many of the others I've inflicted.

But it would be a shame to stop this now.

I'm torn. I want Sage gone so badly. This is what she deserves. But then I could potentially use her to get to her stalker and kill them both.

But her tongue feels so good . . .

I stare down at her, watching as she lathers my cock in her saliva. She smiles and winks before wrapping her lips around the tip. I let out a moan and feel my knees wobbling as she sucks gently, taking more of my shaft in her mouth.

"I thought you might like that," Sage says, then smirks as she does it again. Her tongue swirls delicately around my tip while she sucks on it, teasing the sensitive nerves there. She works me in her mouth, opening her jaw wider to take as much inside as she can.

Spit drips from her chin onto the floor, and I do my best to ignore it while she sucks me. She moans as she bobs her head up and down, careful not to get cut, letting her tongue graze along the underside of my cock. Each moan sends a small vibration through my dick that only heightens the sensation.

After a minute I'm not thinking about killing her anymore. She got lucky. My thoughts are no longer on how I would love to spill her blood on the floor, then going through my meticulous cleaning process to rid my home of any trace of her. All I can think about is how incredible her mouth feels around me.

She continues blowing me, moving slowly for a few minutes just to bring me close to the edge. She pulls her head away, staring at my twitching cock with admiration. She sticks out her tongue, gently teasing the tip as she sees how close I am to exploding.

"Are you going to finish what you started?" I ask, feeling the desire to come taking hold. I need this. Every moment with her mouth not wrapped around my dick feels like a moment wasted.

"I'm just admiring my handiwork," she jokes, licking the tip of my cock again with a soft giggle.

Pulling the knife away from her throat, I drop it and lower both of my hands to her face. Running my thumb over her wet lips, I pull down her jaw, opening her mouth wide for me. "I want you to take all of this in."

Sage nods and lets her mouth hang open wide as I move my hand away from it. I shove my cock in her mouth, loving the way she gags on it as I grab the back of her head and hold her steady. I pull her head closer, feeling how her throat clenches around me. Regardless, she stares up at me with an eager glimmer in her eyes.

"You like the way I fuck your face?" She can't speak, and she can't nod, but I see acknowledgment in her eyes.

I hold her head steady in my hands and start thrusting myself against her, letting my cock go as deep into her mouth as it possibly can. She gags on it with every thrust, the sensation of her throat bobbing up and down further pleasuring my aching cock.

"I want you to swallow every last drop of my cum," I say, staring down at her as I feel my cock ready to burst. The pleasure is overwhelming, and all at once I feel an explosion radiating through my body as my dick pulses.

I watch as my cum falls out of her mouth, mixed with her spit, with each pump as she does her best to swallow my entire load. I hold her steady the entire time, not giving her a moment of reprieve as I fuck her face relentlessly, waiting for every spasm to die down before I finally pull out of her.

Sage gasps for breath, immediately bringing a hand to her chest as she sits down on the ground. I stare at her, seeing the mess she made in my kitchen and feeling disappointed in myself. I had my chance again, and I let it slip through my fingers.

She looks up at me with a wide smile on her lips. "That was so hot. I can't wait to do that again."

I look at the knife on the counter one more time and pick it up. "If you don't mind, it's my scheduled dinnertime."

Sage stands up and lowers her shirt before walking out of the kitchen with a wink, leaving me standing there with my veggie lasagna.

Chapter Twelve

As soon as Travis has finished his dinner and put the leftover portions of veggie lasagna in their proper containers, he changes his clothes and prepares to help me gather my things from Ryan's cabin.

I wait for him in the living room and wonder how serious he is about his routines. He's made comments about them before, and a part of me always thought he was joking. Seeing him more intimately in his real life is opening my eyes to the fact that he might not have been.

It makes the fact that he's willing to throw off his entire routine to make sure I'm safe that much more romantic. I've never had a guy *sacrifice* something for me. Sure, asking him to interrupt a few minutes of his schedule to help me isn't that big of a sacrifice, but it's a romantic gesture that doesn't go unappreciated.

When I hear Travis approach, I quickly get up and start folding the blanket on the couch that I ruffled up.

"Oh my god, please stop what you are doing!" he yells as if I just triggered a museum alarm.

"What?" I ask, confused, as he rips the blanket from my hand and starts folding it the same way I did, only he makes sure that all corners line up exactly.

"That's not the proper way to fold a blanket. Please don't touch anything else unless it has step-by-step instructions." He finishes folding and places the blanket back on the couch.

"Sorry," I mumble, still not sure why everything has to be so perfect.

"Now, let's go," Travis says, looking at his watch as he hurries to the door. "I've only got an hour and fifteen minutes before I have work to do."

I jump to my feet and follow him out of the house. He unlocks the car, and I'm surprised when he doesn't open the door for me. Honestly, I'm glad he doesn't. If he had, he would have been *too* perfect, and I might have to try to find some kind of flaw with him.

I hop into the car and look around, impressed at how tidy it all is. Not only is the car in near-pristine condition, but it also smells like it was just cleaned. Considering how immaculate Travis's house is all the time, I can only imagine how detailed he is with his car.

Travis takes a seat behind the wheel, and I watch as he goes through a checklist in his mind, inspecting the rearview mirror and both side mirrors, and tests to ensure the blinkers make the proper sound when he signals. When he's done, he buckles his seat belt, adjusting it slightly around the neck, and looks at me with a blank stare.

"Seat belt." Travis watches me as he waits for me to comply.

"We're just driving right down the street. I have really sensitive skin, and it will chafe my neck," I say, brushing off the suggestion.

"Statistically, over fifty percent of accidents happen within twenty-five miles of home. Short trips give a false sense of security. The risk doesn't disappear because the destination is nearby." Travis pulls his hands from the steering wheel and rests them in his lap while he waits for me. "I wasn't asking you to put the seat belt on. I was telling you."

I don't argue with him. It's hard to bite back the smile as I think about just how much he cares. He doesn't have to say it, and that's what I admire about him so much. Everything he does shows me how much he cares about me. That whole spiel about traffic accidents is basically him telling me he doesn't want anything bad to happen to *me*.

I buckle the seat belt and stare at him with a smile on my face that I make no effort to hide. "What would I do without you?"

He shakes his head and puts the car in drive. "I can think of a lot of things that I would be doing without you."

I laugh and shake my head as I look out the window for the short but curvy drive. Travis is a meticulous driver. Even though no one else is on the road, when we come to a stop sign, he stops and looks both ways, not once, not twice, but three times to make sure no car randomly appears to T-bone us. He hovers exactly at the speed limit, never faltering and going above or beyond by a mere mile. I can't blame him; he clearly has precious cargo on board.

I've always been prone to the dramatic, and I find myself imagining the two of us getting in a horrific car accident when a deer runs out into the street. The car flips several times, and Travis barely manages to claw his way out of the wreckage. He's on his hands and knees, screaming my name, hoping to find me. When he finally sees me on the ground, I'm just barely holding on so I can cup his face one last time and tell him I'll miss him.

"Let's make this quick," Travis says, cutting through my daydream as he pulls into Ryan's driveway.

I lead the way, heading toward the cabin, unlocking the door and letting him in. He doesn't hesitate, and he immediately makes his way to the bedroom. I wrinkle my eyebrows as I pull the key from the knob and follow him.

He's acting like he's been here before, but Ryan mentioned that he doesn't even know who Travis is. That would mean the two of them never had dinner together or had drinks on the weekend. Travis had no reason to be in Ryan's house. So how does he know where the bedroom is right away?

"Such a slob," Travis says as he kneels in front of my two suitcases and starts throwing piles of clothes back in them. "When you're staying with me, I have rules. One of them is that you cannot leave things lying around like this."

"I'll be on my best behavior," I say, holding my hands up in front of me innocently. "I'm surprised you knew where to find everything so quickly. I didn't think you and Ryan were very close."

Travis stops what he's doing and looks at me, raising an eyebrow almost suspiciously. "It doesn't take an advanced degree in architecture to know how to find a bedroom. Besides, it was the only door that was open, and seeing all your clothes strewn all over the place, it was a logical conclusion."

I laugh and fold my arms, watching him as he tries to hastily throw my clothes in the suitcases. I can tell the disorganization is bothering him, and I feel a little ashamed, but I brush it off easily enough.

"Is that everything?" Travis asks as we stand by the door with two suitcases and a backpack filled with my laptop and filming equipment.

"Should be. If I've left anything behind, I can always come back," I say, practically pushing him out. I can hardly wait until I'm back in his cabin, playing house.

We get in the car, and Travis undergoes the same driving ritual he did leaving the first time. I put on my seat belt without prompting, and we head back to his house.

Travis hastily brings all my things to a guest room and sets them down before running off to his office, checking his watch the whole time to make sure he's still on schedule.

"I'll be about an hour. Then I want you to show me everything this guy has sent you," Travis says, looking over his shoulder briefly as he rushes into his office.

I stand in the center of his guest room, looking around curiously. I wouldn't expect someone like him to get a lot of company, so I'm surprised he even has a guest room. I plop down on the bed, testing how lavish it feels beneath me. For a room that probably gets no use, Travis spared no expense.

I wonder what his bed feels like. I bet it's perfectly suited for his exact needs, meticulously tested in an actual factory lab and not some hybrid memory foam mattress he got through a deal on Amazon. I don't know when, but Travis is eventually going to let me see it. After all, I'm going to be waking up next to him every day for the rest of our lives.

"Sage!" Travis calls from the other side of the door, jolting me out of my thoughts. I lost track of time daydreaming about the two of us, and I hurry to grab my laptop and meet him in the living room to go over all the details. "I have to go to sleep in two hours, so we don't have much time."

I open the laptop and pull up my Instagram account to show him everything. "I've been a content creator for two and a half years. I don't remember exactly when DarkHours99 started messaging me, but it couldn't have been long after I started."

I open our message exchanges, highlighting how he would often send me several messages in a row without any response, leaving me paragraphs upon paragraphs talking about how beautiful he thinks I am.

"He comments on literally everything after I post it. If I were to post something right now, within five minutes he would leave a comment, possibly even message me privately."

Travis leans forward on the couch, resting his elbows on his legs as he analyzes the messages between us. His eyebrows are furrowed, as if he's concentrating deeply. It warms my heart to see how much he cares about what I'm going through. He's truly interested in this issue of mine, and I'm thankful for that. Not a lot of women can land men who genuinely care about what's going on with them.

I guess I'm just one of the lucky ones.

"And all of the messages are this suggestive?" Travis asks, sitting up and looking at me with a hint of frustration in his eyes.

I have to bite the inside of my cheek to keep from squealing from excitement. He's actually frustrated—maybe even angry. He sees that someone has been harassing me, and he feels so connected to me that it bothers him too. I have him right where I want him. It's only a matter of time before he's falling head over heels for me.

I nod and lean forward to load up my profile to show him some of the comments being left on my public posts. As I do, I scroll to the bottom and see a new message I haven't read yet from him. **Why won't you answer me? Are you with him?**

Travis looks concerned again as he stares at the message.

"What am I supposed to do? He might know where I am, and he can do something to try to find me."

"He's not going to hurt you," Travis says with confidence in his voice that has me believing it. I look at him, feeling more appreciative for his presence than I ever have. I can read between the lines. He's going to protect me. He's never going to let this man do anything to harm me.

"I'll try to figure out where he's sending you messages from in the morning." Travis takes a deep breath as he stands up and stares down at me. "You should try to get some sleep tonight."

He turns around and walks away, presumably heading toward his bedroom to sleep for the night. *Alone. Tragic.*

"Thank you," I call after him, standing up and biting my lip as he turns around and nods. "Thank you for everything. You have no idea how scary it is to be alone. There are all kinds of bad people out there, and I'm glad I have you to help."

He smiles at me without saying anything and walks away.

I go back to the guest room and climb into bed, trying for what feels like hours to fall asleep. All I can think about are the messages DarkHours99 has sent and the possibility that he'll show up somewhere in town to confront me. I think about him breaking into Travis's house, and Travis taking care of the situation for me.

It puts a smile on my face. I just feel safe with him in a way I haven't with many other people. So, naturally, when I can't fall sleep, I go find him. I crack open his bedroom door, being as quiet as a church mouse, to find him sleeping on his back with the blankets perfectly tucked around him and his arms flat beside him. I don't know why I would expect him to sleep in any other position.

I tiptoe across the room and carefully pull up the blanket and climb in bed next to him. He doesn't stir at all. I don't want to wake him. He looks more peaceful now than he has ever since I've known him. Instead, I lie next to him, studying every inch of his face until I fall asleep.

Chapter Thirteen

I don't normally dream. I know it's a strange thing, but when I rest, it's silent. It's one of the only times I'm not thinking about my schedule and routine. I'm not thinking about killing. That's why dreaming about Sage is so strange.

We're sitting on the couch, completely naked, and I'm telling her all the ways I'm going to kill her online stalker, and out of nowhere she straddles me and starts grinding herself against me. It feels incredible, and the ecstasy surges through my body as she moves her hips against me.

"Tell me you want to be inside me, Travis," Sage's sultry voice meets my ear. Somehow she sounds both far away and nearby.

Nodding, I mumble, "Yeah." My cock slips inside her wet pussy, and I groan in pleasure.

I'm about to come when something feels off. I can't put my finger on it until I notice the couch is slightly crooked. "We have to fix that," I murmur, and to my surprise Sage agrees eagerly. We get up, and I move the couch while Sage fixes the rug. Then we sit back down on the couch without a word.

What a strange dream.

Sage rubs herself against me, and as I'm getting closer to my orgasm, I feel very real sensations in my body. I haven't felt anything like this since I was a teenager.

Somehow I manage to pull myself out of the dream realm and ground myself in reality to bring an end to it before I make a mess of my bedsheets. But then I open my eyes, and I'm not entirely convinced the dream is over.

With her shirt completely off, Sage is on top of me, fully seated on my cock as she moves her hips. Her eyes are closed as she tilts her head up, biting her lip hard as the pleasure starts taking hold of her. I blink a few times, dumbfounded at the situation I find myself in.

Sage has truly infiltrated every aspect of my life. First I couldn't get any work done because of her incessant need to bother me. Then she stole a kill away from me by ruining my chance when I planned on going out. Now she's forcing her way into my dreams, ending my sleep before I plan to myself.

"What the hell are you doing?" I say, grabbing her waist and holding her still as her eyes jolt open and she looks down at me in surprise.

What the fuck is she surprised about?

The surprised look on her face shifts into a smile as she grinds her hips more against me, bouncing up and down ever so slightly to tease herself on me.

"Isn't this how you wanted me?" Sage asks, and I find myself nodding. She grabs my hands and lifts them from her waist to her breasts, letting me hold them as she resumes her movements. "You can have me however you want. I just wouldn't want this morning wood to go to waste."

When I don't respond, she presses her hands against my chest and slides them under my shirt to feel my muscles. Her moans get progressively louder as she moves up and down on me, letting me feel just how wet she is already. I don't know how long she's been at this, but it can't have been that long. On average, nocturnal penile tumescence lasts for only a few minutes.

I want to push her off me and end this. I know what I really want to do with her, and the fact that she can't seem to keep her hands off me is only complicating the matter. But fuck . . . she feels so good.

Her pink hair is hanging around her shoulders, tousled from the night's sleep and moving freely as her body rocks. Her tits are perfect too. My hands are still on them, and I can't help myself as I squeeze and flick my fingers over her hard nipples. She gasps and smiles, moving her hips a little faster.

It feels amazing, and from the way her body is twitching and shaking, I know it feels good for her too. But even though I'm enjoying the sight hanging over me, it's not what I want. Sage needs to know that I'm the one in control.

She's ruined enough things for me. I'm not going to let her ruin this as well.

I push her off me, immediately grabbing her and tossing her down on the bed. She squeals with excitement, spreading her legs wide for me to see her pussy on full display. She's glistening from everything she's done so far, and it takes a lot for me to hold back.

I position myself between her legs, immediately shoving my cock deep inside her. She closes her eyes and cries out as she takes every inch of me. My hands climb up her body, stopping briefly to admire her tits once again. My eyes linger on her neck.

I could do it now. Bring an end to all of this.

Nobody's going to be looking for her for a while, and that would give me all the time in the world to properly clean up the crime scene and dispose of her. She won't even know what's coming.

My hands find her neck, and I squeeze gently, feeling how her throat tenses and bobs up and down at the pressure. The sight of her neck completely swallowed by my hands is invigorating, and I harden even more.

But when I look into her eyes, I'm disheartened. I expect to see fear and anxiety, but I don't. She's excited. She moves her hands to hold mine, almost encouraging me to grip tighter. I'm a man she barely knows, and I'm choking her in bed, for God's sake!

What the hell is wrong with her?

I thrust my cock in and out of her, feeling how her pussy clenches around me, begging me to keep going and give it some release.

I'm at a crossroads. I want nothing more than to grip tighter until she's clawing at my arm to fight me off. I can perfectly imagine it. I stop moving and put all my weight on her throat, squeezing even tighter until I see her lips turn purple. Her fingers dig into my arm, and she tries to fight me off, but she can't. At the very end, she'll realize that it was me she should have been worried about all along.

But for some godforsaken reason, I can't bring myself to do that. As much as I tell myself I want that, I can't do it. I've had every opportunity to end her life, and I found some kind of excuse not to. And now she's here, staying in my home, splayed out before me once again, ready to have her life stripped away from her, and I can't do it.

"That feels so good," Sage moans through everything I'm doing. I feel her throat bobbing under my grip, her voice vibrating against her skin. "I like things a little rough."

I stare at her, gripping her neck a little tighter with one hand as I push her leg up with the other. I slam my cock into her as hard as I can. The headboard shakes and bangs against the wall with each thrust. I'm glad I don't have any neighbors, because I would have a possible noise complaint on my hands if I did. Sage is screaming at the top of her lungs as I fuck her.

With each thrust of my hips, I feel my frustration growing more and more. The only thing I want to do, I can't. I have a mental block I would give anything to get rid of. But if I can't kill her, I can at least have this.

I lose myself in the motions, squeezing her neck tighter and releasing, giving her just enough time to gasp for breath before gripping her again. Her eyes practically roll back in her head, and her entire body spasms below me when she finally comes.

Her pussy convulses with each thrust and sends me over the edge, pulling every drop of my cum deep inside her. When I'm done, I let go of her throat and pull out of her. There's a clear handprint on her skin, a small but temporary reminder of what I couldn't do. I sit on the edge of the bed with my elbows on my knees, staring at the floor.

What the hell has gotten into me?

Sage moves closer, her hands climbing up my back to gently massage my shoulders. "You know, you're the only man I've ever met who's more stressed out after sex than before."

She doesn't know the half of it. I take a deep breath and look at her, seeing the afterglow of our morning escapade coloring her cheeks. Her eyes are pale blue, glimmering in the sunlight. I can just make out the speck of brown in her iris, a minor flaw in an otherwise perfect appearance. She looks peaceful. Happy, even.

"I guess I'm too busy thinking about the person who wants to kill you," I say, keeping my voice monotone. The smile on her lips falls, and for the first time I see worry clouding her eyes. There's a storm of anxiety brewing behind them that tastes like victory to me.

She sits up and rolls off the bed, her feet padding against the floor somewhere behind me. I smile to myself. Once again, I have control.

Reaching for my phone, I google "is it normal to be horny and homicidal at the same time?" Before reading the first listing, I abort. I clear my search history just in case the NSA is watching. Plus, I have more important things to do. I need to analyze this dream state I was in earlier.

I grab a notepad and pen from my nightstand and start scribbling everything down, complete with threat levels and a totally unnecessary arousal chart. Only to rip it all up and throw it in the trash. It's all compromised data anyway. Plus, I really should be worried about the mystery man who tailed me at Scoops instead.

Chapter Fourteen

After the blow job last night and morning sex that ended with a somewhat unsavory conversation, the last stop on my thank-you tour is breakfast. Maybe I can make him a soft, buttery croissant—hot, flaky, maybe a bit moist, and yeah, definitely leaving some crumbs.

Wait. Am I comparing sex to a pastry?

I blush at my own internal thought.

Travis can butter my biscuit any day.

Don't get me wrong, if Travis wants to make me blow my back out every day while I'm in Lake Lure—or for the rest of my life, for that matter—he can. But these acts are the only thing I can really give him to thank him for stepping in and helping me out.

Travis's kitchen is stocked. His fridge is filled with a myriad of fresh meats, vegetables, fruits—just about any healthy stuff you can imagine. To absolutely nobody's surprise, it's meticulously organized. In such a way that I actually have trouble finding things.

"Come on, he's got to have tomatoes here somewhere," I say to myself, shaking my head at the organizational system while I dig through a crisper drawer of vegetables.

"You won't find any fruits in the vegetable drawer," Travis says over my shoulder.

"Please don't tell me you're one of those guys?" I close the fridge and look at him with feigned exasperation. Travis looks confused as he puts on a pot of coffee. "You know, one of the *tomatoes are fruits because it has seeds* people."

"Is that why you think tomatoes are fruit?" Travis raises an eyebrow and leans against the counter while he waits for me to answer. I just shrug. "Everything in the fridge is classified by what it is. There are larger subsections: meat, dairy, fruits, and vegetables. Each of those has their own subsections, to be more specific."

Travis pushes himself away from the counter and walks over to the fridge, opening it to point to everything as he explains. I watch, genuinely intrigued by whatever process this is.

"Tomatoes are fruits because they grow from the flower of a tomato plant—"

"And they have seeds," I interrupt, standing my ground that it is a characteristic of a fruit.

"In my house, you'll find them with the berries," Travis continues, not paying my comment any attention. He opens a drawer in the fridge filled with your typical berries: raspberry, strawberry, blueberry, etc. Right next to them, where they undoubtedly should not belong by any normal person's standards, are tomatoes.

I know he has his reasoning, and I'm not one to argue, so I leave it at that. I smile and walk toward him, reaching into the berry bin and grabbing a few tomatoes. "I hope you worked up an appetite this morning, because I'm making shakshuka."

"What's the caloric content of that?" Travis stares at me with genuine curiosity that I almost think is a joke.

"I'm not entirely sure," I say. "But it can't be much. It's mostly water-dense vegetables and eggs."

I can see that Travis wants to say something else, but he thinks better of it and goes to the counter and picks up his phone. There's no doubt in my mind he's googling the average calories in shakshuka.

"Do you like to cook?" I ask, chopping the tomatoes on a cutting board while I glance at him eagerly. He doesn't say anything right away. I clear my throat, and he looks away from his phone and nods. "I bet you're really into healthy eating and all that stuff, aren't you? It's funny how most rich people are like that, right?"

He looks at me and nods, not being forthcoming with the conversation at all.

"Do you have a favorite meal?"

"Eating to me is a necessity, not something I particularly enjoy." The coffee maker beeps, and he jumps to his feet to pour himself a cup of black coffee.

"If only I could be like that." I laugh; throwing together the rest of the ingredients for the shakshuka and putting them in a pan to sauté. "It would make life so much easier, wouldn't it? I could just eat healthy all the time, and I'd never have two a.m. cravings for McDonald's."

Travis leans against the counter and sips his coffee, nodding as I speak. Ever since I've known him, which admittedly has been only a week, he hasn't been that much of a yapper. Compared to me, anybody seems like the strong silent type. I love to talk; I practically haven't stopped since I said my first word. I've never been one to appreciate a moment of silence either. But right now, as I watch Travis looking like a sexy snack, I can't help but imagine him shirtless.

With my mind clouded, I reach for the paprika, taking a whiff of the spice. I realize too late it must have been cayenne pepper I grabbed, because the next thing I know, I'm thrown into a coughing fit.

My eyes are watering by the time I'm done, and Travis is watching me like I'm crazy.

"Spice of love, baby," I manage to rasp out, making Travis only shake his head at me.

It takes another few seconds before I'm back to normal. Then I do what I do best. Talk. "Well, I love to cook. It's something I've always enjoyed. Food was pretty bland back in the compound. That's the real reason I left." I laugh and stir the onions and garlic in the pan, looking at him as if I'm holding for applause. "So I started taking over meals in my household. I did everything I could to spice up the bland, boring meals we were always eating. I found a real love for the craft while I was doing that. It was especially cool because everything was farm to table. It's a fully self-sustaining commune."

Travis perks up at that, setting his mug of coffee down on the counter and staring at me. "The commune has animals there you raise for consumption?"

I nod, focusing on the next step of the cooking process. "Oh yeah. Granted, most of the residents are vegetarian or vegan, but they didn't want to be restrictive on types of diets. The founders of the compound cared more about the practices of the meat industry than the act of eating meat, anyway."

Travis nods again. I can tell he's losing some interest in my story, and I feel almost desperate to get it back. Having him hanging on my words is a dream come true, and even if he's a little shy, I'm savoring every moment of this conversation.

"In the homeschooling program the commune enrolled us in, they have rotations with the animals," I say. He perks up again, and I feel my heart jitter. "It was one of my favorites. We got to work in the barns and see the whole process of raising these cattle. There was a time I wanted to be a farmer too. It was nice. It felt like they were pets for a time."

"I was never allowed to have pets growing up," Travis says. *Finally!* I want to drop to my knees and thank the Lord above that Travis is finally sharing something with me. "My sister was for a while, then I killed her hamster, and our parents never let her get another."

Okay. Not exactly what I was imagining we'd be talking about, but I guess I'll take it.

"Oh god, your sister must still hate you for that." I laugh and brush it off, not wanting to make him feel weird about admitting to that.

"She's dead too." His voice is cold and monotone as he says it. I feel a chill run up my spine, and I can't shake it off. Travis is still leaning against the counter, his face completely stoic as he sips his coffee once again.

I never thought I would say this about Travis, but that was a bit of a red flag. I suppose everybody has some of them. Lord knows I'm not perfect. But the way he so bluntly and emotionlessly said that made the hair on the back of my neck stand up.

"Did you ever get to see any of the animals being butchered?" Travis gives only a brief moment of pause between these statements.

My throat goes dry at the question, and I shake my head without saying a word. Why would he ask me something like that? I just told him how much I loved those animals, how they were like pets, and that's what he chose to ask?

That's two major red flags standing up at exactly the same time.

"You seem really interested in that." I laugh nervously, trying to shrug it off as best as I can. "Honestly, it's giving off serial killer vibes."

I force a laugh and nudge him on the shoulder, expecting him to break character and join in the laughter. For him to tell me it was just a joke, and he was yanking my chain to see how I'd react. But he doesn't do any of that.

Instead, he just stares at me and sips his coffee while I turn off the stove burner and prepare the next step of the recipe. I can't ignore the crawling sensation all over my body. All my life, I've heard countless stories of people who have been in the presence of danger and haven't trusted their gut instinct quick enough. But that can't be what's happening right now.

I slept in his bed last night. He has had ample opportunity to do something to hurt me, and he hasn't. I might just be overreacting.

My phone dings on the counter, and I jump, nearly dropping the steaming pan of vegetables on the floor. Travis watches as I set it down on the counter and grab it to look at whatever it is. I'm desperate for a distraction.

My heart stops when I see who the notification is from. DarkHours99. If I can't have you, nobody can.

There's nothing else. Only a message he sent yesterday that I haven't responded to. I feel a chill creeping over me again, and I know I must look as pale as a ghost. This message is undoubtedly a threat. Before, I could have been reading into things too much, but I know for damn sure I'm not now.

"What is it?" Travis says. He walks toward me and grabs the phone out of my hand, looking down at the message for himself. He lets out a slow exhale before running his fingers through his hair.

"This is serious now, isn't it?" I gulp as I try to grapple with the severity of that message. "Maybe I should just go to the police. They have resources to find him, and they can stop him wherever he is."

Travis shakes his head and sets the phone down on the counter, forcing a calm look on his face. "You don't have to worry about him."

For the first time, I can see the subtext in his words. There's a hidden meaning in what he's saying that is all too clear. Does he mean that he could hurt him? Is Travis a dangerous man?

There's a chance I have inadvertently come to the worst person for help in this situation. Sure, I've googled him and scoured every corner of the internet to learn everything I can about the reclusive man standing before me. That doesn't mean I know him.

If he could hurt a stranger, does that mean he could hurt me? I look down at my hands as the thought races through my mind. No, he wouldn't hurt me. He's had plenty of chances, and I'm perfectly fine. In fact, I'm better than fine. I'm here, cooking breakfast for someone I truly care about.

If Travis wanted to hurt me, he would have. I have to trust him.

Chapter Fifteen

Sage's breakfast is surprisingly palatable. I've never had shakshuka before, but I wouldn't be opposed to having it again. After all, the recipe was relatively simple, and it is a very healthy and fibrous breakfast. She doesn't say much while we eat. I know that's from her own worries about the message from her stalker, but it is a pleasant change of pace.

It makes me think that even with her here, I might have some semblance of normalcy. For the briefest moment, I think things might not be all bad with her around. As long as she stays out of my way, I think we'll be fine.

The thought has barely entered my mind when Sage reaches for the pepper in haste, knocking down both the salt and pepper shakers, spilling grains everywhere.

"I'm sorry!" Sage blurts out before adding, "You look like I just killed your dog."

This is worse.

Okay, maybe I'm being a tad dramatic here, but this feels worse. Sage tries to get up to clean it, but I stop her, knowing she won't do it right anyway.

"I'll Venmo you for emotional damage," she says when I'm done cleaning her mess.

"You can't afford me."

She giggles. "Yeah, probably not."

After we finish eating, I promptly clean up her mess. She attempts to help, but her attention to detail is clearly not as defined as mine.

"Leave me your log-in information. I'm going to try to find who this guy is," I say as I take a towel that is meant for drying hands away from her before she wipes the counter with it. "You should spend some time outside. Leave me to my work for a while. I turned the hot tub on this morning, so it should be perfect now."

Sage nods, taking a few deep breaths. "I could really use that right now."

She offers me a smile and squeezes my forearm before bounding off toward the guest room. I don't want to think about the mess that has probably swallowed that room whole since she's been here. It hasn't even been a full day, and I feel it's safe to assume the worst.

I'll wait until she's outside before I go to my office. The last thing I need is her walking in and disrupting me while I'm in the middle of preparing for something that will help her. She's already been enough of a distraction. This is my chance to get back to my routine. She better not fuck this up.

Sage walks out of the guest room in a skimpy pink bikini she's almost spilling out of. The blood immediately drains to my cock as I watch her saunter through the living room and make her way out the door.

It's not time for that. I force thoughts of her away and shake my head before heading to my office.

I take a seat behind the desk, sinking into my plush leather desk chair and letting the anticipation for what I'm about to do fill my chest. This is the part I love. The planning, the prep work. Finding out everything I can about someone and figuring out how to use it against them.

I live for this.

Sage gave me her Instagram account log-in information, so I start there. Her stalker has a faceless profile. I immediately know this man uses some kind of burner account to keep his online proclivities private. More often than not, with accounts like this, you'll find some kind of clue as to who they really are.

People are often vain enough to follow themselves with their burner accounts because one extra follower on their main will make them look that much more appealing to the people in their real lives. If they're not following themselves, they might follow people they know in real life. I wouldn't put it past a man like this to follow female coworkers and friends with this account just to contact them personally and harass them, thinking he can get away with it.

I start digging. I look through every post on the profile, most of which are memes and inspirational quotes that lean heavily toward the red pill community. Not surprising. There are no personal photos on the entire account, nor is there anything he has been tagged in. That means there's no indication through the content alone of who this man is.

I look through his followers list to see it's mostly bots that mass follow random people, with a few up-and-coming OnlyFans models following him too. The list of people he's following is much greater. About a third of the people are famous actors and comedians, and the rest are all women. Some profile pictures look harmless, which I think could be people he knows in real life. Some of them are obvious influencers, like Sage.

After skimming through the list, I don't think I'm going to find anything, other than the fact he might have some kind of pornography addiction.

If I can't freely get information on him, I'll lead him into a trap. It doesn't take long for me to throw together a website for Sage. Honestly, she should probably have one already, but that's a conversation for another time.

I saw him mention the possibility of Sage creating a wish list for her fans to purchase things for her. Clearly, he thinks that will buy him some favor with her, and he desperately needs that because he doesn't get validation anywhere else in life.

I open the chat exchange and start typing a message to him. Sage doesn't respond to him a lot, but I do my best to mimic her voice as I type. Hey! Trust me, you've nothing to worry about. In spite of everything I believe in, I attach an emoji that's blowing a kiss. I've just been really busy filming some new content. I think you might find this especially interesting.

She uses a lot of emojis. I cringe as I attach another to the message. I attach the link to the end and open the software I have and wait.

The message is read almost instantly, which comes as no surprise. I can imagine this man seeing a message from her pop up and immediately dropping everything he is doing to read it. His self-worth hinges entirely on this, and I pity him.

Immediately after, I get a ping on my software, letting me know someone has clicked on the link to the website I created. "People make it too easy."

I smile to myself as his IP address is given to me freely. All I had to do was throw together a mediocre website with a few pictures of her embedded in it.

Not seeing any new content here. But I can't wait to see what you have to show, babe! he replies.

Eli Morrow. Thirty-five, lives in Birmingham, Alabama. He works from home as a social media and data analyst for a men's health vitamin line that has far too many bought followers on Instagram and Facebook. I would assume their sloppy business is Eli's doing, knowing what I know about him.

He doesn't look anything like I pictured. I was imagining some grimy man-child in a basement, but the pictures I see of him standing in front of his Christmas tree with his fiancée don't look anything like that.

"I bet Carol doesn't know anything about your little indiscretions, does she?" I shake my head as I scroll through years of pictures detailing his life. He lives online. He has thousands of friends and followers on his main account, yet nobody but his fiancée has tagged him in anything.

I can read him like a book. He lives for online validation from strangers because if people who don't know him think he's great, that must mean something. In real life, he's sad and lonely. He might be engaged, but neither of them is happy. Eli isn't bad-looking, but he's not good-looking enough to go out and get anyone he wants, so he's happy to settle with someone he thinks will stay with him. I'm sure Carol thinks he is the charming, loyal man he's portrayed himself as for so long.

A squeal of laughter from outside catches my attention, and I look up from the computer to see Sage in the hot tub. She's standing up with a wide smile on her face, looking not at me but at a squirrel in the distance, water dripping down her perfect body, making her glisten in the sun. I lick my lips, staring at her, not thinking any better of it.

Her tits are practically begging to be free from that bikini top, and I want nothing more than to go over and untie it myself. She lowers herself back into the water and calms down when the squirrel scampers off. I watch as she closes her eyes and relaxes against the side.

I try to turn my attention back to my search, but my mind is tainted with images of Sage once again. I think about waking up this morning with her riding me, how good it felt to have her pussy wrapped around me like that. How much she liked when I choked her.

"No," I say. I clench my fists and focus on the screen, trying to force every thought of her out of my head. I thought this was done. I thought I was going to be able to do my research without her intruding on it.

Maybe I can't have her around after all. It's never going to work. As long as she's here, I'm going to be distracted, and that's going to ruin me. I'll do it after Eli.

When he's gone, I'll kill her. I close my eyes and think about exactly what I want to do. I imagine walking through the front door with a knife in my hand. She's asleep on the couch as I approach, ready to plunge the blade into her chest.

But as I get closer, the image shatters. It's ripped away from me before I can get to the most gratifying part. I try again, imagining strangling her while she's in the shower, but just as my hands wrap around her throat, the image morphs into the memory of this morning.

I'm going crazy. I'm losing my fucking mind.

No matter how many times I try to imagine what her face looks like when the life slips away and her eyes turn cold and dead, the image dissipates before it comes to fruition. I can't kill her. Not even in my own fucking mind.

Frustration spreads through every vein in my body, and I feel a prickle behind my eyes, needing to relieve it. That's normally why I kill. The urge gets unbearable, and I don't know how I can go on without conceding to it.

The alarm on my watch rings, letting me know that my research time is over. I have an hour of free time. I don't know what I want to do with it, which is frustrating in and of itself. It's an entire block of my day that I don't have planned out like I normally would.

I stand up and walk out of my office, lingering in the living room for a few moments as I try to come up with a plan. My mind bounces between Eli and Sage and Kevin and everyone else who came before them.

Footsteps on the deck catch my attention, and I look up to see Sage standing outside the hot tub, waving at me. I ignore her at first, taking a seat on the couch and turning on the TV. If I can't focus on killing, I can at least focus on current events.

I try to watch the news. Bombings, terrorism, billionaires acting in their own self-interest, panic over mass recalls of car parts. Nothing new. Sage keeps her eyes on me as I try to avoid looking at her.

Eventually I give up and can't take my eyes off her. She walks around casually, admiring the tree line as she leans against the railing.

Maybe I can push her off the balcony. It's not a big fall, but it could possibly break her neck. If not, she could hit her head on a tree stump and die that way.

My eyes land on the curve of her ass, and that thought fades away like all the others. She turns around and smiles at me, waiting a moment before walking toward the door and opening it.

"Are you just going to watch, or are you going to come join me?" Sage asks, flashing me a coy smile.

I turn off the TV and stand up, following her outside. I don't know what it is, but it feels like I'm in a dream when I'm around her. It's like she has some kind of spell over me and I can't control what I'm doing.

Sage is temptation. Something intangible that has somehow manifested into a living, breathing creature walking around and dictating what I do. How the hell am I ever supposed to resist this?

"I'm not wearing a bathing suit," I say as I stand in front of the hot tub.

Sage shrugs and reaches behind her to untie the top of her bikini. Her tits are completely free, nipples hard against the cool breeze flowing around us. The bottoms are next to go, and she runs her hand along the curve of her ass while smiling at me.

"Neither am I."

I slip out of my clothes and climb into the hot tub behind her, acutely aware of how naked we both are. Sage sits across from me, spreading her arms out over the back of the hot tub and letting me get a full view of her tits . . . before she starts rubbing them slowly.

I don't like this. As I watch her, she has a control over me that I can't explain. My body reacts to the slightest provocation of hers, and suddenly I'm putty in her hands. I can't have that. She needs to know I'm the one in control.

"I want you to suck my cock," I say. Sage raises an eyebrow as I stand up and walk toward her. My cock is already stiff, and she takes it in her hand to rub it without saying a word.

"I thought you'd never ask," she says moments before her tongue is wrapping around me again.

Within moments, her lips envelop me, and she's sucking my cock deep into her throat. She's enjoying every second of this, and for some reason that irritates the fuck out of me. No matter what I say or do, she is impossible to control.

Her head bobs up and down on the length of my shaft as I run my fingers through the mess of pink hair she has piled in a bun above her head. I pull the clip off and toss it aside, letting her hair fall free as I grab a bunch of it in my hand.

She moans as I grip it tight, pulling it slightly as I push her head closer to my groin. Sage stares up at me, unable to smile, but if I had to guess, she would if she could.

I watch her, trying to ignore the thought of her enjoying what's happening as I savor the unintentional sounds escaping her throat as she swallows my cock. My fingers lace through her hair as I hold her against me, feeling how I throb more and more as I get closer.

When I let go of her head, she immediately backs away, gasping for air as she stares at my still-hard cock. Her tongue is on it, tracing the shaft hungrily, like she can't wait to taste every part of it. One of her fingers slides between her legs, and I watch as she inserts it inside herself.

"I never said you could touch yourself," I say. She raises an eyebrow, stilling the motion of her arm before pulling her fingers away from her pussy.

That's more like it. For once she's doing what I want her to do. She's listening to me, and I have some control in this situation.

"You'll come when I tell you that you can," I say, grabbing her head once again to bring it back to my cock.

She wraps her lips around it again and takes all of it in her mouth, moving her head up and down faster as my body reacts to her touch. It doesn't take long before the pleasure overtakes me, and I have to steady myself against the back of the hot tub as I explode down her throat.

Sage swallows every drop of my cum, and when she's done, she stares at me expectantly. I know she wants it to be her turn. I'm not going to give her that satisfaction.

"My free time is almost over." I climb out of the hot tub and grab one of the towels to dry off before walking back to the house.

I feel good that I've regained some semblance of control, but when I look over my shoulder, Sage is smiling at me eagerly. I can't fucking win with her.

Chapter Sixteen

SAGE

Travis is too busy working to spend a lot of time with me after our brief hot tub rendezvous. It was such a turn-on, and I'm a little bit disappointed we're not doing anything else because he's busy. But the more time I spend away from him, the more time I have to think.

We don't have dinner together because he locks himself in his office doing God only knows what in there. I don't know what he's working on. He's a genius, so there's a chance he has something more up his sleeve. But I have a sinking suspicion it's something else.

I open one of the kitchen cabinets, trying to hunt down some snacks, but instead I stare at an entire shelf of notebooks labeled "Knife Maintenance Log." Slightly freaked out, I walk back upstairs to rest for a little bit.

I lie awake in the guest room, staring at the ceiling as I run through recent events in my head. His comments at breakfast have stuck with me all day, and I can't shake them, no matter how hard I've tried. On top of those comments, there's undoubtedly something off about him.

I can't take it anymore, so I grab my phone, searching for any information I can about Travis's sister. I don't know what I'm looking for, but I need some kind of clarity that he had nothing to do with her death.

Even though Travis is a public figure, I don't find much about his family. I have to scroll for a while until I find an obituary for Leah Blacksburg. My heart stills as I click on the link and skim through the article, searching for the cause of death.

A car accident. Travis was in the car with her when it happened, and he survived. Leah didn't.

I feel a tear come to the corner of my eye, and I'm not sure if it's sympathy for Travis or relief that he didn't have anything to do with her accident. Even though I know he's innocent of that, I can't stop thinking about everything else. Once the thought takes hold of my mind, it's like an infection I can't shake off.

Every interaction we've ever had replays in my head as I carefully analyze each moment to figure out what it is. I sit up, wrapping the covers around my shoulders to stave off the evening chill while I think.

The first time we met, our meet-cute, he told me about Ryan as if he knew him, and Ryan had no idea who Travis was. Okay, that's a little strange, but in Travis's defense, he is a very wealthy public figure. It's beneficial for him to know who he surrounds himself with—personally and geographically.

After we got off on the wrong foot, I brought him cookies, and I saw an awful lot of bleach in his house. Now, his house *is* immaculate, but it was already squeaky clean when I saw it for the first time.

Then there was the night he almost killed me with his car. He was wearing leather gloves, dressed in all black. He looked like a sexy cat burglar.

A chill runs down my spine as I think about the footage I have of him standing behind me and watching while I filmed. I grab my phone and look for it, zooming in on his face once again as he watches me closely.

"I was there to strangle you," I whisper, remembering what he said to me when he found me on his fence after I asked why he was sneaking around Ryan's house. I jump to my feet and shake my head.

This can't be true. What are the odds I meet a possible serial killer in person, really? They can't be that big.

I think about all the cases I've listened to on the true crime podcasts I love. My blood runs cold when I remember the *Pretty Grim* podcast about Lake Lure and all the missing people.

"What the fuck?" I say to myself as I pace back and forth in the room. "Missing people in a small town, large quantities of bleach, breaking into Ryan's house, and a perfect kill outfit. Oh my god."

I run my fingers through my hair as I tiptoe out of the room. The evidence is already astounding, but it's human nature to try to make connections where there may not be any. There could be perfectly logical explanations for all these things that I just don't see. I need more evidence.

The Travis I know wouldn't do anything like this. He's helped me many times already. Hell, he could have killed me at any moment since I've been here, and he hasn't.

All the lights are off throughout the house, and Travis's bedroom door is closed. I assume he's in there sleeping, and I'm careful to be as quiet as possible. The last thing I need is to wake up the person I suspect of being a serial killer while I'm snooping for evidence. That's bound to go well.

I start in the kitchen, not finding anything of use aside from the extremely sharp knife set. For someone who's not a big fan of cooking, that is a little strange. The living room is a wash. It barely looks like Travis even uses it, so I don't find anything there.

Eventually I tiptoe my way into the garage and start looking around. Of course, it's a big garage. Travis has two cars here, one small and environmentally friendly electric car and an oversize SUV—notably the one he was driving when he almost ran over me.

Along the side of the wall is a stack of something covered with a gray tarp. Everything in here is as clean as the rest of the house, which would strike me as odd if it were anyone but Travis I was snooping on.

I hold my breath as I approach the tarp, carefully pulling it off the pile to reveal countless bottles of bleach stacked up near each other.

"Why would anyone need this much bleach?" I ask. The question is rhetorical because I already have a good idea. Next to the bleach are bundles of rope and packs of zip ties he's purchased in bulk.

I turn my attention to the SUV, which I'm almost positive he was planning something nefarious with the night he almost hit me with it. In the back, lining the trunk, is plastic sheeting that I have no doubt is specifically there to make his life a little easier. At least, it'll be easier for him to dispose of evidence.

I got what I came here for, but I still don't understand. A stone forms in my chest before it plummets into my stomach, and I feel like I'm going to be sick.

How could I have been so wrong? I've put so much trust in Travis, and he's not who I thought he was.

My eyes widen at the idea of him coming in and spotting me, knowing he needs to get rid of me before I cause a problem for him. I cover the bleach as quickly as I can and turn off the light to hurry back to my bed. I don't exactly feel safe right now, but I need to play along with the status quo until I can get away. He can't know that I know anything about this.

As soon as I close the garage door, the lights in the hallway turn on, and I freeze. I turn around to see Travis staring at me with his arms folded in front of him. By the panicked look that is no doubt on my face, he has to know exactly what I just saw.

I take a deep breath and prepare for the worst. *No use sugarcoating this now.* "Are you a serial killer?"

The words are out, and there's no way to take them back. I'm suddenly acutely aware of how much larger he is than me and how I'm standing in the middle of *his* house, which he knows like the back of his hand. How could I be so stupid?

"And what if I am?" Travis says as he slowly steps toward me. His face is completely calm and stoic, unbothered by my discovery.

"Are you going to kill my stalker?" My heart is pounding in my throat, and I flex the muscles in my arms to keep them from trembling.

"Yes. I'm planning on it." Once again, his voice is emotionless. He just confessed that he's planning a murder, and there isn't a flicker of regret or even excitement on his face.

The next question I need to ask is difficult. I feel the words bubbling in my chest, and I struggle, pulling them free. Travis watches me, waiting for me to say what he knows is coming, but I can't bear to ask.

"I'm not planning on killing you anymore."

"Anymore?" I'm shaking now, and he can see that, which makes me angry. The man just told me he was planning on killing me, and now I'm cowering in fear. I have no doubt that feeds into whatever fantasy he's had.

For the first time, I see emotion on his face. Annoyance.

Travis sighs and shakes his head, walking toward me as my body tenses. "You're cutting into my sleep schedule now. We can talk about this in the morning."

He opens the garage door and walks over to the tarp. He dismisses me as casually as someone calling to check in about a spreadsheet.

Travis walks back out with zip ties in his hands and puts his hand on my back to push me into the hallway. My head is spinning, and I can't make sense of any of this. Not only did I just find out Travis, the man I have been obsessed with—and sleeping with—is a serial killer. But now he's leading me to his bedrooms again.

With zip ties.

I stop when we approach the guest room, and he shakes his head, leading me toward his room. "You're sleeping with me tonight."

We approach his bed, and he wraps a zip tie around my wrist, the other around his, and links them together. Both of us lie down on his mattress, and I stare up at the ceiling, trying to think of the most rational thing for me to do right now. Attempting to escape without a solid plan would be plain stupid, and knowing Travis, he would track me down before I could make it across state lines.

I scratch the idea of a getaway off my what-to-do-next list while trying not to think about Travis being so close to me.

I wanted to spend the night with him, but this isn't exactly how I imagined it.

Travis rolls over and closes his eyes, his entire body relaxing almost instantly as he falls asleep. I look at the zip tie on my wrist, realizing I'll have to get comfortable with it. I'm resigned to just staring at the ceiling all night, but my mind is working like unpaid overtime.

Travis's admission of previously wanting to kill me remains in the forefront of my thoughts. Maybe he was joking or simply misspoke? No, that doesn't seem like Travis. My brain is probably just trying to make me feel better, but I'd like to believe Travis kills only bad people. Like a sexy vigilante.

Holding on to that idea for comfort, I try to come up with new scenarios of the future.

I have to figure out a way to survive this. Hours have passed when an idea forms in my head. It's a bad idea, a really bad one—but it might be the only one I've got.

Chapter Seventeen

My alarm clock rings, and my eyes jolt open, the memory of Sage finding out the truth about me still lingering in my mind. I promptly reach over to stop the ringing, tiredness making me sluggish. I'm annoyed that I'm tired too. I grab the alarm clock and throw it on the floor. It shatters on the hardwood, and I make a mental note to leave a one-star review later.

How dare this clock shatter in my time of emotional need?

Sleep is yet another thing Sage has disrupted in my life. If it wasn't for her snooping around, I never would have gotten the motion-sensor notification on my phone that disrupted my slumber last night.

Ugh, if I wanted random surprises in my life, I'd adopt a cat.

She's still beside me, and I know there's a conversation we need to have. I'm simultaneously impressed by her and disappointed in myself that she could find me out. I've killed thirty-eight people so far, and besides the person who is seemingly digging into Amelia's disappearance, nobody has ever discovered evidence linking me to their deaths. How did Sage, of all people, put the pieces together?

I look at her, surprised to see she's awake and staring at me. I expected to see fear or anxiety in her eyes, but I don't. She and I aren't made the same way. My mind is vastly different from hers. I try to put myself in her shoes and see what she might feel like after I confessed to being a killer. I just can't do it. I expect she felt betrayal, fear, and stress. But her face doesn't show any of that.

"I've been thinking about . . . *it* all night," Sage says. She takes a deep breath and looks at me with an annoyingly earnest gaze. "I'm in."

"In . . . what?"

"I'm going to help you kill this guy," she promptly replies. She sits up and looks at me with a half smile on her face. She must be mistaken, because there was no invitation for her help. This isn't a fun activity to do with friends. I'm extremely meticulous, and I won't lower my standards for her to join me.

"I never asked for help," I say, sitting up and glaring at her. "I've killed thirty-eight people so far, and I've never needed help."

I study her face as I give her my number, and she gives no indication of being alarmed by it. She hears that I've killed that many and isn't fazed. Even I know that's not a normal reaction.

Sage might just be in worse shape than I am.

I turn away and open my bedside drawer, pulling out one of the knives I have stashed away there. I flick it open and turn around to show it to her. I hope to see her eyes wide with fear, but they're not. I use it to cut the zip ties around our wrists.

"Why would you want to help me?" I can't wrap my head around it. This isn't a hobby a friend recommends you pick up. It's serious. It's not something anyone can do.

"Because maybe something good can come out of your . . . hobby. There are bad people in this world, and those people can do whatever they want and get away with it. If I can help right those wrongs—balance the scales between good and evil in the world—then I *want* to." She has a hopeful look in her eyes as she speaks, and I feel my distaste growing.

I'm not surprised. Sage is delusional and naive, so she likely thinks I'm some *Dexter*-inspired killer. She thinks all my previous victims have been child molesters and killers themselves. That couldn't be further from the truth.

"That's not why I do what I do." I squint at her as I take a deep breath. "I'm not saving the world from evil. I *am* evil."

"I don't believe that," she says immediately, but I can see the crack in her veneer. She's trying to see good in me, which contradicts what she knows about me now. I smile at her naivete. It would be interesting to see the world through her eyes. Believing in the best even when you're presented with evidence against it.

It's such an innocent mindset, and I can't help but want to shatter it.

"You have no idea how easy it is for me." I rest my hand on her leg, tracing a small circle on her thigh with my finger. "Before I sold my company and had billions of dollars to throw into these proclivities, it was a little hard. But most people don't know where to look. That's what I love about it. The planning. You should know, I'm very detailed. One doesn't get away with thirty-eight murders without having a detailed plan.

"Three months ago, there was Cal." I smile as my hand creeps up her leg, slowly inching toward the warmth of her pussy. "I met him panhandling outside of a Speedway, and I offered to buy him a hot lunch. I sat down with him, talked about his life, and learned how he got where he was. After that, it wasn't hard to follow him around and map out his routine. He was homeless, addicted to pain pills mostly. When he couldn't get his hands on those, he took anything anyone would offer. When he saw me again two weeks later, after I had already studied his every move, he trusted me enough to get in my car. Instead of going to the diner, I brought him to an old paper mill."

My hand reaches the outside of Sage's crotch, and I start rubbing it. She is hesitant for a moment, but she spreads her legs wider for me. All she's wearing is a pair of pajama shorts, thin enough for me to feel every part of her.

"You'd be surprised how many abandoned factories litter this part of the country." I laugh and shake my head as I move the fabric of her shorts aside to rub her bare folds. "For the most part, they are a liability.

You can buy them through shell companies dirt cheap, and most of the time the local government is practically begging people to take them off their hands. From there, it's not hard to get the rest of my supplies."

Sage watches me cautiously, her mouth hanging open as I trace my fingers along her labia. Her chest rises and falls heavily, a sign that she's clearly interested in what's happening. I didn't expect that, but I don't expect a lot of things about her.

"So, I brought Cal to the paper mill and tied him up with rope while I let my knife slice from his chin to his navel. It wasn't deep enough for him to die right away, though."

Disgust flashes over her features. "That's terrible," she mutters.

My finger rubs against her clit, and she gasps, leaning back slightly as she sinks into the warmth of my touch. "He begged me to let him go, promising never to tell anyone about meeting me. He told me about his family, how they'd be looking for him. I knew that wasn't true. They'd all but written him off years before. I knew I could savor the kill. I started with his arms, cutting into skin and fat and watching as blood spilled freely on the plastic sheeting. Then I moved to his torso and held him to the ground while I sliced into the less vital organs."

"Travis! I don't want to hear that!" she blurts out, but she doesn't pull away from my touch. I can see the inner turmoil written all over her face.

Her breath quickens as I slide a finger inside her, feeling how wet she is from what I've been doing to her so far. I'm surprised she's as turned on by this as she is. There's something broken in her, in the same way it is in me. That's the only explanation for this reaction.

I listen to her moan as I think of the other details of my kill, pumping my finger in and out of her faster and faster before stopping altogether and keeping her just on the brink of orgasm as she listens with rapt attention.

My cock stiffens in my pajamas, threatening to break through and show its head again. This is new for me. Normally there's nothing sexual about my kills. Of course, it is very gratifying, and when I'm done my adrenaline is pumping and I'll often pleasure myself. But the act itself is not rooted in sexuality.

"After I stabbed his kidney, I knew that I only had about fifteen minutes before he was dead. Until then, I could have my fun," I continue, moving my finger in and out of her as she lies back on the bed, keeping her eyes trained on me.

Her hands reach for her shirt to slide it up. I reach out and grab one breast, then the other, running my fingers over her nipples while she moans.

"In the end, I slit his throat, and the little blood that was still pumping through his veins spilled out like a geyser." Her pussy tightens around my finger as she gets closer, and my cock stiffens even more. "I sat there for a moment staring at his face as life faded from his eyes."

Sage is whimpering as her pussy clenches around me, and she comes on my finger. "Oh, fuck yes!"

"I killed six more people in that paper mill before I had it demolished," I say, moving my finger quickly in and out of her as I pinch her nipple. "Nobody can ever find what doesn't exist. That evidence is buried under fifteen tons of rubble."

Her body trembles and shakes against the mattress as I keep working her with my finger. More wetness coats my hand as she writhes against the mattress. I watch her lose control of herself, feeling more powerful in this relationship than I ever have.

By the time her body is still, my head is clear. She breathes heavily, a hand over her forehead, as she stares up at the ceiling with a hint of confusion on her face.

Once again, I have confessed something to Sage that I shouldn't have. I told her every detail of a kill, even where the evidence was buried. Of course, it would be nearly impossible for her to get that evidence, but whatever remains of Cal and the other six I killed there could be found.

I've made a mistake, and I have no way of rectifying it. I never go back on my word, and I already told Sage I wasn't going to kill her anymore. What the hell am I supposed to do now?

I get up and walk into my bathroom, closing the door behind me, and I lock it just in case she gets any ideas about following me. Grabbing my toothbrush, I look at myself in the mirror. My hair is all messed up, and my eyes look tired as my hand tightens on my toothbrush.

I know what I need—a pep talk.

"You are in control," I say quietly. "You are a weapon. You are superior to all . . . and you definitely do not care about the girl," I tell myself before I break the toothbrush in half.

Dammit.

"You absolutely care about the girl."

Chapter Eighteen

Sage

I know I should run. I know I should grab all my things and flee Lake Lure and never come back. Even if I wanted to, it's not like it would do me any good. Let's be real. Travis has confessed to killing thirty-eight people. He's confessed to stalking them meticulously before each kill and creating a routine they probably didn't even know they had.

At first I let myself fantasize that he was taking out only bad guys and people who deserved it, but when Travis told me about killing an indisputably innocent man, my stomach churned. I don't understand how I was still able to come apart at his touch. Confusion over that swirls around my brain.

I should definitely leave, but there's nowhere on God's green earth I can go that Travis isn't going to find me. There's absolutely no point in running. Plus, I definitely didn't pack enough cute clothes for a life on the run.

Yeah . . . there's no way I'm getting hunted in Crocs.

Besides, I don't know if I still want to get away.

Despite Travis's revelation about his prior kills, I'm warming up to the idea of killing Eli—calling him by his real name instead of DarkHours99 feels surreal, but in a way, it's helping all this. He's threatened me, and he's delusional enough that he might actually act on it. If I can do something to stop him from hurting me, and possibly other women like me, I should.

Travis says that isn't the reason he kills, and the idea of that makes me a little nervous. Still, I can't help but wonder if I can help him. I know, I know. The whole "I can fix him" mentality doesn't typically work. But I do think it's possible in this case. Besides, he wanted to kill me and then decided not to. That's progress. He is totally fixable, and I'm going to be the one to do it!

There's something in Travis making him act this way, and if I can figure out what that is and redirect that energy to something else, then that could be a great thing.

My phone chimes, and I look at it; immediately my heart drops at seeing a message from Eli, but I open it and prepare to respond. For the time being, I need to keep him calm. Travis told me it would be the best thing to do until we can be with him in person.

He's coming up with a plan, and I'm eager to make myself useful. I have to prove that I can be of value to him before he revisits the idea of killing me. God, I desperately need to convince him to change the way he chooses his targets. Innocent people don't deserve this.

I see the weather is beautiful out there! Any chance you're gonna go for a swim? Eli messages with a tongue-out emoji. Knowing that he's sending me this while simultaneously having a fiancée back home is frustrating. I feel bad for her, but this problem will be out of her hands soon enough.

I'm DYING to lol!!! I'll make sure to send pics. Maybe I'll go skinny dipping … I reply, feeling the ick run through my body at the idea. I shake it off and put the phone down, turning my attention to Travis's pantry.

It is stocked with food, but it is not stocked with food I want to eat. You don't get a body like Travis's without eating disgusting whole-grain meals all the time. But some of us aren't built like Greek gods. I need carbs, chocolate, fat, and salt.

"If I'm going to be staying here, we have to go to the store," I say over my shoulder. Travis is sitting at the counter, drinking his coffee and reading the news on his iPad. Ever since his confession, he's barely let me out of his sight. "If it's not on your schedule, I can go on my own. You can trust me."

Travis sets the iPad down and shakes his head. "I'm not taking any chances." He looks at his watch and thinks for a moment. "I have an hour and forty-three minutes of free time remaining before I get back to work. We can go, but if you tip anyone off about what I've told you, I'll be forced to reconsider killing you."

I laugh and smile at him, leaning against the counter. "I wouldn't dream of it."

His eyes narrow as he stares at me, but he has to know I'm being truthful. I really wouldn't. To my knowledge, I haven't met any other killers, but I don't think I could look at them the same way I do Travis. I want to know more about why he kills. There's something in him that's driving him to do this, and I want to learn everything I can.

Both of us get ready to go to town, and after his driving ritual, we make the short trek there. Travis opts to shop at a small mom-and-pop grocery store. I'm surprised this place can even survive in an area like this.

It's smaller than your typical Whole Foods store, with aisles that are narrow and packed with name brands as well as local wares. I marvel at the bakery section, seeing all the homemade goods from countless small businesses nearby.

Travis follows me around and watches my every move as I navigate the aisles. We get to the baking section, and I stand in front of the brownie mixes, trying to figure out exactly which one I want. It's been a long time since I've made weed brownies, and I remember there's one brand that clashes particularly badly with the weed butter I make.

"They're all the same," Travis says, tapping his watch to remind me we're on a schedule.

"This coming from a man who probably hasn't had a brownie in ten years." I grab two boxes and look at them to study the ingredients.

"Try twenty-eight." His phone rings before I can tell him how ridic-ulous that is.

"We're going to have to change that," I whisper to myself while he pulls the phone from his pocket.

He stares at it and looks at me cautiously before looking back at the phone. "I need to take this. You better not do anything stupid."

He slides the answer button to the right as he turns to walk away. I barely manage to catch a glimpse of the name Peter on the screen. "Hello?"

Travis walks away, looking over his shoulder at me one last time as he leaves the baking aisle. I hesitate for a moment, knowing that I want to eavesdrop. Travis warned me not to do anything to expose him, and I don't think this would.

I set the brownie mixes into the basket and follow him. He didn't go far—he is just an aisle away, talking in a hushed voice. He's not looking, and he doesn't hear me tiptoeing up behind him as he whispers into the phone.

"Any surveillance from the rental shop?" Travis asks.

Surveillance? Is this about a potential kill? Eli, maybe?

But who else would know about this?

"He has to have given a real ID somewhere. The man's not a ghost," Travis continues, running his fingers through his hair. There's a long pause on the other end as Peter tells him something else. "So he's still in the city?" There's a hint of hope in his voice, and I think this has to be about a kill. "All right. Keep me posted if they move anywhere."

He hangs up the phone and turns around, his face immediately falling in disappointment as he sees me. "What did I say?"

"You didn't say anything about eavesdropping," I reply, shrugging casually. "What was that about?"

Travis huffs and shakes his head, grabbing my arm and leading me toward the cash register. "Can we not talk about this here?"

He grabs the basket from my hand and sets it down on the register, neither of us saying anything to the cashier as they ring up each item. Travis hands them the bank card, chivalrously paying for all the junk food I'm buying. He might be a killer, but he's still a gentleman.

We pile into his car, and he checks his watch one last time before pulling out after his routine. I know we're cutting it pretty close to his scheduled work time, and I feel a little guilty about this impromptu outing.

"So, who was on the phone?" I ask while his hands are glued in the ten-and-two position while he focuses on the road.

"You know, I stepped away because it was a private phone call."

"You're tracking someone, though, right?" I pull my leg up underneath me as I turn to stare at him. "Do you normally outsource the tracking to someone else? Who else knows about . . . your *hobby*?"

Even though Travis doesn't look at me, I can feel him rolling his eyes.

"It's a genuine question! If I know about this, I am liable in a way. I need to know about these things. If there's someone else out there who understands what's going on, then I should be filled in."

Travis sighs and shakes his head slowly as he rolls up to a red light. He finally looks at me with resignation in his eyes.

"I have a private investigator on payroll. He has had some indication someone is looking into me, and he's helping me find out who it is."

There's no emotion in his voice, not even stress. If I were him, I would be terrified someone was looking into me. He is, after all, a *serial killer*.

"How does he know this?"

"Someone has been searching for my name in some unusual ways. On top of that, I've seen somebody watching me. When we were at the ice cream shop, there was someone in a car clearly keeping an eye on me. They weren't trying to hide it either."

I feel sick. How can he be so calm about this? Someone knows what he's up to, and they're looking for him.

"What if they have evidence? You said you do the whole thing with the abandoned factories, and maybe that's traceable in some way. Someone could have gone on to one of those sites and obtained something to implicate you," I say. I'm nervously rambling off every fear that pops up in my head. "They could capture you. It could either be a police officer who is ready to arrest you and throw you in jail, or possibly even give you the electric chair. Does North Carolina still have the death penalty?"

He opens his mouth to reply, but I don't even give him a second to speak. "What if it's worse? It could be someone who's been following you and wants to blackmail you with this information. They can take everything from you. Maybe even make you kill other people on their behalf like some kind of hit man."

"And that will be worse than lethal injection?" Travis laughs for the first time all day, and I stare at him, almost surprised to hear the sound. "You do realize almost anyone else in the entire world would think this is a good thing, right?"

He's absolutely right. Most people would not be worrying about a serial killer being caught. They would be cheering on the police officers or vigilante heroes helping to throw them behind bars. But I'm not. The thought of somebody barging into Travis's house and throwing him in handcuffs makes me want to vomit.

"Well, I'm not like anyone else."

"I'm starting to wonder if you're more dangerous than I am," Travis says with a small chuckle at the end.

It's supposed to be a joke, I think. But maybe he has a point.

Chapter Nineteen

Sage has completely disrupted my schedule for the day. However, I do have to take some accountability for that. If I'd have killed her when I had the chance, this wouldn't be a problem. Now there's someone in the world who knows explicit details about some of my kills and can opt to use that against me.

So I have to keep a close eye on her. At least until I get an idea that she's to be trusted. Right now she seems like she is. She's less bothered about the fact that I'm a killer than I would have thought. I can't understand how she's as calm as she is about it.

I get what she says about her being liable for this now. I've brought her into my world, and I don't know how much longer I can keep my history from her. She's bound to find out about my kills eventually. She already knows about Cal, and if she has any sense about her, she can easily find a string of other missing people that might connect to me. She knows more than any police officer on the East Coast.

The alarm on my watch rings, and I stand up from the kitchen table, my makeshift office for the time being. My actual office has too much sensitive information for Sage to be trusted in there. I keep that locked at all times, even when it's just me at home. You can never be too careful when you have skeletons in your closet.

"It's time to exercise," I announce. I close my laptop and walk from the dining room table to the living room, where Sage is lying on the couch and scrolling on her phone.

I considered taking her phone away from her as well, but she has too much of a following online for that to be wise. Some of her loyal followers would notice if she stopped posting, and with Eli knowing where she is, that's a recipe for disaster. I might not be able to monitor what she does online, but I have to trust it's in my best interest.

"Have fun with that," she says with a smirk. She settles into the couch more, making it clear she has no interest in joining me.

"I don't know if I've made it clear to you, but I don't want you out of my sight." I fold my arms as I stand above her, waiting for her to comply. "You're coming with me."

She stares at me and lets out a small exhale before standing up and conceding to follow me to my home gym. I open the door and spot her face in some of the mirrors on the wall, showing just how surprised she is by my setup.

"Isn't this a little much for a home gym?" She looks around at the machinery like she's trying to figure out how some of it is used.

"It has everything I need for my regular exercise rotations."

She takes a seat at the overhead press and tries moving the weight I have preset with no luck. I smirk as she runs and looks around to try to figure out what she's supposed to do, not realizing she's just too weak for the amount of weight.

"Maybe you can start on the treadmill, or something better suited for you," I suggest before making my way to the elliptical. This exercise block is specifically for strength training, but it's always best to begin a workout with cardiovascular warm-ups.

"I'm not really big on exercising," Sage says as she takes a seat and watches me. "I don't mind a show, however."

I ignore her as I begin my workout, moving up and down on the elliptical until I feel my heart pumping in my chest. All the while, she sits on my rowing machine, sliding back and forth as she holds her chin in her hand and keeps her eyes glued to me.

Even if I couldn't see her reflection in the mirror, I could still sense every movement of her eyes on me. They burrow into my back, digging their way through me. I don't understand what she's looking at. It's like there's something specific about me she's trying to analyze.

"Could I paint one of the rooms?" she suddenly blurts out.

"Paint as in with color other than white?" I question, slightly out of breath from my workout.

"Yes, maybe a Blush Whimsy and Sunset Linen. Or what about . . ." I tune out the rest of her ridiculous suggestions, once again regretting not killing her when I had the chance.

When I'm done on the elliptical, I move to the bench press, taking off my sweaty shirt and tossing it aside. This catches her attention even more, and she raises her eyebrows and smirks at me. With every movement of my arms, her gaze follows. I feel it tracing every peak and valley of my muscles.

I'm not used to this. One of the reasons why I have my own gym at home is for privacy, and having someone here, staring at me, is infuriating. Normally, when I exercise, I use this time for mindfulness. It's important to pay attention to your body and how it reacts while you're using it. Right now I can't focus on any of that.

"Isn't there something else you could be doing?" I snap, sitting up and staring at her. I'm frustrated, and I'm not holding back anymore. "I can't concentrate on my exercise with you constantly watching me. What's going on?"

"I was just wondering if any of your victims felt you watching them the way you clearly feel me watching you," she says. She sits up straighter and doesn't look away from me. She sees how anger morphs my face, but she doesn't react.

How could she be so flippant about this? This isn't a casual situation. I know she might think I'm some callous, cold-blooded murderer—and to an extent, I most definitely am—but I take this seriously. It's not a joke to me, and her treating it like one pisses me off.

I stand up and bridge the gap between the two of us to stand in front of her, glaring down. "I don't want to hear you talking about this anymore."

"Why not? It's all out in the open. There's nothing to hide," Sage replies, standing up to try to meet my gaze.

"It's not about hiding, it's about my process. I don't talk about the things I do. I think about them, I plan them, I study them, but I don't make jokes!" I clench my fists as my voice rises. My frustration is overwhelming, and the same burning behind my eyes that I always feel when I'm getting close to a kill rears its head. "This is my life. I work hard, and I won't have you here making light of it."

She doesn't have to say anything. I wouldn't be able to hear her even if she did. The floodgates are open, and the emotions I usually feel as I'm killing spill out of me. I need to do something to get rid of them, but I can't hurt her.

I grab her by the arm and drag her to the bench press. There's a flicker of fear in her eyes, and I can practically taste it wafting off her as I bend her over the cold bench.

"If you want to make jokes, I'm going to punish you for it," I say. I pull down her pants, tossing them to the side before ripping off her panties.

Sage gasps, and I see a smile on her lips in the mirror that only irritates me more. Seeing her bare ass on display, the folds of her pussy just barely visible, makes my cock twitch in my pants. I don't waste a moment pulling it out, running my hand along my shaft a few times to make sure I'm good and hard.

I kneel down behind her, grabbing her waist tight enough that my fingernails dig into her soft flesh. As I shove my cock inside her, I imagine what it would be like to squeeze her hard and rip her apart.

"Oh, fuck!" Sage shouts, her voice echoing in the room.

It takes only a few moments before I can feel her getting wet around me, and I quicken my pace as I thrust in and out of her. I'm grunting and quickly losing control of myself as I slam against her with as much force as I possibly can.

The fury in my veins empowers every movement, and I practically tune out her screams. I meet her eyes through the mirror as I see her staring at me, her mouth hanging open as her skin flushes from the heat building between us. She's still watching me, even after everything. Her eyes don't leave my reflection, and I force mine to stay on hers.

I move my hand from her waist, smacking her ass hard with my hand before rubbing it and massaging the red spot. In the mirror, I can just barely see a red welt forming. Sage cries out, moaning and shaking as I fuck her.

"This is what you get for going against what I say." I smack her other ass cheek. She cries out at the force, and I massage it again, watching through the mirror as her skin turns bright red. "Tell me you'll listen to me from now on."

"I will," she says through a strained moan. She bites her lip hard as I thrust in and out.

When I feel myself getting closer to release, I slow down and make more long, purposeful thrusts. Sage squeals, and her entire body shakes as she comes, her pussy convulsing around me as it throbs from pleasure.

My eyes never leave hers as I finish with an explosion of cum bursting out of me and filling her completely. Both of us are breathless when I pull away, and I stare at her as she turns around and looks at me again. Neither of us says a word.

We sit in silence for a few minutes, recovering. Sage's phone alerts, and she stands up to see what it is. Both of us know it's Eli without even looking.

The last thing we need is him getting suspicious about something happening, so I told her she needs to be on his good side. I have an idea brewing of how to get him to Lake Lure, and Sage might just need to be the temptation for that. I know she doesn't like it, but talking to him is a sacrifice she has to make.

"What's it say?" I ask, resting my elbows on my knees as I wait.

"'If I was there with you, we would hardly be leaving the bedroom,'" she answers, handing me the phone.

I feel rage boiling in my veins as I look at the message. I knew that Sage was humoring him, but I had no idea the conversation was sexual in nature. She's doing exactly what I asked of her, but seeing it is infuriating.

As I'm looking at their messages, Eli sends a picture of his dick completely unprompted. I shake my head in disbelief as I hand the phone back to her. She rolls her eyes and sends him a reply that I have no doubt is flirty and sexual, telling him how great it looks.

"What did you reply?" I ask, almost regretting when she sighs before answering.

"'If only you were closer, I could see what that tastes like,' with a bunch of drooling emojis." Sage rolls her eyes once more and flashes me a nervous smile.

Her phone chimes once again, with an almost immediate response from Eli. Sage reads it out loud. "'That can be arranged, babe.'"

Eli fully believes her when she says she's interested in him. In his mind, there's a reality where he and Sage will wind up together, living happily ever after. I can't wait to take that from him. He doesn't get to have that with her.

She's mine.

I can't wait to rip this guy's fucking heart out of his chest.

Chapter Twenty

Travis is in his office once again, doing all kinds of research he refuses to tell me about. I take advantage of the time spent out from under his watchful eye and get to work in the kitchen. I preheat the oven and start putting my brownie mix together. I leave everything but the butter out of the bowl. Then I start making my cannabutter mixture.

Believe it or not, this is a recipe my hippie parents taught me ages ago. As soon as I was eighteen, they were more than happy to share their weed recipes. I guess that is a perk of growing up in a commune.

I add the butter to a pan and stir it constantly before adding in the weed. The familiar musky scent wafts to my nose, and I inhale with a slight smile. Since I've been in Lake Lure, I haven't gotten properly stoned, and I am looking forward to it. With everything going on with Eli, I could use a break.

I strain the weed out of the butter when it's finished and add the remainder to the brownie mixture before pouring everything in another pan. Travis walks out of his office just as I put the used buds in the trash can. He looks around suspiciously, sniffing the air before his eyes land on an open window in the living room.

"You have to leave the window shut," Travis says with an annoyed sigh as he walks toward it and closes it. "We're in the middle of the woods. There are countless critters running around. I don't like to smell skunk in my home."

"Sorry," I reply, smirking to myself because he really doesn't know what I'm doing. Travis always knows what I'm doing, but he doesn't right now. "It won't happen again."

His eyes land on my filming equipment, unpacked and strewn all around the living room. "What's this?"

"Sorry, I'm about to move it all, I promise. I post travel vlogs on my YouTube channel every Friday, and I have to film some content for that." I set a timer on my phone for the brownies before running around and gathering up everything.

Without prompting, Travis helps. I've always wanted a man who doesn't need to be told what to do. Travis sees something that needs to be done, and he steps up. He might have his flaws, but he has a lot of good qualities too.

"Don't get my house in the shot," he advises as we walk outside, and I start setting up my camera. I nod and point the camera at the woods instead.

While I'm in the midst of setting up the ring lights, adjusting the microphone, and making sure my battery is at 100 percent, my phone alarm rings. It takes only a minute to pull the brownies out of the stove and put them on the counter to cool. As I catch my reflection in the oven glass, I give myself a little pep talk.

"Okay, don't be weird. Just be cute and chill."

I can smell the weed butter, and I'm tempted to dig right in, but I stop myself.

When I get back outside, Travis is sitting in a chair behind the camera. "Am I going to have an audience today?"

"I'll admit, I'm curious about what you do." Travis leans back and gestures for me to take my spot in front of the camera.

I never film while anyone is watching me. Honestly, it makes me feel a little self-conscious about what I do. When I'm alone, in front of a camera, I can turn on the charm with ease. But having Travis watch me makes me wonder if I'll do and say the right things.

I take a deep breath and press the record button on the camera. "Evening, travelers! Welcome back to my channel. I'm coming to you today from beautiful Lake Lure, North Carolina!"

I smile and wave, almost immediately forgetting about the eyes watching me as I delve into my internet persona. I go on and on about my journey to Lake Lure, how I hitchhiked to get to the Airbnb I've been staying in, and about the disappearances from the true crime podcast, playing it up to seem over the top rather than suspicious—like maybe there's a curse or some haunted ground rather than an impossibly sexy murderer living nearby. I'll need to go back to Ryan's place and film some B-roll of his yard and the interior of his cabin. That's how I'm able to review the Airbnbs the way I do.

People like Ryan see my content and want free advertising for their homes, so they let me stay in them as long as I post about them on my social media. Then, after that, they have more clicks and bookings than they did before. I don't have to pay any bills, and they get some free advertisements. It's a mutually beneficial arrangement. Because of that, though, I skipped over Ryan being a creep when I first met him.

I also don't say anything about meeting Travis during my travels. That one goes without saying. I can't exactly admit to falling in love with a serial killer who is going to hunt down and kill my stalker, now, can I?

"I can't recommend coming to Lake Lure enough! So if you're looking for an East Coast getaway, look no further!" I stand motionless in front of the camera for a few brief moments, holding the smile on my face before letting it fall completely and stopping the recording.

I flip through a notebook I have and stand in front of the camera again, ready for a second round of filming. This time I'm more aware of Travis's eyes on me as I move. I take a few deep breaths and go over some of the points I have for this recording in my head.

I turn on the camera and do the exact same thing over again, this time talking about hiking trails in the area. Travis watches me, squinting as he studies my every word.

My ears burn hot, and I'm thankful for the camera-ready makeup caked on my face to hide the redness I'm sure is there. Travis doesn't say anything or offer any critique while I'm filming. I catch my mind straying from my travel guide to wonder what it is he's thinking.

"What do you think?" I ask him when I stop the second recording.

Travis sits up straight in his chair and takes a deep breath while he looks me up and down. The way he looks at me makes me feel like he is some kind of scientist, discovering a new species for the first time. It doesn't feel good. It's not how I want him to look at me at all.

"I thought I was good at putting on a persona, but I'm nothing compared to you." His eyes scan my face, and I'm not sure what he registers. I think I should feel offended by the comment, but he's right. That's exactly what I do when I'm behind the camera. "Nobody would ever expect there's something different about you. They don't know what's swimming beneath the surface."

"And what's that?" I fold my arms across my chest and raise an eyebrow at him. He stares at me with a smirk on his lips, clearly enjoying the challenge I'm giving him.

"Darkness." A chill runs through me, and I try to shake it off, but I can't.

Maybe he's right. There could be something about me that resonates with him; that's why he's let me in the way he has.

My phone rings in my pocket and jolts me out of my introspection. I look at it, surprised to see my parents FaceTiming me. It's not Sunday yet, and they don't normally reach out if it's not part of our regularly scheduled time.

"Hello?" Both my parents are on the screen with wide smiles on their faces, waving at the camera. "What's going on?"

"Oh, we were just calling because Gemma had an idea about having you film the annual solstice festival for your channel, and we wanted to see if you were interested," Mom explains.

"Of course, we also wanted to see how you were doing," Dad adds. "How is that fella of yours?"

I jump at the mention of Travis and smile, immediately clicking the camera reversal button on my phone to show him sitting behind the camera. My parents' faces light up, seeing him for the first time.

"This is Travis! He's helping me film some content for my channel right now, actually," I say. A smile beams across my face as my parents take him in.

I see Travis in the small rectangle in the corner of the screen, stiffening, his face completely blank as he awkwardly raises a hand to wave. My stomach twists, and I immediately realize I shouldn't have done that. I got carried away.

I click the button again and take the camera off Travis while forcing a smile.

"Tell us about yourself, Travis," my mom says with a curious grin on her face. My dad is mumbling unintelligibly about something, which I think is him commenting on how cute a couple we make.

Travis doesn't move from the chair, but I see how uncomfortable he is. I wish I could take it back. At some point he'll have to meet my parents, but that has to be on his own terms.

He's also a dangerous man, and I need to be careful giving out information about him. Especially considering there's somebody nosing around, trying to look into him.

"He's being shy," I say, stepping away from Travis and trying to redirect the conversation away from him. "Wait, I think I might be able to film the festival. When is it, again?" I ask. Thankfully my parents are very easily distracted, and they don't ask anything else about Travis as they start bombarding me with information about everything they've done. I feign interest for a while longer, and eventually I manage to hang up the phone.

Travis is still sitting down behind the camera, and his hands are gripping the arms of the chair. He might be mad, and I completely understand why he would be. There's a devious hope that he might punish me for what I did, just like he did in the gym. I cautiously approach and take a seat across from him.

"I'm really sorry, Travis. I wasn't thinking. I totally understand if you're mad at—"

"I'm not mad." Travis's grip on the chair loosens, and he takes a deep breath as he looks around. "I was actually thinking about my parents. I was just comparing everything you told me about yours to mine. They're just so different."

I wait silently for him to elaborate, but he doesn't. He just stares off into space while he thinks. I want to ask more, but I know that would be pointless. Travis is guarded, and I doubt he's going to willingly give me information about his life. He didn't even tell me what happened to his sister when he mentioned her the first time.

I can't help but wonder if I'll ever meet his family. If things go well between us, I know that I want him to meet mine. What if the two of us end up getting married? Are we going to have the big wedding of my dreams, or just a small courthouse wedding between the two of us so he doesn't have to integrate me into his life fully?

"I'm all finished filming for the day," I say, packing up my camera and tripod. Travis stands up and helps me before we walk back inside.

I set everything down in the living room before packing it into its proper place, not wanting to get on Travis's bad side with the mess of it all. After I zip up the camera bag, I remember the brownies on the counter.

I run over to them and see that they are completely cooled, and I immediately cut into the pan. Travis watches me as I put a small piece on a plate for myself, and a smile creeps onto my lips.

Travis has been guarded since the moment I met him, and this could be my way to break his walls down. My special ingredient might just be his kryptonite.

"Remember how you said you've never had a brownie? Well, that's about to change," I say as I cut a piece for him and put it on a plate.

This should be interesting.

Chapter Twenty-One

TRAVIS

I don't understand the point of brownies. I look at the plate and see a brown glob of gluten, sugar, and fat that is only going to disrupt my perfectly coded digestive system.

Sage approaches me with a small plate with a brownie on it. I look at it and shake my head. "I've already told you I have no interest in eating that."

"Come on," she continues, looking up at me and batting her eyelashes as if she is going to seduce me into eating a superfluous treat. "I worked hard to make these. Just a couple of bites is all I'm asking."

"You followed instructions on the back of the box. A five-year-old could do the same thing. I wouldn't exactly call that *working hard*."

Sage rolls her eyes and inches closer, biting her lower lip seductively. Clearly, she thinks sex is going to sell this brownie, and that won't work.

"I made them for you. You have to try them." Her finger lands in the center of my chest, and she traces a small circle around it. I raise my eyebrows and shake my head again.

"A single brownie averages around two hundred calories and has excessive sugar. They provide no value in terms of nutritional value or micronutrient density." I push the plate away, but she still doesn't take the hint.

"Okay, you're built like a marble statue. I think you can afford a few empty calories every now and then." She holds the plate out to me once again, this time losing the seductive edge she had before and focusing more on being annoying. "Sure, these may not be good for you nutritionally. But brownies are good for the soul. They're warm, with ooey, gooey chocolate that provides immeasurable joy."

I stare at the brownie like it might explode. Lowering my face, I sniff it. It doesn't smell bad. Quite the opposite, actually. Still, I'm not convinced.

"Joy isn't a dietary category. I eat for function, not pleasure. My daily caloric intake is specifically calculated to my dietary needs, and consuming that much sugar will cause a spike in my blood glucose levels, disrupting my insulin regulation and interrupting the metabolic rate I've maintained for the past ten years."

Sage's face does not change when I explain my reasoning. She simply doesn't care. She might be a heathen who eats whatever she wants, whenever she wants, but I'm not. I have my schedule, and that doesn't apply only to time—it applies to every aspect of my life.

"Believe it or not, life is about more than data points and spreadsheets."

"This has nothing to do with spreadsheets—"

"Just try one bite! That's all I'm asking." Sage shakes her head in exasperation as she holds the plate closer.

I roll my eyes. "You're not going to shut up about this until I eat it, are you?"

"Of course not." She smiles innocently as she nudges the plate closer.

Sometimes in life, you have to choose your battles. And right now I'm exasperated. Only to make her leave me alone, I sigh and nod. The smile on her face grows as I take the plate and hold the fork over the brownie before stabbing it in and loading a bite onto it.

She watches intently as I bring it to my mouth and let the flavors explode on my tongue. My normal diet consists of organic, whole foods with a myriad of protein vegetables and healthy carbs. I very rarely have sugary treats like this. The taste is incredible, and Sage can read that on my face even though I try to hide my enjoyment.

"Are you happy now?" I ask, handing the plate to her after only one bite.

She pushes it back against me with another eye roll. "Come on. I can see that you like it. Just live a little."

I do as she says and eat the rest of the brownie. She smiles and happily eats her own as we take a seat on the couch in the living room. It's 5:00 p.m., which means it's time for the evening news, so I turn it on to watch.

The brownie leaves a strange aftertaste in my mouth that I don't understand, and I think back to Sage in the store talking about the different brands. I see what she means now. I drink some water to force it away, but I can't seem to drink enough.

After a while, my throat starts to feel dry, and I drink more water to quench it. My head feels light, as if I am floating in a pool on a sunny day with my eyes closed, letting life pass me by.

Sage leans against me, and I rest my arms on her, running my fingers through her soft hair as our gazes are glued to the TV. The evening news ends, and I realize I didn't pay attention to a word they said. A nuclear bomb could be coming directly to Lake Lure, and I would be none the wiser.

A sitcom I've never seen before comes on, and I can't help but laugh at the countless faux pas the main characters find themselves in. Sage and I both laugh uncontrollably as one of the characters gets locked out of their apartment and gets caught by the police while trying to sneak in through a window.

"That's something you would do," I say to her as I try to stop laughing.

It seems like we sit in silence for hours, but I know that can't be true, because the sun is still up outside, and the show hasn't ended yet. I don't know why, but this moment is extending forever.

At one point I find myself staring blankly at the wall, a weird feeling arising in my body. "I can feel my organs getting soft."

My comment sends Sage into a laughing fit. "I sometimes feel like my eyeballs are shrinking," she says once she catches her breath.

She sits up and crosses her legs in front of her, looking at me with a warm smile on her face. "You said you were comparing our parents earlier. Why? What was so different about them?"

I open my mouth to reply, surprising myself. I stop, thinking that this is something I wouldn't normally tell anyone. But I can't explain it. I want to tell her. Right now I feel like I need to. Sage already knows so much about me; it makes sense that she know everything.

"Does it have something to do with what happened to your sister?" She grabs my hand and traces small circles along my palm as she waits for me to reply.

My heart aches, hearing her mention Leah. I try not to think about her if I don't have to, but the sudden mention of her brings everything back up. The memory is at the front of my mind as if it happened yesterday. I relive it constantly, and I close my eyes while I try to fight it off.

"It's all my fault," I whisper as Sage squeezes my hand tight.

"What is?"

"Leah's death." I pause and open my eyes to look at her. She looks alarmed at my confession, and I feel the same pain I felt the night it happened all over again. "She was only twelve years old. She had her whole life ahead of her, and it's all my fault that she was taken. I was just a kid. I didn't know what I was doing."

"What did you do?"

I can't tell if there's fear in her voice or not. Sage already knows who I am, and she has accepted me. Why would this scare her now?

"We were driving home from school, and she was in the front seat next to my dad. I was in the back, angry that I wasn't allowed to sit up front when she was. I called shotgun, but because she was older, my dad let her sit there. I was angry, and I was distracting my dad while he was trying to calm me down. He didn't see the deer that walked into the road."

Sage gasps and squeezes my hand in hers as she lifts the other to her chest. I can't bring myself to look at her as I relive the story.

"It's all my fault she died. I killed her." I shake my head and close my eyes tight as the emotions swell through my system again. I hate this. I hate retelling the story. I hate the way it makes me feel. I don't have control over myself, and it makes me feel weak.

"You didn't kill her," she says, grabbing my face in her hand to force me to look at her. "It was an accident. You were a child, and you were acting the way children act. Don't blame yourself."

"My parents think it's my fault too. I could always tell they blamed me. When I would tell them I felt guilty, that I was upset because it was my fault, they never denied it." I lean back on the couch and let out a long exhale. "As soon as I left the house, they stopped reaching out. They lost two children that day."

When I finally look back at Sage, tears are streaming down her face, and I wrinkle my eyebrows at her. I don't understand how someone could cry so easily at someone else's pain. I don't even cry at my own.

After the accident, I remember being heartbroken. The crash was scary enough, but the memory of Leah's death haunts me. I remember my father rushing out the driver's-side door to pull her broken body from the car before he collapsed on the ground with her in his arms. He screamed and cried, and he begged God to bring her back. I stood there in shock, watching. When it finally registered, I started crying too. I didn't stop crying for days. Eventually my father kicked the door to my room open and told me I didn't get to cry. I didn't have any business crying because I didn't get hurt in the accident. I didn't lose what he lost.

I haven't shed a tear since then.

Looking back, I know that's why I'm the way I am now. I couldn't control my anger before the accident, and I couldn't control my tears before he told me to stop. Now everything in my life is rigorously controlled. There's no room for outlying emotions. And I can't get hurt if I don't let anyone in.

"Why are you crying?" I ask Sage when I shake off the remnants of the memory.

She shakes her head and dries her eyes before taking a few deep breaths. "I just can't imagine letting a child feel that way. They should have told you it wasn't your fault. They shouldn't have let you bear that weight for so long, and I'm so sorry for all the pain you've experienced." More tears fall from her face as she tries to choke back sobs. "I wish I could take it all away from you."

This is the first time anyone has said anything like that to me. I realize now I've almost been waiting for an apology from my parents that will never come. This is new, and I don't know how to react.

Sage climbs into my lap, and I hold my arms out, not knowing how to react to her sudden proximity. Her arms wrap around me, and I feel my defenses waning. She kisses my cheek and runs her fingers through my hair, burrowing her face in my neck as she tries to stifle her tears.

I hesitate for a moment, but I wrap my arms around her, too, completely enveloping her. This is strange. I haven't hugged anyone since I was a child. It's not something I've thought about, but looking back, the last person I hugged was probably Leah.

My entire body is tense as she holds me, and as the memory fades, I relax into it. Maybe this isn't so bad. Two weeks ago, the idea of somebody hugging me would have sent chills down my spine, but now things are different. Sage is different.

I don't know how much time passes, but the two of us sit on the couch together, letting our bodies meld as we hold each other. I have to admit, I kind of like it.

Chapter Twenty-Two

I don't remember going to the bedroom last night, but I wake up with a hand zip-tied to Travis's headboard. Travis has been doing that to keep an eye on me, but normally I'm zip-tied to his own wrist. He's not in bed beside me, and I start feeling like I did something wrong.

With a huff, I close my eyes again. While I wait for Travis to come and get me, I daydream about starting a fashion line for bedazzled zip ties. Maybe there is a market out there. I should find a support group for women who've been held hostage by a hot guy.

I try to sit up, and the headboard rattles against the wall as I move. Travis must have ultrasonic hearing, because he storms into the room mere moments later with his arms crossed in front of him and a scowl on his face.

Yep. I should have predicted this would happen, but I didn't.

"What the fuck is wrong with you?" Travis asks, standing at the foot of the bed while I wiggle my arm. "You can't just go around drugging people without their consent."

My mind is a little foggy because the pot brownies were much stronger than I intended them to be. I shake my head and try to recall the memory of the night before. It all comes flooding back to me as I think about Travis sitting on the couch and telling me about his sister's death. I still feel awful for him.

I did what I did because I needed him to open up to me. Now that he has, we're closer than we've ever been. It was a good thing, but he doesn't see it that way. I know he might come around in the future, and I can hardly wait for that.

"Come on, you never would have loosened up if it weren't for the brownie," I say, arguing my piece.

He just shakes his head with a disgusted look on his face. "I didn't want to tell you those things. They're my private memories that I chose to keep from you. You can't just make a decision like that for me. I shared that information unwillingly." Travis raises his voice as he speaks, and I shrink away from him. He lost control last night when he was telling me about his past while high, and he's losing control right now.

"I'm sorry," I say, hoping to placate him. Honestly, I'm not sorry at all. Travis needed that—we needed that for our relationship.

Speaking of . . . My wrist is still zip-tied to the headboard, so I casually ask, "Are we, like . . . in a relationship now, or is this just your weird version of a sleepover?"

He just shakes his head and walks over to me, pulling a pocket-knife out of his jeans and opening it. For most people, a serial killer approaching them with a knife might be a bad thing, but believe it or not, I trust Travis.

He cuts through the zip tie and frees my hand from the bedpost. I immediately reach for the waistband of his pants and look up at him with an eager smile.

"Let me make it up to you," I say, then bite my lower lip. Travis doesn't hesitate when he pushes my hand aside and walks over to the door.

"Not now. It's planning time."

I jump to my feet, and he stops in the doorway, turning around and staring at me with an exasperated sigh. I smile as I walk toward him. "We'll plan together, then."

I follow him to his office even though he has forbidden me from going in here before. I confidently move a chair to sit beside him, behind the computer.

"You in my office is a one-time thing," Travis says before he begins to ignore me as he logs on to all the different databases he needs, plus my Instagram account. I haven't looked at my phone yet today, but I see I have several messages from Eli.

"I traced some of the messages he sent you yesterday, and it appears he's moving closer to Lake Lure," Travis explains. He copies some information into his databases and searches for one of Eli's recent locations. "Looks like my hunch was right. He's here already."

My stomach twists, and I feel a surge of nervous energy that could even be confused with excitement. Travis is focused, with a stoic look on his face. I wish I could crack his skull open and see what's inside. I want to know what he's thinking, and he's almost impossible to read.

"So he's here. What do we do now?" I ask. Travis points to the computer screen, where he is using some kind of information that Eli has inadvertently given us to pinpoint exactly where he is.

"It looks like he's staying at the Lodge. He arrived yesterday evening, I think."

"Is he alone?" I remember his fiancée, and I feel guilty. I know that Eli is a bad guy, but I wonder how she would feel knowing everything he's getting himself into.

"We have no way to know right now, but if he came here just for the chance of finding you, I would imagine he is," Travis replies. He grips the mouse tight as he grimaces at the idea of my stalker coming to find me.

I pull out my phone to see what new messages Eli has sent. Surprisingly, he doesn't say anything about being in Lake Lure.

I'm confused.

I thought the whole point of me sending him the seductive messages was to convince him to come here under the guise of us hooking up.

"If he made all the effort to come here and not even tell me, what was the point?"

Travis looks at me, and a dark expression falls on his face. I feel like there's something I'm missing, and I stare at him expectantly.

"Trust me, I've noticed that too. I don't think he has any intention of letting you know when he plans on visiting you," he says.

I feel like I'm going to be sick.

I already knew there was a possibility my stalker was a very bad person. But somehow, seeing pictures of him with his fiancée made him seem disarming. If what Travis is insinuating is right, then Eli wants to assault me. It's not enough that he knows where I'm staying and that I've been seemingly into it. There's something much more sinister lying beneath the surface.

Just the idea of that gets rid of any doubt I might have had before. This man is dangerous, and I want him gone. I don't care about his life back home, his fiancée, or his family. If he's willing to fly across the country to come here with the intent of raping me—or worse—he can die.

"Where do we start?" I ask.

Travis must see the fury in my eyes, because the corners of his lips turn up as he looks back at the computer.

He delves into everything he knows about Eli. For the first time, I can see how his rigorous schedules and eye for detail are a benefit. He's able to predict almost exactly where he can find Eli, and he has a plan for what to do.

"Have you ever felt like somebody has been on your trail while you do all of this?" Everything he discusses involves meticulous stalking. To me, it almost seems impossible that somebody wouldn't catch him.

"Never," he replies, as confident as ever.

I raise my eyebrows, but he doesn't budge. I happen to remember him telling me about somebody possibly being on his tail right now. He doesn't seem concerned about that, though.

"So tell me about what you have planned for Eli," I say with a smirk. Excitement swells in my chest as he scans my face and probably sees the eagerness in my eyes.

Travis and I recognize something in each other. I've never felt this with anyone else before.

"Well, we're going to start with you luring him somewhere quiet." Travis's voice is low as he talks, and he leans back in his chair as if this is relaxing to him. "Then I'll come out of hiding with a needle and incapacitate him entirely. He'll wake up in a damp basement, not understanding why he's restrained to a table."

"Basement? You're not using one of the factories like the others?"

"That's not my only mode of operating." He leans forward with a smile, grabbing his pocketknife. He opens it and twirls it around his fingers like it's a fidget spinner. "Not only do I have factories, but I own a crematorium. It's closed down and situated on a plot of land you can't even see from the street. It used to be a pet cemetery. We'll bring him there, and while he's in the basement, we'll make him realize the error of his ways. I'll take my time killing him before loading him into the oven and turning him to ash."

An excited glint shows in his eyes. He holds the knife in his hands as I watch him. He scans my face, lowering on my body as he bites the inside of his cheek. Staring at him, I see something switch in his eyes. It's like he can taste the kill already.

Without warning, he moves swiftly and stands up, wrapping an arm around my neck and holding the blade of the knife to my throat. My breath catches as I feel the cold metal press against my skin.

"It's easy, you know," Travis whispers in my ear. A chill runs through my body, and I'm not so sure it's a bad thing. My heartbeat quickens, and I bite my lower lip as I strain my eyes to look at him. "I could kill you right now. All I have to do is swipe this knife along your pretty little throat, severing your carotid artery. You would die within a matter of minutes. I know how to clean up blood too."

His voice is cold, and despite everything telling me I should be afraid of this, I'm not. I shiver as warmth rushes through me, flooding between my legs. I stare at him, savoring how this makes my entire body tingle.

"You wouldn't hurt me," I say, knowing it's going to get a rise out of him. And that's exactly what I want.

He moves around me and presses the knife harder against me. He kneels in front of me as he stares me in the eyes. "I don't know if that's true."

Before I can say anything, he gets up and pulls me to my feet, slamming the knife down on his desk. His hands are around my waist as he pushes off my pajama bottoms. *Fuck. Yes.*

My hands immediately find the buckle of his jeans, and I undo them, shoving them aside. I feel frenzied as he pushes me back on the desk and spreads my legs wide. His fingers trace my slit as he feels just how wet I already am for him.

Travis is as hard as a rock, and I can't help but wonder if it's entirely from holding the blade to my throat. "I knew you were into knife play," I tease.

He doesn't say anything as he shoves himself into me. I arch my back on the desk and cry out from the pleasure shooting through my body. My breath quickens, and it takes me a moment to adjust to the feeling of him inside me again. It's incredible, and I almost wish he would never leave this spot.

His hand wraps around my throat and he squeezes, forcing me to stare up at him as my body starts to tremble.

"I could snap your neck," he says in a cold, murderous voice as he pumps himself inside me. I see the truth in his eyes, and I trust that he won't, but the desire is still there.

His words echo in my mind, telling me he was in Ryan's cabin to kill me. Something changed, and I know he's not going to hurt me now. That doesn't take away the little bit of fear I feel as his hand squeezes my neck harder.

Something about that danger excites me. I'm dancing on the cusp of death every single day with him, and I'm beating it. It's intoxicating.

My heart rate quickens as I struggle to breathe under his grasp. Every sensation in my body is heightened as he grips my thigh with his other hand and his cock fills me entirely.

I moan, the sound coming out ragged. He seems to notice this, and the devilish look in his eyes only grows. "Do you want me to stop? To let you go?"

His grip tightens while he waits for my answer. Instinctually, I nod. Though I don't know if that's what I really want. I'm starting to feel the rush of adrenaline swimming through my head as every nerve in my body is on high alert. It feels like heaven.

Travis smirks at me and shakes his head, looking down at my body before him. I grab hold of his arm, attempting to push it off me. Maybe Travis likes having a bit of a fight, so I'll give him one. My grip is weak, which I sense is even more of a turn-on for him as he holds his arm steady.

"I'll let go of you when I'm good and ready," he says as he pumps into me harder and harder.

I can't take it much longer, and within moments, my entire body is spasming on his desk. My legs spread wider, and he pushes them even farther apart with the hand that was on my thigh a minute ago. He relaxes his grip on my throat only slightly before tightening it again. Ecstasy rushes through my veins as my head spins from the choking. I try to moan and whimper, but every noise I make is stifled.

Travis sees this and loses control completely. He doesn't hold back as he comes and fills me with every drop. As he thrusts inside me, he pounds his hips against me. The desk rattles and shakes below us, and I'm afraid it's going to break.

When the pleasure fades, he releases me from his grip, and I fall back on the desk, pushing papers and utensils aside inadvertently. I gasp for breath, and my chest heaves as I will myself to recover. Travis sits down in his desk chair, his pants pulled back up and buttoned.

Eventually I sit up and look at him. "I want to go with you when you kill him."

He nods and gestures for me to get off his desk so he can put everything back together.

He spends the rest of the day stalking Eli on his computer. I watch from time to time, but I have my own work to do for my channel.

When bedtime rolls around, I climb into bed and hold my wrist out for him to zip-tie, but he doesn't. I smile at him, knowing this means that he trusts me. At least more than he did previously. Finally, we're making progress.

Chapter Twenty-Three

Over the next few days, I gradually make room for Sage in my life. I've come to the realization that no matter how hard I try to scare her away, she won't leave. Not even my body count fazed her too much, and if I can't get rid of her, I have to keep her close. Maintaining my former schedule would be impossible with her constantly hanging around, so I had to make *adjustments*. I cringe at the word.

As painful as it is to admit, it's not as bad as I thought it would be. Sage is more energetic than I am, and she talks almost nonstop, but I've learned to tune her out most of the time. Her voice is like white noise to me now. Plus, she is very interested in the planning process for everything I'm going to do to Eli.

He keeps messaging her, still not telling her he's in Lake Lure. I've been watching him, though. Not physically, but digitally. I've managed to track his phone to see where he goes and what he does, all thanks to his need to speak to Sage.

She is in the living room with her feet kicked up on the couch and a paperback book in her hands when I find her. "What did I say about putting your feet on the furniture?"

She sits up and makes a show of planting her feet on the carpet as she smiles. "Won't happen again."

"Get dressed. We're going to pay a visit to the motel our friend is staying at," I say before walking back to my bedroom and riffling through my drawers for appropriate attire. I hear her moving around the cabin and know she's obeying.

Because we're not actually killing Eli tonight, we can't wear anything suspicious. We have to blend in and go unnoticed as we approach the hotel to spy on him. If he sees me and Sage in the car together, then it's going to raise some red flags. I can't have that.

Kevin slipped out of my fingers because of Sage, and I won't let this kill go. Every hour I go without gratification is torture, and I desperately need to quench this thirst.

Soon enough I'll be able to fully relax, at least for a time. Then I'll delve into finding my next victim and begin this whole ritual all over again. Now that Sage knows about my proclivities, she won't be able to hinder me anymore.

She's waiting for me in the living room when I finish getting dressed, and I sigh, taking in the clothes she chose.

"What?" she asks, looking down at herself.

She's wearing a pair of denim shorts cut extra short and a vintage oversize Harley-Davidson T-shirt that is tied in the back to fit her.

"People are going to be looking at you," I say, shaking my head. The idea makes my blood boil, and I try to fight against the feeling. It's no use. The idea of another man looking at her—and God forbid, touching her—is infuriating. "Let's just go. We're staying in the car, anyway. And I'm going to need you to put a hat on—your hair is visible a mile away."

"Okay, rude," Sage jokes as she grabs a baseball cap from her bag and puts it on. She follows me out the door and climbs into the passenger seat of my car, putting her seat belt on without prompting. "So what are we doing, anyway? I thought we were waiting to kill him."

"First of all, we are not *killing* him." I pause to adjust the mirrors on the car, ensuring I have clear visuals of everything around me. "And all we're doing is making sure he's staying where we think he is. I haven't actually been able to get eyes on him, so I have to make sure he's alone. I can't afford any unexpected hang-ups."

Sage turns on the radio as we're driving and starts singing along to some sugary pop song that grates on my nerves. I have a choice. I can either turn off the radio and drive in silence, and Sage will drone on and on about something I don't care about, or I can leave the music on. With the music on, I can at least think without distraction.

Another song comes on, and Sage starts babbling about fruit trees and bees. I slowly increase the volume of the music using my steering wheel controls.

We make it to the Lodge, where I believe Eli is staying, and look around the parking lot for any sign of him. Sage lowers herself in her seat, leaning back incredibly conspicuously. I roll my eyes but don't say anything.

After a few minutes of driving around, I park the car at the end of the lot so we can keep a close eye on every other car we see.

"Maybe I can try to lure him out of his room?" she offers.

"No, if he sees you, that might be strange. We can't have him thinking anything could go wrong while he's here."

My phone buzzes in my pocket, and I pull it out, seeing a text message from Peter on the screen. Heads up, it's likely someone is tailing you right now. Be careful. I'm looking into it.

Fuck.

I've gone this long without being caught, and whoever it is who's following me—the same person looking into Amelia—they're going to throw a wrench in this whole plan. I grip my phone and see my knuckles turn white as I get lost in thought.

"What's wrong?" Sage asks, sitting upright and staring at me with concern.

I look at her while trying to hold back my anger. If I'm being tailed, in the parking lot of the hotel my next victim is staying at, it's because of her. If this is going to lead to my downfall, it's all her fault. I'm going against my routine because of her. I'm looking into Eli because of her.

I'm in this car right now, woefully unprepared for my next kill, all because of her.

I don't answer right away, and I look around the parking lot for any sign of John Doe's car. I remember the license plate number, but I don't see it anywhere. Of course, if this guy has any sense, he will have returned that rental car and gotten a new one.

"Talk to me," Sage urges. She squeezes my arm, and I yank it away.

"Someone's following us."

She immediately turns around, not being subtle in the slightest as she looks for whomever it is.

"Will you stop that? It's already bad enough that somebody might have seen us driving around the parking lot. If Eli comes up missing, this will be his last known location, and I'll have been seen here."

She sinks back in the seat and lets out a slow exhale. She turns to me with a half smile on her lips and her eyebrows raised. "What's there to worry about? It's not like you're here to kill anyone."

I know it's a joke. The look on her face tells me as much. But even knowing that, it doesn't make it any less annoying.

"Is this just a game to you?" I shout, slamming my hands against the steering wheel. "This is real for me. I don't take any of this lightly, and I need you to take it seriously."

Sage stiffens in her seat beside me as I watch her, feeling the fury in my veins. She's not afraid of me, but she seems shocked I would yell like this.

"Okay, then we give a valid reason for being here." Instead of cowering away from me, she's trying to help me cover for this mistake. I almost feel bad for lashing out. "Maybe we can rent a room. If anyone asks, we can say a breaker went out at the cabin, and we booked a room for the night because the hardware store was closed."

I take a deep breath and grip the steering wheel between my hands. She's right. I rack my brain trying to think of another plan, but the one she is suggesting is solid.

Never in my life have I met someone who's been able to calm me down when I feel like this. I'm amazed at how Sage is able to get through to me. Maybe having her around isn't so bad.

"Let's do it," I say after a moment, and I pull the keys from the car. We hop out and start walking toward the entrance of the motel to book a room for the night.

Sage stares up at me like a kicked puppy, but I try to ignore her.

"Maybe we can even have a little fun while we're here." She pokes my arm and crawls her fingers up to my shoulder in an attempt to seduce me. "Perhaps a little bit of role-play. I'll be the French maid who walks in looking for a big tip and—"

"I can't think about this right now." I shake my head and push her hand aside. I continue walking to the entrance of the motel, but she stops. I turn around and look at her expectantly, waiting for her to just give up and follow me.

A group of people walk out of the motel lobby, and I hear their tipsy laughter as they chat among each other. I don't turn around to look at them right away, but I see Sage's eyes flitting over my shoulder at them.

"Oh, mami!" a man's voice calls in our direction. "Those shorts look good on you. Come over here and let us take a better look."

The other guys all laugh, high-fiving each other as they stare at Sage. This is great. Now we have witnesses.

"Maybe I should go over there and talk to them. At least they seem to want my company," Sage says, crossing her arms as she stares at me.

I look over my shoulder at the group of guys, seeing how they're licking their lips and letting their eyes crawl all over her body. Jealousy taints my blood. I feel it slither from my chest and spread to my fingertips as I clench my fists. I look back at Sage with a hardened expression on my face.

"You're mine." I reach out and pull her into my arms, holding her close to me. My lips crash against hers before she can say another word. The guys behind us all boo at the scene, mumbling to themselves how lucky I am. I ignore them as her lips part to let my tongue fill her mouth. I pull away after a moment, seeing the satisfied look on her face. "I'll kill anyone who even threatens to put a hand on you."

I'm serious, and Sage knows it as well as I do. It puts a smile on her face, and she grabs my hand to walk toward the entrance. I wish I could know what was going on in her mind, but seeing how pleased she is by the idea of me killing for her, I know I'll never fully understand this woman.

Chapter Twenty-Four

The night has finally come. I've worked hard to mentally prepare myself for what this means, but now that I'm mere hours away from helping murder someone, reality is setting in. I don't have cold feet, but I am nervous.

As I mentally prepare, I have a full-blown fashion crisis over what to wear to help commit a murder. "Okay, leather feels like I'm trying too hard. Denim? Too chill! Maybe a hoodie? People distrust hoodies."

In the end, I pack three outfits. *You know, options.*

Whenever the idea of backing out crosses my mind, I remind myself of everything Travis has told me about Eli. He's stalking me. He found out where I am staying, and he traveled all the way here without letting me know because he wants to hurt me.

God, if he could do this to me, imagine who else he could do this to! There's a strong chance I might not even be the first woman who's caught his interest like this. Maybe there are dozens who came before me, and plenty who will come after. What we're doing is a service to countless other women who might fall victim to him.

Travis and I both dress in all black. He's wearing the sexy cat burglar outfit I saw him in once before, leather gloves and all. I'm careful not to say anything to disturb him as he gears up. I've been with him long enough to know that he has his ritual, and I don't want to do anything to mess that up today.

Ultimately, I decide to put on a pair of black leggings and borrow one of Travis's black long-sleeve shirts. It's oversize, but if anyone were to see me in it, they wouldn't think I was wearing anything other than my boyfriend's shirt. Definitely not a kill suit.

Travis moves swiftly through the house, gathering everything he needs, and I can feel the tension radiating off him. He's in the zone preparing for this. I watch him, studying his movements. His dedication is admirable.

"Are you ready?" Travis asks me when the SUV is all packed and ready to go. I stand up and nod, following him to the garage, where we both climb into the car.

The trunk is loaded with bleach, plastic wrap, tarps, zip ties, and plenty of cleaning rags. We drive in complete silence. I don't turn on the radio, and I keep my eyes glued to the dark road ahead as Travis seems like he is getting lost in his own mind.

Even though knowing what he's thinking is impossible, I assume he's going over the plan countless times, searching for any weaknesses. I do the same, but I get sidetracked thinking about different scenarios of how this could go wrong.

When we pull up to the diner near the motel, my heart drops in my chest. This is it. Phase one of the plan to find Eli and kill him.

"You know the plan?" Travis stops the car and looks at me, his eyebrow raised as he studies my face.

"Check in online and wait. I'll order a drink. It's quick and inconspicuous. When he shows up, lure him away." I take a deep breath and steel myself for what I'm about to do.

"I'll be waiting around the restaurant." He stares at me as I hesitate to open the door and leave. "Everything is going to be okay. I'm not going to let anything bad happen to you."

I smile at him and leave the car. Travis drives away, leaving me standing in front of the diner alone. I take a picture of the bright neon sign, making sure it's aesthetic and good enough to match the rest of my grid.

I check out the pictures. *Okay, if I die tonight, at least this lighting is insane.*

The LakeHouse is adorable, which makes this an obvious hot spot for tourists and travel influencers alike. I head inside and take a seat at the bar, ordering a watermelon mojito from the server.

While I wait, I take a couple of cute selfies, ignoring the people glaring at me while I do. Nobody likes people taking selfies in public, something I am all too aware of as an influencer.

When I'm done, both pictures are on my Instagram story. I refresh it constantly, looking for any sign of Eli liking the images, as he usually does. This time, instead of messaging me about them right away, I notice that he sees the Instagram story but does not comment.

A few minutes after my mojito arrives, I start sipping on it and stare straight ahead while I wait. Soon enough, someone sits down beside me, and I look to my left to see Eli.

My heart beats rapidly in my chest. It's really him.

This whole plan actually worked, and he saw the picture and came to the diner.

I force myself to look away because Eli doesn't know I know who he is. He has a faceless Instagram account, and if I make it known that I recognize him, it's bound to raise his suspicions. So I do what most women probably do when they see him—I ignore him.

And by *ignore*, I mean act like I'm deep in thought about solving climate change via TikTok dances. Convincing, I know.

"Excuse me," Eli says as he leans on the counter and stares at me nervously. "Do I know you?"

I do my best to paint a clueless look on my face as I shake my head. "I'm sorry, I don't think so." I pause, then shrug. "Well, I have a YouTube channel, so maybe you've seen some of my videos?"

Eli snaps his fingers and nods. "That's exactly right. I follow you on Instagram, actually."

"Oh really? That's so cool. This is kind of funny. I've never been recognized in public before." I laugh and do my best to sound flirty. I force a wide smile on my face as I turn the barstool, letting my entire body face him. He looks down at me with a smile, raising an eyebrow at my outfit.

"I have to say, I'm a little more used to seeing you in the dresses and bikinis." He laughs and blushes, looking down at the menu in front of him. "It looks like you're about to do a heist or something."

"Well, maybe I am." I lean forward and smile, biting my lip softly. "There are some priceless artifacts around here that my little fingers need to grab. But you have to promise not to tell on me."

"Of course, you have my word," Eli says, crossing his heart. "And if you're ever looking for any extra crew members, don't hesitate to reach out."

As much as I don't want to do this, I look him up and down with a hungry smile as I reach out to squeeze his arm. His mouth hangs open as he flexes his muscles under my grip.

"I am always looking for some muscle," I say with the most annoying giggle I have ever made. "I might just have to take you up on that offer."

Eli is clearly at a loss for words, because he doesn't say anything right away. The tips of his ears turn red, and I look down to see his dick straining against his pants. He quickly readjusts himself, but not before he sees me noticing. He laughs nervously, and I scoot even closer to him.

My hand lands on his thigh, and a shiver runs down my spine. I lean in to whisper in his ear, letting my breath graze against his neck, "It would be a shame to let that go to waste."

He backs away and widens his eyes as he looks me up and down. "Are you serious?"

I nod, biting my lip with a coy smile. "What can I say? I kind of have a thing for strangers."

Eli clears his throat and readjusts himself once more in the seat, looking over his shoulder at the door. "I'm staying at the motel right down the street."

"Then what are we still doing here?" I stand up and grab a twenty-dollar bill from my pocket and slam it down on the counter. Eli jumps to his feet and follows me to the door.

When we're outside, we walk around the building to where I know Travis is waiting. I turn around and walk backward with an eager smile on my face, my eyes falling to the bulge in his pants.

"I don't think you can wait to get to the motel, can you?" I bite my lip and stop in front of a parked car. "I might need to take care of that right now."

"Here?" Eli laughs incredulously, looking around nervously. "I'm sure I can wait a couple of minutes."

"Why not now *and* at the motel? I can't wait another second to taste you." I walk toward a dark corner of the parking lot.

Eli is hesitant, looking at the darkness, then back at his car. I know what he's thinking. The things he needs are in the hotel. If he really wanted to do me harm, he needs me there.

"I like things a little naughty," I whisper, inching closer and pressing my hand to his chest. His breath hitches in his throat, and I know he's exactly where I want him. "Trust me, it'll be fun."

I turn around and walk quickly into the dark corner, not bothering to look back at Eli, because I know he's following. He mutters something under his breath about not believing this is actually happening. He jogs to catch up to me, and I stop just before we reach the dumpster. From the shadows, Travis gives me the universal "ready" signal—which, in his case, is an enthusiastic thumbs-up like we're about to do a trust fall at summer camp. I nod back like this is totally normal and not, you know, kidnapping someone next to discarded cheeseburger wrappers.

"I've never done anything like this before," Eli says, closing in on me. "Believe me, I've had some fun with your pictures, but I never imagined you'd be this filthy."

I don't take my eyes off him as I lean my back against the wall of the diner, beckoning him to come closer. Travis moves behind him as quietly as a mouse, a syringe in hand.

"Tell me about all the things you've fantasized about doing to me."

Eli moves closer, pressing a hand against the wall beside my face. He thinks for a moment, opening his mouth to give me whatever filthy answer is on his mind. But before he can say a word, the needle sinks into his neck and his eyes close as the drugs take instant effect.

Eli collapses on the ground, and I stare at him with a scowl on my face. I wish I could wash off the feeling of his breath on me, and I can't wait for the rest of this plan to unfold.

"You did good," Travis says, smiling at me. That little bit of reassurance is all I need.

He hardly needs my help loading Eli into the trunk of the SUV.

With Eli in the car now, all I can think about is the possibility of him waking up and scrambling across the car, grabbing the steering wheel, and sending all of us crashing to our deaths. Travis doesn't say anything as he heads directly to the crematorium he owns.

I'm surprised at how secluded it is when we arrive. Travis told me it was far from the road, and he was right. It is a cemetery—there are hundreds of small gravestones for pets on the lot—and it feels eerie. The building is completely obscured by heavily wooded area.

Travis unlocks the door and brings out a stretcher to load Eli onto while he's still unconscious. I help him strap Eli's limp body to the metal before we roll it inside.

I stand back and let Travis take the reins once we're in the basement. He checks the ties before ripping Eli's clothes off entirely so he's naked in front of us.

Travis is focused—more so than I have ever seen him before. While he moves, there's a faint smile on his lips, showing that he is deriving pleasure from this. Before arriving, I tried to prepare myself for what I'd see. But standing here now, I can hardly believe it.

It feels like I'm sitting in a movie theater watching something unfold on-screen. It doesn't feel real. I know that it is, and I know that I had a hand in this. But I can't force my brain to register this as something actually happening to me.

My body feels light as I watch Travis work. I forget where I am, what I'm doing, everything that has led to this. My throat goes dry, and every hair on my body stands up. It's like I'm having some kind of out-of-body experience.

When Travis is done carefully inspecting everything, he sits down on a stool while he waits for Eli to wake up. Neither of us says a word to each other.

It feels like ages before Eli's eyes slowly open, and he looks around the room, trying to remember what happened. Both Travis and I watch as the memory of him running into me, having the meet-cute he thought he orchestrated himself, runs through his mind.

Now he's here, tied up and vulnerable. He looks just as afraid as he probably wanted me to feel. A flicker of excitement runs through me at the idea.

"I bet you're wondering where you are," Travis says, forcing Eli to look at him.

Eli tries to say something through the cloth stuffed in his mouth, but he can't.

"Remember Sage? The woman you flew all the way to Lake Lure in the hopes of meeting. Is that where it was going to end, Eli? Were you only going to run into her at the diner and tell her how big of a fan you are? Or did you plan on luring her back to your hotel room and tying her up? I bet it feels really awful having the tables turned so suddenly."

Travis stands up and grabs a knife he placed on the table beside Eli. Eli sees it for the first time, realizing that this is the end for him. He squirms against the metal stretcher, screaming into the cloth that stifles every sound.

My heart thuds against my chest as Travis traces the knife along his body. It's delicate, almost tender, as it scrapes against Eli's chest and lands right above his heart.

"Did you think you could take what's mine?" Travis leans in closer, almost pressing his mouth to Eli's ear as he speaks in a hushed, chilling voice. "I'm going to enjoy this more than any other kill."

Eli screams again, his eyes bulging as he pleads with Travis to let him go. Travis's eyes don't leave his as he plunges the knife into his chest. Eli goes still, the muscles that had been tensed and squirming on the stretcher suddenly limp. Blood pools around the knife and drips onto the metal table below him.

My mouth hangs open as Travis looks at me with a grin. "It's over."

It's over. His words echo in my mind as I'm trying to process everything I just witnessed. Honestly, between Eli's corpse and Travis's unnerving crime scene confidence, I'm not sure which one disturbed me more. Probably Travis. Eli at least had the decency to pass out before things got weird.

The realization of Eli being gone settles in, and a sense of relief washes over me. On top of that, I feel empowered. He was going to hurt me . . . possibly kill me, but now the threat is gone, thanks to us. In an odd way, Travis and I will forever be connected. As I look up at him through my lashes, I feel that connection buzzing between us, growing stronger by the minute.

Travis reminds me of an avenging angel, my dark knight who will kill for me. There is something so primal about him right now. I don't know if it's that thought or the adrenaline pumping through my veins, but I suddenly have the urge to jump Travis's bones and show him just how grateful I am.

Chapter Twenty-Five

Sage moves out of the shadows in silence as she takes in the scene fully. It's one thing to talk about killing someone. Hell, it's even one thing to plan it. But actually plunging a blade into someone's flesh is something else entirely. She's in shock, and I know she'll come out of it eventually.

I look away from her without saying a word and check the temperature on the oven to make sure it's high enough. The last thing I need is a medium-rare corpse. That would really ruin my Yelp rating—if serial killers had one.

Thankfully, it is. I don't like to linger with the bodies for too long. It's best not to dwell on what I've done. It only makes my lack of guilt feel more prominent.

I move the body to the mouth of the oven and slide it into the opening, letting it fall into the fire as the flames swallow it whole. I close the door when I'm positive it's fully inside and dust off my gloved hands.

I take a few deep breaths, savoring the energy in the room as if I could feed on it. The adrenaline has kicked in, and I feel like I'm high. I feel powerful.

Sage is still staring at me when I turn around and wait for her to say something. Being quiet isn't something I'm used to with her. I know her mind must be racing, and I'm steeling myself for the questions already. But she doesn't look traumatized or even upset. She looks . . . completely turned on.

I unstrap one of my black leather gloves, and Sage holds a finger up to stop me. "Can you leave those on a little longer?"

I nod, furrowing my eyebrows as I strap the glove back on. Or at least, I try to. The strap slips out of my hand, and I awkwardly restrap it.

Sage quirks a brow and says, "First time?"

I deadpan back, "No, I'm just not used to engaging in foreplay next to a cremating corpse."

She giggles like I made a joke, before lifting her shirt over her head and tossing it aside. She looks at me with eyes glazed over as she kicks off her shoes and slides out of her leggings. She's not wearing any underwear, and the bra she chose is practically see-through.

My cock immediately stiffens in my pants, and I unbutton them to free it. I've never had sex after a kill before. The high usually lasts hours, and I've jerked off toward the end a few times. As I've said before, killing isn't a sexual thing for me.

But seeing Sage now, completely naked, while Eli's body burns in the oven, I might have to change that.

"Get on your knees." She does as I say and opens her mouth as I approach her. When I'm close enough, she immediately wraps a hand around my cock and starts licking the shaft.

Every movement of her tongue is incredible, the feeling heightened by the ecstasy I already feel from the kill. She moves quickly, almost frenzied, with each flick of her tongue over the tip of my cock. She moans when wrapping her lips around it, taking more of me in her mouth.

"Slow down. I want to savor this," I say as I lace my fingers through her hair, pushing her head farther down on my cock. She takes all of me in her mouth, gagging on me as I hold her against my groin. I close my eyes and relish the feeling of her throat closing around me.

After a few moments I let go, and she backs away entirely, gasping for breath. "Fuck me," Sage says, staring up at me with hungry eyes. She falls back on the ground and spreads her legs wide.

I take my shirt off and toss it on the ground, climbing on top of her and positioning myself between her legs. She's already wet when I hover around her pussy, and I shove myself inside her.

"Oh my god, yes!" she cries out. Her arms wrap around my neck, and she digs her fingernails into my back as she holds me close to her.

I stare down at her chest and lower the cup of her bra to see her nipples. I take a breast in my mouth, swirling my tongue around her hardened bud and gently nibbling it. Sage arches her back as I touch her, moaning uncontrollably with every flick of my tongue.

My cock moves in and out of her, twitching and throbbing as I get closer to coming. I keep myself right on the edge, slowing down and stopping altogether before bursting. Every thrust is incredible, feeling more intense than it usually does. I don't want this to end.

I sit up on my knees and grab her waist to lift her off the ground slightly. I pull out of her mostly while holding her tight before slamming myself into her while gripping her waist. She screams as I pull her closer with each thrust, fucking her hard while I keep her on the brink of orgasm.

I feel her pussy throbbing around me, desperate for release, but I don't let her have it. For the first time since being with Sage, I'm in control of myself. I stare down at her body, seeing how eager she is for my touch, and I savor every moment of it.

"You want me to make you come?" I ask, reaching up and squeezing her nipple between my fingers.

"Yes!" Sage cries out, attempting to grind her hips against me to make herself come. I laugh and stop her.

"You'll come when I let you." I wait for her pleasure to recede before pumping myself into her again. "You're so fucking wet right now. Is that because of what I did?"

She looks at me, nodding while she bites her lip, hard. "Yes."

I pump into her harder, letting her know how much I approve of her answer. As I get closer, I start losing control of myself and sink into the pleasure. My cock throbs as she clenches around me, almost pulling me deeper inside as her orgasm ripples through her body.

I don't stop fucking her until every last drop of my cum is drained from me. Sage screams the entire time as she twitches below me.

When we're finally done, I pull out and stare at her with a satisfied smile. She watches me with interest, no doubt recognizing how relaxed I am for the first time since meeting me.

"We should finish up here." I button my pants while she stares at me, and a moment later she puts her clothes back on.

I've never done anything like that before. It's not part of my plan, but I feel too good to dwell on that.

The body is almost done in the oven, and the two of us finish cleaning up. After a while, I turn off the oven and wait for it to cool before pulling the stretcher back out to see nothing but ash remaining of Eli.

I find my bag and pull out a small glass vial, the same ones I use for each of my victims. Sage watches curiously as I scoop a small amount of ashes inside and stare at it with a smile on my face.

"What?" I ask, realizing this is the first time someone has ever seen my ritual. Nobody knows about my morbid keepsakes but me.

"I just never expected you would be the type to have trophies." Sage shrugs.

We finish cleaning the room and sweeping Eli's ashes into a box. When I'm confident there's no evidence remaining, we leave the basement and head back to the car. I empty the box of ashes as the wind blows, and they flow away, melding with the earth around us.

The drive back home is quiet, but the tension that was there before is gone. Both of us are calm and relaxed. A pleasant buzz in my head forces a smile on my lips. This was an incredible kill. I have Sage to thank for that. I never would have found Eli if it wasn't for her, and I wouldn't have yearned for his blood if it wasn't for her either.

Sure, I missed out on killing Kevin because of her. But that kill would not have compared to this one.

When we get home, I lead her into my office, where I grab the vials of ashes from all my other kills and show them to her. This is the last part of who I am that she doesn't know.

She picks them up and looks at them, carefully analyzing each one before putting it back. I can see the reverence in her eyes. These were people at one point. Living, breathing people whom I have killed.

She isn't afraid.

Chapter Twenty-Six

I'm surprised by the calm I feel this morning. Well, maybe *calm* isn't the right word. I feel energized by what we did. The power of being able to make Eli follow me into that dark corner, knowing what was going to happen afterward, is intoxicating. If I could do that for him, I can do that for countless other people.

I feel like something has awoken inside me. Never in my wildest dreams would I have imagined I would have a hand in something like this. Even days ago, I thought I'd want to run for the hills when everything was done, but I don't.

Travis is still asleep when I wake up. That in and of itself should show that something has changed. I stare at his face and study just how serene he looks. For the first time since I've met him, there's a weight off his shoulders. There's a lightness surrounding him. He's at peace for once.

He's sleeping so soundly I'm tempted to poke his cheek just to see if he's still breathing. Not that I'd want him to be dead—but if he were, at least I'd get to use my new crematorium skills again.

I tiptoe out of bed, being careful not to wake him. After everything we did last night, he needs his rest. It's almost 8:00 a.m., and I know he's going to be waking up any minute now.

In the kitchen, I pull out the ingredients to make a celebratory breakfast. I don't care about Travis's calories for the day. I'm going to shove bacon and eggs down his throat if it's the last thing I do.

I hum to myself, practically dancing behind the counter as I crack eggs and mix them in a bowl. Bacon is frying on the stove, sending the salty and fatty aromas through the room. My stomach growls, and I realize I didn't eat anything yesterday. I was far too nervous about the kill.

"What are you doing?" Travis startles me, and I nearly drop a bowl filled with shredded potatoes. I exhale a sigh of relief when I see it's just him.

"I'm making us breakfast. And you're going to eat it." I wave the spatula like a sword. "You have two options: scrambled or scrambled with a side of 'I don't want to hear it.'" When a fleck of grease hits the counter, I salute the mess with the spatula. "Breakfast combat casualty. He died bravely." Travis immediately grabs a paper towel and wipes it up.

He grabs another spatula while I'm in the middle of mixing the shredded potatoes with the seasonings and some freshly diced onions and flips the bacon in the pan. I keep humming under my breath as I sway my hips back and forth. Travis just watches me with an amused smile.

"What?" I ask as I dump the potatoes in a hot pan.

"You confuse me." He shakes his head as he speaks, and I roll my eyes. "You're not like most people."

"Neither are you." I nudge him with my elbow, and we stand in silence for a few minutes while we cook together. "How do you feel?"

He pauses and sets the spatula down before looking at me. I can see the heaviness creeping back into his face, and I almost regret asking.

"I feel relieved. It's sort of like spending a day out in the heat, covered in sweat and dirt, and taking a cold shower. I feel fresh, renewed." He pauses, and his eyes graze over me. "It feels good."

"Is it normal to feel this good the morning after?" I gesture around me to the mess I've made in the kitchen while cooking. He laughs and shakes his head again.

"If you want to know about normal, I'm not the person to ask."

"Is it always like this for you?" I idly stir the potatoes while I stare at him and wait for an answer. "You know, I want to know if this is the norm or if it's an outlier before it happens again."

"Again?" Travis wrinkles his eyebrows and leans against the counter, crossing his arms.

"Yeah! Look at what we did together. We worked incredibly well, and this doesn't have to be the first and last time." I take the potatoes off the stove when they've fried up enough. "Eli isn't—wasn't—the only internet creep out there. I have hundreds of guys in my DMs telling me disgusting things, and I'm sure a lot of them have similar motives."

I pull out my phone and open the messages, scrolling through them so he can see just how many men write to me. His eyebrows rise, but other than that, I don't see any signs of him eagerly agreeing.

"We can track other people down and eliminate them just like we did Eli. We'd be doing the world a favor. It's a net-good situation, you know? You can get what you need by murdering people, but the people we're choosing deserve to die."

His eyes harden as he looks at me. "I've already told you, that's not why I do what I do."

"What difference would it make?" I feel myself getting a little defensive, so I take a deep breath to calm down. From what I understand, he targets someone without any reason. Of course, there are more transient people who might not be as easily missed, but that's about it.

"This isn't some game I'm playing. I'm not out to be some vigilante hero making the world a better place. There are bad people in this world, and I'm one of them," he says. His voice is final, like he doesn't want to hear any more of this.

I huff and finish cooking breakfast while he starts cleaning up the mess behind me. I can't stop thinking about what I said. It's the perfect situation. Travis can help me make the world safer. Would anybody really miss some internet troll hiding behind their keyboard and threatening women?

I whip my head around and stare at him with my hands on my hips. "What about us? What do you see in our future, then?"

Travis pauses and stares at me with a blank face. His eyes move around quickly as if he's trying to compute the right answer.

"If you don't want to help me, I'll just use what you taught me and go off on my own."

He raises his eyebrows and shakes his head slowly. He tries opening his mouth to speak, but no words come.

"I can do it. I'll be a one-woman killing machine."

"You're threatening me to become a murdering team with you?" Travis is dumbfounded. I bet he never imagined this is what would happen when I accidentally knocked on his door the first day we met. Hell, neither did I.

I don't know how to make myself more clear to him.

"Travis, I've seen how you operate. You plan everything down to the last detail. What's your plan for me? I know your secrets. You told me how you kill and how you dispose of the bodies. I could be a danger to you."

He backs away from me while trying to wipe the surprise off his face. Maybe I shouldn't have told a serial killer I can potentially spill very incriminating information about him, but here we are.

"I don't have a plan for you," he finally says. His eyes lock on mine, and my heart tightens in my chest. "You're unpredictable. I never could have planned on meeting someone like you."

I don't know if that's a good thing or not. All I know is that I care about him, and I don't want to go off on my own. But after last night, I don't know how I can go back to normal. He's unlocked something inside me, and I'm going to find a way to use it to do good.

I drop the conversation for now. We'll have to figure this out eventually, but we can at least enjoy breakfast.

Chapter Twenty-Seven

Several days pass, and I feel the itch coming back. It's not strong enough to disrupt my daily life, but it lingers. If I'm quiet for too long, I start dreaming about killing. I think about the thrill of the chase, finding someone and watching them. Waiting for them to show me their routine so I can properly stalk them from a distance.

I have some time before I need to find a victim, but I always keep my eyes peeled. You never know when the perfect person is going to fall right into your lap.

"Is there anything you want to eat?" Sage asks as she throws together a grocery list on her phone.

"I normally alternate between veggie lasagna, chicken and broccoli, and salmon with quinoa and brussels sprouts."

She flashes me a dirty look as she shakes her head. "Maybe now that I'm here, you can try to change up your food habits. You can be a little less rigorous every now and then, right?"

I raise an eyebrow. "Like what?"

"I don't know—Thai curry? Tacos?"

"You mean food that doesn't come with a low glycemic-index rating?"

She rolls her eyes and pulls out her phone. "You are a nutritional war criminal."

"I'm just saying, if kale was a person, I'd marry it. Stability is sexy."

She throws a baby carrot at me from the fridge drawer before she stares at me with hopeful eyes, and I reluctantly nod.

"I'll keep my schedule the same, with the exception of Saturday and Sunday."

She smiles wildly and immediately starts searching for recipes on her phone.

I've made a lot of adjustments in my life for Sage, and it's hard. Some of them come more naturally, but some have the potential to upend my life. Something as simple as letting her cook me dinner two nights a week is a relatively small sacrifice to keep the peace in the house. I figure if I give her freedom for these things, she can leave me to my own devices and allow me to keep my schedule intact otherwise.

Plus, if she's going to be making an overly complicated dinner, that gives me time in my office to focus on my kills. Stalking Eli and killing him with Sage was interesting. She didn't force her ideas on me—she let me take the reins. But now she wants to be a team. I didn't ask for that.

We drive into town to buy some groceries and household supplies. Sage has a list, so I give her my platinum card, and she eagerly runs inside ahead of me to grab whatever exotic ingredients she needs for her ideas. I follow behind with a faint smile on my face at how excited she gets. It's hard to admit, but she is fighting her way into my heart.

"Excuse me," someone says nearby. Turning, my eyes widen as the perfect victim walks toward me. She's young, probably nineteen or twenty, if I have to guess. Her clothes are tattered and stained with dirt and sweat. Her hair is pulled back in a ponytail, but I can see how matted and unkempt it is. "Do you have any change to spare? I'm trying to buy a bus ticket home."

I freeze for a moment as I stare at her. She offers me a kind smile, and I do my best to force one on myself. I wasn't expecting to find a victim so soon, but sometimes fate has other plans. The itch is strong, practically pulling me toward her like a magnet. It's begging for me to do it now. To wrap my hands around her throat and strangle her.

I fight back against it and reach into my pockets to dig around for change. I grab my wallet and open it, finding a few bills inside. I've been approached by countless homeless people peddling for money; almost none of them are really looking for bus tickets home. But on the off chance she is, I don't want to give her much money. Maybe a few bucks, but none of the $100 bills in my wallet will work.

"I'm so sorry. I don't have anything on me right now." I flash her an apologetic smile and look toward the door of the store. "What's your name?"

"Nicole, and I don't mean to be any trouble—"

"Nonsense!" I keep smiling at her and shake my head fervently to let her know she's not a bother. "Are you going to be around here for a while? I can get some when I leave and bring it back to you."

She smiles and looks nervously over her shoulder toward an alleyway across the street. "They don't really like me staying around the grocery store. It makes the customers feel weird." She laughs nervously and looks down at the ground. "I'm just across the street, though. Again, I don't want to be too much—"

"Don't worry about that." Putting my wallet back in my pocket and thinking about how good it'll feel to slice through her throat. "If you're over there, I'll come find you when I'm done shopping."

I wave goodbye, throwing on the kindest persona I possibly can. All I can think about is how incredible this is. She's exactly what I'm looking for. She's young, so I assume she must be some kind of runaway. If her story is accurate and she's just trying to get money to go back home, her family is not in touch with her. It will be weeks, possibly even months, before someone notices she's gone.

I can taste the excitement on my tongue as I walk into the grocery store. Sage is lingering by the door with her eyebrows wrinkled, and I can already read what she's thinking.

"Friend of yours?" She grabs a basket and waits for me to reply.

"I think she would be perfect for a project of mine," I whisper, raising an eyebrow.

She inhales sharply but turns around before saying anything. We walk through the store, and she silently fills the basket with ingredients while I walk behind her, fantasizing about the kill.

At the end of an aisle, a salesperson is handing out samples of some kind of fish sauce. Sage grabs a sample cup, gives it a suspicious sniff, and recoils. "This smells like Poseidon's armpit."

I chuckle. "You're the one insisting on 'flavor.'"

We turn a corner, and I nearly knock over a tower of avocados stacked like a Jenga death trap.

"This store is a lawsuit waiting to happen," I mutter, catching a rolling avocado with the toe of my shoe.

"You say that like it's a bad thing," she says without looking up from her list.

The store isn't busy, but there are a few customers straggling around and throwing items haphazardly into their carts. Sage seems to take inventory of each of them as she leads me through the aisles toward the back of the store, which is completely empty.

"You can't hurt that girl," she whispers. Her eyes are sharp and adamant, but I'm almost shocked by her reaction. With how excited she was with Eli's kill, I would assume she would be happy that I found another. "She doesn't deserve to die."

"How do you know that?" I inch closer and lean down slightly so the two of us can converse more discreetly. "Neither of us knows anything about her. She could be just as bad as Eli."

She rolls her eyes and drops the basket on the ground to cross her arms in front of her. "She's just a kid. She doesn't even look like she's old enough to buy alcohol. You can't go after someone like her. There are countless other people who deserve to go."

I clench my fists and sigh, shaking my head. "Don't put this on me. The vigilante idea was all yours, not mine. This isn't about who deserves to go. It's about who I choose to vent the energy inside me. It's always in me. I have to get it out, and I can't always wait until we find the right person."

Sage is silent as she sees how resolute I am. With each word, I feel myself growing more frustrated with her. After everything we've done, I thought I could expect her to be more understanding of the risks involved.

"I have a choice. I can either find some anonymous person nobody's ever going to miss and kill them, or I can find someone else who I track down and interact with, which will lead to me getting caught," I continue, gritting my teeth as I speak. "Regardless of how you're looking at it, someone's going to die either way. I'm not a hero, and you're not going to make me one."

She looks away from me, and for a moment I feel bad about snapping. I know she has good intentions, but that's not my responsibility. She's already come into my life and changed it so much; I am not willing to budge on this. This is who I am. She knew this before she got involved.

"Let's get out of here." I turn around and storm out of the store before she says anything else. My anger is boiling over, and I can't risk the two of us having an outburst in public, not when so much is on the line. I expect Sage to follow me. Normally, when I tell her to do something, she does. But when I get to the car, I turn around and she's not there.

It feels like the ground has been pulled out from under me. She's always there. I've gotten used to her following me around like a puppy dog all day long. It's part of my new routine, and her not being there is yet another way she has disrupted it.

That's not even mentioning the fact that she knows everything about my kills. She knows the names of the people I have tracked down, where I've killed them, and where I keep their ashes.

I open the driver's-side door just to slam it shut as I storm toward the store entrance once again. How could I be so fucking stupid? Never in my life have I been trusting with anyone, save my sister when we were children. Why would I give such sensitive information to someone I barely know? If I don't do what Sage wants, is she just going to rat me out to the police?

Of course they would believe her. She can make up any lie she wants, and they'll believe her. She has that ability to charm people. She can tell them I forced her to help me, that she was a victim just like everyone else I've killed. I can't have that.

I briskly walk through every aisle, trying to find her. She's not hard to spot with her vibrant pink hair. But no matter where I look, she has practically vanished. I feel my frustration starting to boil over. On top of that, I'm worried she's run off to someplace I'll never find.

The last place I look is the bathroom. Thankfully, the store is empty enough that nobody else is in the ladies' room aside from Sage. She grips the counter as her shoulders shake with every sob she lets out.

I freeze. I've seen her cry only once before, under much different circumstances. It stirs something in me that I don't recognize. My heart aches, and I feel like it's pushing me toward her. It's unfamiliar, and I don't know how to act.

"You're crying," I say as I slowly inch toward her. She looks at me with blotchy red eyes and a scowl on her face. She's never looked at me like this.

My brain is completely still, refusing to cooperate with me. I know how to put on a facade to seem like I'm the same as everyone else. The only problem is that facade works only for typical situations like what to say to a clerk at a grocery store checkout. Not how to console a crying woman in a bathroom.

I hold my hand out and place it on her shoulder. My entire arm feels heavy, like I'm doing the wrong thing and forcing my body to go against itself. Sage looks at it, then back at me, and rolls her eyes.

"Is this . . . helping?" I ask, my hand awkwardly hovering in midair like I'm waiting for a high five from a statue.

"You look like you're malfunctioning," she says, sniffling.

"That checks out." I retract my hand and wipe it on my pants like it caught feelings.

"Do I pat your head now? Or fetch tissues? I've seen people offer tea during emotional events."

"Unless it's laced with bourbon, I'd pass," I retort.

"Noted for next time. Bring booze and avoid touching."

"I'm sorry." I pull my arm away and step closer. "I don't know how to respond to emotional outbursts from other people. This is all new to me."

"How about I give you some pointers, then?" Sage says as she whips her head around and glares at me. "When somebody reaches out to a person they care about and tries to connect with them and be a part of their life only to be rejected, they might react this way."

My body stiffens, and I take an inadvertent step back as I study her face. I never thought her suggestion was coming from a place of caring about me. My assumption was that she wanted to have fun. She liked the high she got from being involved in Eli's murder, and she wanted to feel that again. I thought it was childish. Even the idea of being some kind of vigilante hunting down sex offenders felt foolish to me. But now I see things from her side a little better.

Looking back, I realize how I was wrong. She was coming from a place of caring about me, someplace real.

Her face softens when she sees my reaction, and her shoulders slump.

"I'm sorry," I say. I look behind me at the bathroom door and think about the possibility of someone else coming in and finding us here. This conversation should not be had in public, so we have to get home. "I see where you're coming from, and I shouldn't have shut you out the way I did. I promise I'll think about your idea, but only if we can leave right now."

She agrees and follows me out of the bathroom. We forget just about everything we even came to town for and climb into the car to go home. Our grocery trip was completely derailed, and now that part of my day has been ruined.

I can sense that Sage feels triumphant. She stares out the window, the passenger-side mirror revealing a faint smile on her lips. She thinks that she's won this argument, but I'm not so sure she has.

For whatever it's worth, I'll let it go for now. But as we drive, my eyes linger on the roadside Nicole pointed to, and I can't help but wonder what it'll be like to follow her. I'll genuinely take Sage's advice into consideration. It's not a bad idea—it's just not what I'm used to. But I have to keep in mind that my safety is paramount. I can't sacrifice that just to appease her.

Chapter Twenty-Eight

I can't stop thinking about our argument in the grocery store. We only just killed Eli, and Travis is already looking for someone else. Now, that energy could be an incredible thing if we were directing it where it needs to go. But targeting a young homeless girl—he said her name was Nicole—who has already probably had a pretty rough go of things is just wrong. I'm worried about her.

Travis can get stuck in his ways, and I don't know how I'm going to fix the situation. I thought I could change him, and for a while it was looking like a possibility. But now, everything every woman has ever said about it being impossible to change a man is making sense.

You would think it would be unfeasible to keep a secret from me now that I know his deepest, darkest ones, but I'm not so sure. I never know what he is thinking. Plus, when he has his scheduled times for work, I don't know if he's lying to me. That's a part of his routine I'm usually not privy to. Eli was an exception because I was so involved in that. But Travis has made it clear he doesn't want me involved in his other kills.

I hover around him as much as I can. I'm paranoid, and I know it. There's just a very real chance he is doing something I have asked him not to. He told me we'd talk about it, but he hasn't been receptive. I know it's going to lead to an argument, and I try to avoid it for the sake of that. But there are other ways to find out what he's up to.

"Hey, I was thinking we could go for a swim later?" I say as I walk into the office. He's leaning back in his desk chair and looking at me as I walk around to sit in his lap. Yes, I would like to go for a swim with him at some point, but I'm also trying to get a look at his screen.

I don't know if I expected to see him watching surveillance camera footage of someone, but he has spreadsheets and a notepad document with code typed out. "I have free time in two hours," he says, his expression unreadable.

I kiss him on the cheek and walk out of his office. I even think about spiking some brownies again and getting him to confess to targeting Nicole while he's high. I doubt he would take any more brownies from me, though.

While I wait for him, I plop down on the couch and start searching for my own information on the phone. While the guys in my DMs provide some promising targets for Travis's energy, I'm sure there are some local victims who might be more enticing.

I pay for a monthly subscription on the Citizens app to see how many sex offenders are registered in the area. Surprisingly, this gives you their names, faces, and their addresses, which makes it easy to find them on social media, where they stupidly share everything about themselves. My mouth hangs open when I see just how many there are. It's a really sick world we live in. One guy's profile picture is him holding a lizard, like that's supposed to soften the blow of being a garbage human. "Ladies, he's a perv—but hey, he loves reptiles," I mutter to myself. "Swipe left, but keep your terrarium locked."

I tap on a few listings for very promising ones. These are disgusting men who have abused children and definitely don't deserve to breathe the same air as everyone else. I screenshot the information, planning on showing it to Travis at some point. If he isn't looking into Nicole as a victim, these are perfect choices. Maybe I can distract him from her long enough for him to forget she even exists.

Two hours pass, and Travis is still in his office. He's looking at his computer, and I have a sinking feeling in my stomach that he's doing something I don't want him to do. He never ignores his schedule. The only reasonable excuse I can come up with is he is so caught up in stalking Nicole that he's lost track of time.

I distract myself by going into the kitchen and preparing dinner. It's not a Saturday, which is one of the days Travis gave me to cook for him, but I do it anyway. I know he cares about his routine, but if this throws off his routine just enough to buy Nicole some more time to get out of town, I'm happy.

I start throwing together some Marry Me Chicken. My mom used this recipe when she was young to convince my dad that she really was the one, and they've been happily together ever since. If she could do that, maybe I can use it to convince my future husband not to kill a specific person.

After a while, when the savory smell of the food in the oven permeates the entire house, Travis peeks his head out of the office.

"It's Thursday. I have chicken and broccoli on Thursdays, so you're not going to convince me otherwise," he warns, flashing me a half-hearted smile.

"Wait, it's your chicken day?" I stand up and feign an apologetic look. "I think I used the last of the chicken. I'm so sorry."

Travis looks frustrated, but he doesn't let it get to him too much. "What is this, then?"

"It's Marry Me Chicken. It's actually my mom's recipe. I would love to share it with you," I say, smiling nervously at him. I walk over to him and place both my hands on his shoulders as I stand on my tiptoes to give him a kiss on the cheek. It's so obvious I'm lying—about wanting to share it with him right this moment. Subtlety has never been my strong suit.

"What the hell is that?" he asks. His tone is clipped, and he forces a smile. He's trying to adjust, and I am thankful for that, and I feel kind of bad for ruining his schedule. But I need to distract him.

"All you need to know is that it's delicious and ready in ten. Would you grab us some wine? A white will probably be best."

Travis does as I ask, walking toward the wine cabinet and grabbing a bottle and two glasses before setting the table.

I check the temperature on the chicken in the pan before pulling it out of the oven and bringing it to the table. Travis eyes the dish with a mixture of hesitation and excitement. I know he's going to love it—everyone does.

"We used to make this all the time when I was younger," I say as I put a portion on Travis's plate, then one on mine. "The commune was mostly vegetarian, and my parents claimed to be. My mom never gave up meat entirely. Marry Me Chicken was always a cheat meal. She'd make it once a month, and it would be our little secret. Well, the only other person who knew was the butcher in the commune. But Carl was sworn to secrecy because she knew he was cheating on his wife."

Travis gags at the last part, and I can't help but laugh. "So the commune is exactly what everyone thinks it is, right? Just a bunch of hippies sleeping around with each other."

"I want to say no, but that's probably true." I laugh. Travis pours both of us a tall glass of wine, and I take a sip as I watch him take his first bite of the food. He closes his eyes and chews slowly, savoring every flavor. "See? Didn't I tell you that food serves a bigger purpose than just nourishment?"

"I didn't believe you. Maybe now I do." He smiles and takes a drink of his wine, nodding at the perfect combination.

Surprisingly, Travis actually seems to be listening when I tell him more stories about the commune. I've always said it should be the center of some kind of reality TV show. Some of the things that go on there are ridiculous. I remember a winter solstice festival where the Yulemas tree was knocked over by two men fighting over a woman who left both of them for another woman. Travis even laughs as I describe every detail of that iconic fight.

"It wasn't all high-stakes drama, though. It was usually pretty peaceful, and we celebrated holidays within our own family units, for the most part. My parents always made a huge deal about Christmas," I continue, finishing my wine as I progress with the stories. "I stopped believing in Santa Claus when I was seven, but my parents loved that I still believed, so I pretended a few more years for them. They would always leave presents under the tree from them, but just one from Santa Claus. The one from Santa was always exactly what I wanted. A lot of the time, I didn't even put that on a list. They just knew somehow. Did you ever believe in Santa?"

Travis has already finished eating one portion of dinner and is midway through another. His wineglass is empty, and despite his protest, I pour him another. Obviously, I can't drug him with weed to get him to loosen up, so wine is going to have to do the trick.

"Believe it or not, I did for a time." I laugh and raise my eyebrows, trying to conjure an image of young Travis kneeling in front of a Christmas tree, opening his gift from Santa. But Travis's smile falls, and he clears his throat. "Leah actually convinced me he was real. I kind of stopped believing because it didn't seem logical, and when I confessed that to her, she pointed out every flaw in my logic. You know, I didn't understand how he flew around to every child in one night, and she explained what time zones are. She made me think she believed, but she just didn't want to take that away from me."

"That's really sweet." I reach across the table and squeeze his forearm as I see the emotions starting to take hold of him. He flashes me a half smile before drinking a sip of his.

"It was. After she died, that Christmas was when I found out the truth. I didn't get anything that year. Not even a stuffed animal from Santa." He gulps to fight against the emotion, and I feel my heart breaking for him.

I can't help but wonder what he would be like if he had a different family. Would he still be this way if he came from a family like mine? Or maybe if his sister hadn't died at such a young age? He might be an entirely different person if his parents had just been more affectionate with him.

But then again, I came from a family that was overly affectionate growing up, and there's something in me that relates to Travis. So maybe it has nothing to do with where we come from; it's who we are entirely.

"When was the last time you spoke to them?" I ask. I already know the relationship is strained, but seeing him now, I can't help but wonder if he wants more.

"A few years ago, on Thanksgiving. I don't even talk with them over text messages to check in." He shrugs as if it's nothing and he doesn't care, but I can see past that. There's a heaviness in his voice, disappointment. "It's probably for the best. They've never forgiven me for Leah, and I don't want to have to feel guilty every time I'm around them."

I squeeze his hand tight and let him know I'm here for him. Travis clears his throat and stands up, grabbing both of our plates and bringing them to the sink. This conversation is clearly over.

I stand up and bring the casserole dish of chicken to the counter to prepare it for storage. "What do you say we play some cards?" I suggest.

Travis shakes his head. "I'm not really interested in playing games."

"I see you. I hear you. But what if it was strip poker?" I raise an eyebrow, and as he stares at me, something in his gaze shifts.

"What type do you want to play?" Travis asks. I grab his hand and lead him back to the table and force him to sit down as I grab the deck of cards from my things.

"Texas Hold'em or seven-card stud?" I offer.

"I prefer five-card draw," he suggests, and I happily agree.

When I come back, he is waiting eagerly for me with a fresh glass of wine poured for both of us. "You read my mind."

"I figure you'll need a drink if you're going to be stripping," Travis jokes. At least, I think it's a joke.

I deal both of us a hand and quickly realize I haven't played poker in ten years, at least. Okay, there are flushes and royal flushes and . . . other stuff. It's a good thing I'm already planning on getting naked today.

We play the first hand, and unsurprisingly, it does not go my way. "Let's go with the shirt." Travis watches as I uphold my end of the bargain and lift my shirt over my head. I do a little shimmy to tease him, watching his eyes as they drop to my chest.

"Obviously, there's no choice but the pants," Travis says when I lose my second hand immediately after.

"Maybe a gentleman would take his shirt off just out of solidarity," I joke as I slide my pants down.

"If only there was a gentleman here." He smirks and deals another hand for us. Of course he wins. He makes it look easy, and I know from the other side of the table that it's not. It doesn't take long before I'm sitting almost completely naked at the kitchen table while Travis is still fully clothed.

As I sit in my underwear, I grab two pot holders from the kitchen counter and hold them up like makeshift armor. "Fine, but next hand, I'm playing as a medieval knight. Sir Lose-a-Lot."

Travis snorts into his wine, nearly spilling it. "That'll definitely protect your modesty. Maybe even give you a bonus card."

Chapter Twenty-Nine

TRAVIS

I don't normally spend time playing games, but counting cards is nothing more than simple math and probability. I know that there are two queens in the community pool on the table and one in my hand, so there's no way Sage has four of a kind.

The only problem with my current hand is, I have the lowest-possible kicker card with a two of hearts. With three queens already out and forty-two cards left in the deck, there's a little over a 2 percent chance that Sage has the other queen. If she has a queen with any kicker higher than two, she actually beats me.

She squints her eyes at the cards in her hand and tries to make sense of the best move for her. It's cute that she's trying. Has she really not picked up on me counting cards? Or does she really think I'm that lucky?

I stretch my neck and crack my knuckles like I'm about to perform heart surgery instead of play cards. "Math never lies," I whisper dramatically, then accidentally launch a card across the room as I try to shuffle. It hits Sage in the forehead.

"Smooth," she says, deadpan. "Remind me to never let you be the magician at a kids' party."

"Cardio-kinesis," I mutter, picking it up. "It's a strategy."

We count down to one and both lay down our hands, revealing that she has nothing at all. "Three of a kind," I say with a smile.

She shakes her head in disbelief, her cheeks getting red as she huffs. "How the hell do you keep doing this?"

"There's only one thing left to take, isn't there?" I point to her crotch, at the lace thong she's wearing, with a devious grin.

"You have to be cheating. Please tell me you're cheating and I'm not just this bad," Sage pleads, not taking her panties off just yet.

I feign offense and lean back while I shake my head. "You really think I would cheat at strip poker, of all things?"

She rolls her eyes and stands up before sliding out of her panties. She tosses them aside and makes a show of sitting down to hide herself from me. She picks up the deck and shuffles it, clearly not ready to stop.

"Either my eyes deceive me, or you're out of clothes," I say as I lean forward. "By strip poker rules, that means you lose."

"No. I have to win a round eventually, and we're playing until that happens." My cock is already straining in my pants, and I look her up and down before agreeing.

"Okay, but when you lose the next hand, you have to do what I say." She freezes and looks at me, nodding. She has no idea what she's agreed to.

She deals the cards, and I see that I have a five and six of clubs in my hand. I hold my breath as she flips the community cards to reveal a straight flush for me with a seven, eight, and nine of clubs on the table. It's like divine intervention is stepping in and making sure I win.

I can see by the look in her eyes she has nothing. Looking between the community pile and her own hand to try to put something together, but she can't. At the very least, she cannot beat a straight flush. With no royals in the community pile, there's nothing better to play.

Right before revealing her hand, Sage throws on her best poker face—if her poker face was modeled after a melodramatic soap opera villain.

"Prepare to meet your match," she declares, tossing her hair back and staring into my eyes.

"You sure about that?" I arch an eyebrow.

She reveals her hand: a scattered mess of low cards.

"Okay, I'm not your match," she mutters. "Maybe your neighbor's match. Like . . . their dog's match."

I didn't even have to count cards to win that one.

"Okay. You win." She folds her arms across her chest, not bothering to cover her bare nipples. She just pushes her breasts higher, making them more prominent, if anything.

Scooting the chair, I lean back as I unzip my pants. "All right, my prize is a blow job."

She feigns frustration but promptly walks over to me and gets on her knees. I pull out my cock, and it's already upright as she kneels in front of it and licks the shaft.

I smile at her as she gets to work, brushing her hair out of her face so I can admire the view. There's nothing quite like seeing a beautiful girl on her knees with your cock in her mouth.

"Make sure you take all of it," I say as soon as she wraps her lips around the tip. I close my eyes and bask in the sensation. Her mouth is warm and wet, and her tongue teases my shaft as she bobs up and down. Sage is a pro at this by this point, and with every movement of her head, she sends me closer to my orgasm.

As she feels me getting closer, she stops, pulling away with a mischievous smirk and gently teasing my cock with her tongue. "You never told me to make you come," she says.

I grab my cock and press it against her lips, and she opens them wide. I sit up a little straighter and grab the back of her head as I push it down on me. Sage stares up and opens her mouth as wide as she can as she takes all of me in her throat. Even as I hold the back of her head, she moves it up and down slightly, letting her throat gulp to tease it even more.

I feel like I'm on the verge of exploding, so I let go of her and push her away. She catches her breath as a mixture of her saliva and my precum drips from her mouth onto her chest.

"I never thought I'd be so happy I learned to count cards," I say.

Sage gasps and stands up, folding her arms in front of her. "I knew you cheated!"

She slaps me on the shoulder and moves to turn around. Before she can get away, I grab her and push her back onto the kitchen table. She props herself up on her elbows, staring at me with interest.

"I think I can make it up to you," I say before immediately shoving my face in her pussy. She doesn't protest as my tongue explores her folds. Her legs spread wider, and I scoop them over my shoulders while going to town on her clit.

I swirl my tongue around it, sucking it between my lips as her body writhes on the table. She moans and whimpers with every suckle. My hands reach for her breasts, and I rub her nipples, while Sage runs her fingers through my hair to hold me closer to her.

"You're so fucking good," she moans as her muscles tense with every flick of my tongue. I slide a finger inside her, feeling how her pussy throbs around it. I can imagine the feeling on my cock, and it twitches in anticipation.

I keep my tongue glued to her as I wait for her to be just on the brink before pulling my mouth away. Sage pushes herself up, giving me a pleading look. "Please, I'm so close!"

"Don't worry, I'll let you finish. Eventually," I say before standing and pushing my pants down all the way. She stares at me and bites her lip.

"On the kitchen table? Travis Blacksburg, who are you?" She laughs as she pulls my shirt over my head and traces her fingers over my muscles.

Her legs wrap around me to pull me close just as I slide my cock inside her soaking-wet pussy. Both of us moan and let out a long exhale as we feel each other. My lips find hers, and I kiss her passionately, letting my tongue slide into her mouth. I can taste myself on her, and I know she can taste her own juices too. Both of us meld together entirely as I pump in and out of her slowly.

"You make me feel so good," she moans as she tightens her legs around me. "I love how you fuck me."

I grab her legs and move them from my waist, folding them toward her torso. Just as I feel her pussy starting to clench around me, I pull out and listen to her whimper and beg for me to let her finish.

With her legs still folded and her pussy on perfect display, I bury my face between her legs again, teasing her clit just until she's on the edge.

"Please!" Sage cries out, desperate for relief.

"Tell me what you want," I say as I press my cock against her pussy and slide it up and down, soaking it in her juices.

"I want you to make me come," she replies, breathing raggedly as my cock grazes her clit.

I watch her face as I slowly slide my cock inside her again. She lets out a long exhale as she braces for the pleasure bound to overwhelm her.

"Your pussy belongs to me." She whimpers uncontrollably as I move in and out, feeling her throbbing on my cock. "Tell me it's mine, Sage."

"It's all yours!" she screams. Her cries are intoxicating as she inches closer and closer.

"I'm the only one who's allowed to touch you."

"Yes! The only one." Just as she finishes, I lose complete control and fuck her hard on the table. It shakes and moves from its spot, forcing me to try to walk with it. Sage screams as her pussy tightens and grips me, drinking in every rope of my cum as I explode inside her.

Her body jolts up unintentionally as her head hangs backward. I don't stop moving until I'm sure both of us have every ounce of pleasure completely drained from us. When I'm positive that's the case, I pull out and take a seat once again.

"You might have won all the hands, but I definitely think we're both winners in the end," she jokes. I shake my head and lean back in the chair, feeling satisfied. "Can I interest you in a celebratory snack?" she adds, walking to the fridge stark naked and pulling out a string cheese.

"I think we just burned enough calories to justify that," I reply.

"Great. Also, you owe me a rematch." She tosses the cheese stick at me like a gauntlet.

I catch it. "Only if you promise to wear the exact same poker face next time. It terrifies the cards into submission."

Chapter Thirty

I open my eyes and stretch, still feeling the pleasure from last night lingering in my limbs. It takes me a moment to realize my hand is cuffed to the headboard.

"Travis," I mumble, slapping the bed beside me to get him to free me. When I don't touch anything, I look to my left and sigh. Not only is Travis gone, but his half of the bed is perfectly made. "I thought we were past this?"

With my free hand, I grab a pillow and chuck it at the made-up half of the bed, as if it might bounce back with an explanation. "At least leave a note next time, Houdini." The pillow thuds to the floor with the same lack of remorse Travis apparently has for my wrist circulation.

I sit upright and look toward the bedroom door, which is closed. He doesn't normally close it in the morning when I'm here. I know he likes to keep an eye on me because there's still a part of him that doesn't trust me with the information I have. Frankly, I find it extremely annoying. Right now it's his most glaring flaw.

"Travis!" My voice is raspy as I shout through the house. When he doesn't come after a few moments, my mind starts to wander. *What the hell is he doing right now?*

He hasn't been cuffing me to the bed, and after last night I don't understand why he would do it now. Did I do something wrong?

I search my mind for anything that happened last night that might have upset him. I disrupted his dinner schedule, but that's really it. As far as I'm aware, I didn't do anything to upset him and warrant being restrained like this. If anything, he was more relaxed last night than he'd been all day. I made sure of that.

The more I think about it, the more panic sets in. Travis is a dangerous man, and the possibility that he turns around and snaps and decides to break his own word about not hurting me is there, even if I haven't wanted to acknowledge it in the past.

I shout his name a few more times and listen carefully for any sign of him in the house. I don't hear anything. It doesn't sound like he is in his office talking on the phone or in the gym exercising. It's completely quiet—almost eerily so.

I don't know how much time passes, but I sink back into the bed and stare at the ceiling, letting my mind roam. Eventually I hear the front door slam shut, and I jolt upright. "Travis?"

Footsteps approach, and Travis walks through the bedroom door shortly after. I'm only partly relieved to see him, but I force a smile on my face anyway. I jangle the cuff around my hand loudly, silently pleading for him to let me go.

"What's going on?" I ask as Travis walks around the bed and fishes in his pockets for the key to the cuff. He sits down beside me and dangles it in front of my face.

"You looked so peaceful. I didn't want to wake you up." He unlocks the cuff, and I immediately grab my hand to massage my wrist. "I didn't want to leave you alone to roam the house either. My hands were tied."

"Well, that's not true. *My* hands were tied." I roll my eyes and stare at him, studying his face for any inclination of what he was doing. "Do you still not trust me?"

After everything we've been through, haven't I proved that I'm trustworthy? I literally watched you kill a man, and I haven't done anything to make you think I'm going to tell.

He must see the hurt and frustration on my face, because he lets out a soft exhale and offers me an apologetic smile. "I get what you're feeling. I just had some things to do in town, and I was being cautious."

My stomach churns at the idea of him being in town without telling me. I hope it's not what I think. A moment of silence sits between us while I try to read him. It's nearly impossible; there's no emotion behind his eyes at all.

"You went to town? Please tell me you at least grabbed some coffee and breakfast," I say, purposefully being lighthearted about the situation. I know Travis doesn't like it when I cry, but the more I think about him doing something I have explicitly asked him not to do, the more tears threaten to form.

He furrows his eyebrows and shakes his head. "That wasn't part of my itinerary while I was in town. Why would I stop if it wasn't planned?"

Your itinerary? So you had a plan in town. Got it.

"Okay, what were you doing in town without me, then? Why was it so important I had to be tied up here?"

Travis looks away from me and hesitates. That's unusual. He isn't exactly the type of person to regret the things he does. I can see there's something he doesn't want to tell me. My mouth turns bitter as I brace myself for what he's about to say. It's like my worst fear coming to life.

"I was in town doing some reconnaissance work on Nicole." He looks at me with a blank expression, his voice completely emotionless. "I didn't want to tell you because I knew you'd be upset. It made you cry so much before. I didn't want you to feel that way again."

I blink a few times and let his words sink in. He didn't want to make *me* cry? So all this was just a big favor to me, wasn't it?

I do my best to look away from him as I clear my throat so he can't see the emotion on my face. I hoped he'd forgotten all about her. Maybe

I was naive, but a part of me thought he would change his mind after he saw my reaction. I guess I was wrong.

"Travis, please don't do this," I beg, grabbing his hand and squeezing it. "She's too young. She's innocent. I could see it on her face. She has her whole life ahead of her. You can't hurt her."

Travis pulls his hand from me and looks away. I can practically feel the frustration simmering off him. I already know what he's going to say.

I slap his arm lightly and narrow my eyes. "Come on, Travis. She looks like she's one bad breakup away from a poetry phase and a ukulele. You're going to ruin her Etsy-store dreams."

"I don't know how many times I need to tell you, but that's not why I do this." He looks back at me with anger in his eyes. "Whether she's innocent or not, it doesn't matter. You need to stay out of this."

"Are you serious? Stay out of this?" I let out an incredulous laugh and shake my head. "I'm already too far into this. Staying out of it isn't an option anymore."

"I've been doing this for a long time. This is a well-oiled machine for me. If you can't handle this, you can't be a part of it. My methods have always worked in the past, and I'm not going to alter them because of you."

My heart drops and my brain runs at breakneck speed, trying to think of a way to change his mind.

"People know her!" I sit up and lean forward with a glimmer of hope swelling in my chest. "People at the grocery store see her. People *have* to have noticed her. If she goes missing, it might raise some suspicions."

"This isn't my first kill," he says with an exhausted huff. "I'm always completely secure. Nobody is going to notice, because I take every possible precaution."

This is it. I can see how determined he is about this. I don't know how I'm ever going to convince him not to do this. He won't listen to me about pursuing bad people, and I can't change his mind.

My phone buzzes on the nightstand, and Travis reaches for it before I can. Even though he "trusts" me, he still likes to make sure everything is on par and I'm not really ratting him out to the feds.

I watch his face as his lips pull into a tight line and his eyes slowly move from the screen to me. His eyes darken, and I feel a chill run through me. "What the fuck, Sage?"

I pull the phone away from him to see what he's looking at. I haven't done anything wrong, and I don't understand what would set him off like this. I look at the screen and see a notification from the Citizens app of a new sex offender registered in the area.

"Are you capable of thinking, or is that something I have to start doing for you?" He jumps to his feet and paces back and forth in front of the bed, tossing me furious glares.

"I don't understand." I can't help myself from cowering in front of him. I clutch the sheets on the bed closer to me and make myself seem small before him. He's never looked at me this way, not even when we first met and I was constantly annoying him.

"Why the fuck would you make searches like this from an unsecured connection?" He rushes toward me, slamming his hands down on the mattress right beside me. I jump back and press my spine hard against the headboard. My skin is burning hot, and for the first time, Travis is terrifying me. "You're going to be the death of me."

His eyes are pointed furiously in my direction, and I can almost see an alternate reality where I'm one of his victims after all. There was a time when he wanted to kill me, and I think he does right now too. The very thought sends a shiver crawling through my body.

"I didn't know," I say in a meek, hushed voice. There's no remorse in his eyes as he backs away and snatches my phone from my hand.

He walks away from me and lingers in the doorframe, looking back at me with a disappointed frown. "This is going to ruin me."

As the door slams, I mutter under my breath, "Next time I'll google murdery stuff on Incognito like a normal girlfriend." I consider yelling it louder, but I'm not sure if sarcasm would defuse or detonate him right now.

I can hear him stomping around, heading to his office. Travis is acting like an animal with its foot caught in a trap. He's desperate and lashing out. I never meant to do something to harm him, but he doesn't see it that way.

Right now Travis is in self-preservation mode. He's dangerous. I'm realizing the weight of the situation I'm in. If I don't leave now, I might not have a chance to.

Chapter Thirty-One

TRAVIS

How the fuck could I have been so stupid?

I've gone so long without being caught, and I let one stupid girl into my life, and she's going to lead investigators directly to my door. What the fuck was I thinking?

Just to really drive home my idiocy, I stub my toe so hard on the desk leg I nearly see stars. Naturally, I screamed, not out of pain, but in existential frustration. The universe didn't respond. Probably too busy laughing.

Since the moment I met Sage, she has been disrupting my life. Why the hell did I think this part of my life would be protected from her? Letting her in was the biggest mistake I've ever made. I should have killed her when I had the chance.

It takes a while for me to regain my focus after our conversation. I know she's upset with me for pursuing Nicole, but she doesn't understand me, no matter what she tries to tell herself. I hardly get to choose my victims. I met Nicole, and she took priority in my mind. Abandoning this now, on the heels of missing out on Kevin, will leave me unsatisfied and frayed.

I wouldn't be surprised if she's set off some kind of alert with her searches, though. This is why I don't cherry-pick my victims the way she wants me to. Now there is vast room for error. I just can't trust her.

After a few minutes of trying to calm down, I storm back into the bedroom and drag Sage from the bed and back to my office. "I don't want to hear a word out of you," I say as I sit her down across from me.

She slinks down in the chair and stares at me with wide, watery eyes. There's no doubt in my mind she's going to try to play up every emotion she possibly can to get me to go easy on her. She doesn't deserve that, not after the danger she's put me in.

"Is there anything I can do to help?" she asks in a small, nervous voice. I ignore her, focusing on her phone and laptop on the desk in front of me.

I hook them up to my desktop computer and immediately scan both devices for malware. Someone like her, with absolutely no technological savviness, probably has vast amounts of malware on her devices without even knowing it. Sometimes it can be harmless enough, but more often than not, there's some sort of malicious intent.

While I wait for my programs to run, I check out her desktop, which has a background image of a glittery unicorn eating pizza in space. Even her folder names are chaos incarnate—"Taxes?," "Definitely Not Porn," and "Super Secret Stuff (Don't Open Travis)." I almost throw the laptop out the window.

She is so careless about everything. What she probably doesn't know, and could very well be my downfall, is that the US government has trackers on just about every website you can think of. Most of this is just keyword-based monitoring, looking for people searching specific strings of information. Vigilantism is something they look out for. With Sage searching sex offenders in the area, bringing traffic to different databases, and looking at individual sex offenders' information, she has probably set off a chain reaction of red flags.

To absolutely nobody's surprise, Sage is using a vanilla Chrome with a few useless extensions and no VPN. What makes this so much worse is that the IP address is registered to *my* Wi-Fi. All the government agencies that got pings alerting to her searches are going to immediately look at my address.

Why did she leave me such a mess to clean up?

The first thing I do is scrub her internet history entirely, deleting all her browser searches, cookies, and cache files. Afterward, I delete and reinstall Google Chrome as a safety measure. There are probably better browsers for her to be using, but if there are red flags raised, and she suddenly switches to a hardened and much more protected browser, that's only going to raise more of them.

I install a VPN for her. If there's anything I know about Sage, it's that she's stubborn. As much as I want her to give up on this sex offender thing, I know it's not that easy. If she does those ridiculous searches again, it won't be linked to her IP address.

The next part is a little bit tricky. I have my own ways of getting information, but hacking into government databases is beyond my pay grade. Plus, I might be a certified tech genius, but they have the best in the world on their payroll. The only thing I can do is make a honeypot—something to divert their attention away from Sage and her ridiculous searches.

It's not hard to create a bot that searches the same things as her and throws the IP address somewhere else in the state. If red flags keep getting raised, they're likely to think Sage's searches were just a fluke.

The last step in the plan is plausible deniability. If all this fails, though I doubt that is going to be the case, we need an excuse for why Sage made those searches. I can't exactly have her telling the government she was trying to turn my attention from innocent victims to sexual predators to kill. Even if by most standards we'd be doing the world a favor, the judicial system would beg to differ.

"I need you to film a video of yourself talking about all the sex offenders in the area," I tell Sage, not bothering to look at her while I type away on my computer. "Make it look like you were doing some kind of research in the area because you're planning on settling down here. As it turns out, there are too many sex offenders in the area for you to be comfortable."

She steps off to grab her camera, and I keep my eyes on her the entire time. She sets it up in the hallway—where I can see her—and records a brief video, forcing a smile on her face once again. This time I can see that it's fake.

When she's done, she sits back down across from me with a defeated sigh. I stop what I'm doing and stare at her for a moment. A dull ache in my chest begs me to sit next to her and pull her in for a hug, but I fight against it. Just like the tears in the grocery store bathroom, this is my fault. Right now she's not acting like the Sage I know. She's not being optimistic or overly bubbly and cheerful. She feels deflated because of me.

For what it's worth, I wish that things could be different. If I didn't have to worry about the things I do, both of our lives would be much easier. But I can't change who I am, regardless of how many times I've tried to ignore these urges. This is what's best. This is what I know and what I can handle.

I can't let Sage ruin me. I refuse to give up everything I've worked for because of her foolish actions. But I don't know what I'm going to do with her after all this. She's impossible to rein in.

Time flies while I get to work and make sure all our bases are covered. Just as Rome wasn't built in a day, the US government can't be fooled in one either—unless you have access to highly classified software and aren't afraid of Homeland Security breaking down your door.

Sage stays put while I work, and I'm thankful she isn't pestering me anymore. However, I can sense the growing unease surrounding her.

"How about I make us some dinner?" she asks after a while. She holds a hand over her stomach with a pained expression on her face, as if to silently tell me she's starving. I let her cook last night when I shouldn't have, but a wrench has already been thrown into all my plans for the day. What could letting her cook again really hurt?

"Fine. But I'm coming with you," I say as I grab her laptop and phone.

Sage doesn't hesitate to jump to her feet and start walking toward the kitchen. I follow as quickly as I can, careful to keep a close eye on her. On the off chance she decides she wants to fight back against me, I need to make sure she doesn't grab a weapon from the kitchen. I doubt it will happen, but she does really care about me not targeting Nicole. If the thought crosses her mind and she thinks the only way to save her is to hurt me, I have to stop it.

She gets to work at the counter, chopping vegetables and preparing the dish while I sit at the kitchen island and continue covering all her tracks. I look up from the screen only when I hear the knife slicing vegetables to make sure everything is up to par.

While she's cooking, my body tenses when she grabs the knife a few times. I don't know if it's the way she drags it across the cutting board or just the energy she's giving off, but it makes me worry. I could easily overpower her if it comes to it, but I don't want to hurt her. We've come so far.

After a while the aroma of sizzling bacon catches my attention. It smells delicious, though very heavy in calories. It's lucky I haven't eaten anything yet today—otherwise I'd have to decline. Whatever she's making is thick with cream, cheese, and fatty bacon. It makes my stomach growl just thinking about it.

"What are you making?"

"Potato soup." She doesn't look at me when she answers, and I feel a little bit guilty. My reaction is going to put a strain on our relationship, and I almost wish I could take it back.

"I've never had that before." I close her laptop, satisfied that my work is done for now, and watch her finish cooking.

"This is my mom's recipe. Well, almost. She doesn't usually add bacon, but I think it helps the flavors." Her voice is flat and monotone. She can barely even look me in the eye.

She finishes stirring the giant pot on the stove and grabs two bowls from the cupboard, filling them to the brim with soup. "Do you think you can grab us some wine? I think red will work."

I walk to the wine cabinet and look for a merlot before grabbing us both wineglasses and bringing them to the table. Sage is already sitting with both bowls in front of her, dolloping a bit of butter on each of them.

Great, more empty calories.

I sit down and pour us both a drink. We begin eating without saying a word. Of course, like everything Sage cooks, this is delicious. A part of me wants to say something to her about it, but by the sullen look on her face, I don't think she wants to talk.

She's barely eating, more so just turning the soup over and over in the bowl. She takes only a few bites here and there. I feel bad. Neither of us says a word as I finish my bowl entirely.

"Do you want mine? I'm not going to finish it, and I don't want to throw it away." Sage sighs, pushing it over to me. "I guess I don't have much of an appetite after all."

She looks down at her lap with a frown, and my heart aches even more. I accept the bowl and start eating it. I wouldn't normally have more than one serving of food, but I also don't normally go twenty-four hours without eating.

When I'm finished, Sage grabs both bowls and rinses them off before putting them in the dishwasher along with the wineglasses. "I might just go to sleep early, if you don't mind."

I still don't want her out of my sight, and I wouldn't normally go to sleep right after dinner. But today is not a normal day. Besides, I'm tired too. My entire schedule changed after finding Sage's searches, so I might as well go to bed early and have a proper night's rest before tomorrow.

"Let's go." I grab her hand and lead her to the bedroom, careful to be more delicate with her than I was earlier today. She's emotional and exhausted from it, and I don't want to make things worse.

Both of us climb into bed, and I grab a zip tie to wrap around both of our wrists. Sage looks disappointed that I'm doing this, but she doesn't say anything. She just rolls over and faces away from me. Honestly, if I were her, I'd roll over too. If someone zip-tied me every night, I'd at least demand a turndown service and a mint on the pillow.

I almost collapse in bed, surprised at how exhausted I feel. I suppose it's from the stress of thinking I could get caught. I take a few deep breaths and close my eyes, relaxing against the mattress. Sage is breathing softly, and I listen to the sound of her exhales, as if meditating with them in my ears.

My mind is foggy, and my tongue feels thick. I open my eyes in the dark room, almost having to force my lids open because they're so heavy. They fall shut on their own, and a memory comes to the front of my mind.

The last time I felt like this was by Sage's hand, when she drugged me without my knowledge. Before I can reach over and ask her what she did, I slip away to my slumber.

Chapter Thirty-Two

My heart pounds rhythmically against my chest while I wait for Travis to fall asleep. I really didn't think I would have another opportunity—or need—to drug Travis, but here we are. I spent all day sitting across from him, thinking about ways to get out of here. Thank God for the cannabutter I had stored in the fridge.

Weed has never let me down before. Thank you to the weed gods.

I consider lighting a celebratory joint in their honor, but then I remember I'm essentially staging a prison break. Probably not the time to get high-fived by Bob Marley's ghost.

I feel Travis's body going limp behind me, and I lift the arm he zip-tied to him just to test it. He's out cold. Tiny snores signal that it's time to get a move on.

I turn around, moving as cautiously as I can. I don't know how long he's going to be out, but he had quite a lot of weed in his soup. After all, he ate mine too. That was surprisingly easy. I'm just waiting for the other shoe to drop now.

Looking at him sleeping, I almost regret what I'm about to do. I've worked so hard to get Travis to like me. I've spent countless hours fantasizing about our future together, and the idea of not having him in my life anymore is heartbreaking. But I know now that I can't fix him. I can't shape him into some vigilante hero going after sex offenders and child predators. He's going to target whoever the hell he wants to, and I'll have to sit by knowing he's attacking innocent people. I just can't do that.

I hold my breath as I reach across his sleeping body for the pocketknife he keeps on his nightstand. He shuffles a little under me, and my entire body stiffens. The moment he wakes up and sees me trying to free myself, it's going to be over for me. If I can't get out of this now, Travis is going to have no choice but to end my life.

He smacks his lips a couple of times, and a loud snore follows. I almost let out a sigh of relief, but I'm not done yet. There's time for that later.

My hand wraps around the cold metal of the knife, and I flick it open, promptly slicing at the plastic around my wrist to free myself. Step two of my plan is now complete. Travis is asleep, and I'm not bound to him. Now all I have to do is leave.

It's surprisingly hard. Even with everything I know about Travis, walking out of here and knowing it'll be the last time I ever see him is difficult. He's not who I thought he was, but that doesn't take away the love I have for him. Leaving him now is what's best for us both. It's probably my only chance at survival, anyway.

The mattress creaks ever so softly as my weight shifts on it. Of course, now the bed decides to develop a Broadway-level sound system. I half expect it to start narrating my escape like a dramatic podcast—"And then she froze, heart thundering, mattress groaning like a haunted cello . . ."

I never noticed the sound before, but now it seems to blast and echo through the room. I silently curse under my breath. Thankfully, Travis still doesn't wake up.

I tiptoe to the bedroom door and open it just enough to slink out. I don't close it behind me for fear of the clicking noise it'll make. Besides, if Travis is going to wake up, I want to be able to hear it and make a run for it before he finds me.

My phone and laptop are still on the kitchen island. I grab my phone, sacrificing my laptop for the time being. I'm going to have to travel light if I'm going to be quick about it.

I load up my backpack with a couple of changes of clothes and quickly make my way to the front door. I close it behind me and stand in place for a few moments, contemplating whether or not I should go back.

It would be easy to cut the zip tie on Travis's wrist and reapply new ones, pretending like none of this ever happened. Maybe I can even play stupid in the morning when he's mad about me drugging him and make it seem like I mixed up the butter. Someday it can be a funny story we laugh about with our children.

A bitter taste grows in my mouth as I think about the potential future we had together. It's just not the same. Can I really envision my life with someone who kills innocent people? Would I want someone like that raising children with me?

I take off running. I need to get out of here before Travis wakes up.

At Travis's house, I rarely have a signal on my phone when I'm not connected to the Wi-Fi. Because of my searches, Travis has disabled the Wi-Fi in the house entirely. I need to figure out what to do, and a large part of that might involve buying some kind of bus ticket out of here. At the very least, I need to be able to see their schedules.

Luckily for me, Ryan's house has Wi-Fi, and I know the password. So I head there. I know I can't stay long because it might be the first place Travis looks for me, but all I need to do are some quick searches before getting the hell out.

As I'm running there, the cabin in sight, my phone vibrates in my pocket, and I stop to look at it. It's just some Instagram notification, but I have a signal where I am.

I could call the police right now. All this could be over, and I would guarantee myself being able to spare Nicole from Travis's wrath. I wouldn't have to run away and hide for the rest of my life. Everything I know is online. My entire job, my livelihood, is based on me presenting myself on social media.

If Travis wants, he can follow me. If Eli was able to do it on his own, someone like Travis, with all the means in the world, can make my life a living hell. I'll never be able to get away from him.

I stare down at the keypad on my phone with 911 typed in. All I have to do is press the green dial button and at the very least an officer will be sent out for a suspicious call. I just can't bring myself to do it.

"Fuck," I whisper as I shake my head. I clench my fists at my sides and stuff my phone back in my pocket. "I don't know what the hell I'm supposed to do anymore."

Even the idea of turning Travis in makes my heart break. I just can't do it. The only thing I can do is leave and hope like hell he doesn't come searching for me.

It's freezing, and I'm starving. With any luck, he is still knocked out cold in bed. I should have at least an hour to eat a sandwich and buy a ticket out of Lake Lure.

I jog to Ryan's front door and type the code into the lockbox to get the key. When I open the door and flip on the light, I freeze in place and look around with my mouth hanging open. The entire place looks like it's been ransacked. It looks like somebody came just to rip everything apart.

Pillows in the living room are tossed around, ripped open, with their stuffing all over the carpet. Glass vases are shattered, with fake flowers strewn around, their petals all ripped off. Books on the shelves have been tossed around, with pages ripped from the spines. Even the TV in the center of the room has been smashed with some kind of blunt object. And that's just the living room. I can't even imagine what the rest of the house must look like.

Someone was here recently, and I don't know if they're still here. Walking in any farther is putting myself in danger, but stepping out that front door right now is too. I could go back to Travis. After all, whoever did this to Ryan's cabin could still be roaming the woods if they're not still here. I briefly wonder if that could have anything to do with the person digging into Travis, but I decide I have bigger things to worry about. Walking around alone at night with some kind of crazed lunatic is even more dangerous than lying in bed with Travis. Better the devil you know than the devil you don't.

I cautiously step forward and look around with a tight feeling in my throat. My nerves are frayed and on edge as I reach for Travis's pocketknife to pull it out. I've never attacked anyone before, and if it comes down to it, I doubt I'll fare well, but maybe I can scare someone away.

I approach the kitchen and look around to see dishes shattered all along the tile floor, with cabinet doors hanging from their hinges. Whoever was here tore the place apart recklessly, just to break it all. It doesn't even look like they took anything.

Footsteps behind me catch my attention, and I whip around with the knife pointed in front of me. My heart drops when I see Ryan standing in the hallway with a pistol aimed right at me.

For a second I wonder if I should be relieved. He is the homeowner, after all. Maybe he just arrived and came in to find his home like this and thinks it's my fault. But then I remember he's supposed to be out of town for another week. A twisted smile forms on his lips, and my heart drops to my stomach.

"What, did you forget your pepper spray?" Ryan asks as he points to the knife with his gun. He inches closer and steps into the light so I can see all of him. There's blood speckling his hands, no doubt from the glass shards that flew through the air when he broke everything in his home.

He looks me up and down, licking his lips as he takes me in. I shudder under his gaze, wishing I could be anywhere else. Running away doesn't seem like an option when someone has a gun pointed at you. I'm all too aware of my hand trembling in front of me as I hold the knife up and try to look scary.

"What does Travis have that I don't?" he asks when he's only a few feet away from me. He points to the knife with his gun and gestures for me to drop it. I hesitate for a moment, but I do as he says. Even though every part of my body tells me to fight back, my brain says I must comply. It might be my only way of getting out of this.

I don't know how to answer his question to pacify him. Travis has everything while Ryan has nothing, but saying that would make it only worse.

"Travis took something from me. Does the name Amelia ring a bell to you?"

I search my brain and come up with nothing. Though, knowing what Travis does, I can imagine exactly what Ryan means.

"Look, I don't know—"

"Amelia was my girlfriend. My soon-to-be fiancée, actually. Travis killed her before I had a chance to propose." He steps forward with a wicked grin on his face. "I've been waiting a long time to get revenge on him. At first I just wanted to send him to jail, but then I noticed the interest he took in you. So now I want him to suffer more than being locked up. He took something from me, and it's my turn to take something from him."

Ryan steps close enough that I can feel his breath against my skin. He points the gun at the side of my head and looks down at my body. Every hair on the back of my neck stands up straight, and I try to think of a way out of this but fail. Ryan wants revenge, and he is intent on getting it.

"But first we're going to have a little fun." He laughs as he looks me up and down again. "Take off your clothes."

I briefly consider bluffing my way out with some weird performance art. *You ever seen interpretive dance with a pocketknife?* But I think better of it. Not the time to debut my talent for pirouetting under pressure.

A tear slips from my eye, and I slowly do as he says.

Chapter Thirty-Three

My eyes slowly open to a dark room. It takes a moment for everything to come back to me, and I immediately reach over to nudge Sage and wake her up. My head is still foggy, but I have every intention of chewing her out. The only problem is that she's not there beside me.

The zip tie around my wrist is intact, but hers has been cut off. The spot she normally sleeps in is unmade and wrinkled, cold, as if she's been gone for a while. I stagger to my feet, momentarily convinced that I'm in a lucid dream—or possibly a Target clearance aisle, because why else would my head feel like it's stuck in a cotton candy machine? I trip over the comforter I yanked with me in my sudden rise, face-planting onto the floor with the grace of a drugged giraffe. This is not the morning-after vibe I was going for.

As much as I want to run through the house searching for her, I have to take it easy. If I move too fast, I might risk injuring myself and delaying this entire process even more.

The pocketknife I keep on the side of my bed is gone too. I shouldn't be surprised by that, but somehow I am. With Sage's complete and utter obsession with me from the beginning, I never thought she would have something like this in her. I don't like the unknown.

I'm careful to plan every aspect of my life to avoid the unknown. Sage being out on her own, feeling as if what I'm doing is wrong for the first time, invites a lot of possibilities I can't predict.

With her gone, I'm expecting the police to break down my front door at any moment and take me away. All I can hope for is that Sage knows what's good for her and doesn't tell them about me. While I don't want a police investigation, I do have the resources to help me around things like this.

My car is still in the garage, which means Sage more than likely left on foot. She's hitchhiked before in the past, and I doubt she's going to change her ways right now, especially when she's fleeing so haphazardly. She didn't even take all her belongings with her.

If she's on foot, she can't have gotten far. It's the middle of the night, and the woods are rather desolate. There's only one place she could have gone: Ryan's cabin.

I know I need to catch her quickly, but driving right now would be a mistake. I can barely walk without feeling like the ground is pulling me toward it. The last thing I need is to crash my car in the middle of nowhere, waking up in a hospital room with police officers asking me what happened.

Sorry, Officer, I was just out to kidnap my girlfriend . . .

The air feels fresh against my skin, and it invigorates me enough to force some of the haziness in my head aside. Walking to Ryan's cabin takes longer than I would like, and I have to stop intermittently to brace myself against trees and shake off the dizzy spells. The first time I ever had marijuana was when Sage gave me the brownie without my knowledge, and I know now that I took two doses when I finished her soup last night alongside my own. My cannabis tolerance is virtually nonexistent.

Eventually I spot Ryan's cabin in the distance and feel a wave of relief wash over me as I notice the lights are on. Sage is here. That's at least one thing I don't have to worry about anymore. I'll find her and take care of the situation before she does something drastic.

I start thinking about what I'm going to do as I approach the cabin from the shadows. Obviously I have to bring her back to my house, but with me being as high as I am and her presumably sober, there might be some complications.

Even though I'm under the influence, I think I can still overpower her. She's small, and she doesn't exercise. Even with a knife in her hands, I can still best her. Unless she took a surprise self-defense course last week. Or has secretly been watching YouTube knife-fighting tutorials. My luck, she probably has a black belt in spite and a PhD in making me regret things.

The problem is that I promised her I wouldn't hurt her. I don't like to go back on my word, but I fear she's giving me no choice. Maybe I can just lock her in a room until she learns her lesson. Maybe I could tie her to the bed and leave her there. I just need to know she isn't going to do anything stupid.

I freeze as I approach the backyard. The curtains are wide open, and I can see the inside of the cabin as clear as day. Ryan's here.

From the window in front of me, all I can see is his profile and a gun in his hand, pointed at something. Using basic deduction skills, if Sage was on her way here, then logically he would be pointing his gun at her.

I feel the adrenaline kick in, sending a burst of energy through my limbs as I run toward the house to get a better view. When I get closer, I'm careful to be quiet. The likelihood of me having to go in and break the situation up is pretty high, and I'll need to catch Ryan unawares since he has the advantage with a gun.

I tiptoe to one of the windows and peek through, taking inventory of the entire scene. Ryan is standing with a gun pointed at Sage, who is standing completely naked in front of him. She's trying to cover herself nervously, and Ryan is saying something I can't quite hear.

Rage simmers in my veins, and I don't spare a moment waiting. Sage might be a problem, but she's *my* problem. Someone like fucking Ryan doesn't get to put her in danger. I'll end him for this.

I go to the window I sneaked in through the first time I wanted to kill Sage—the first night we slept together and I realized there was something different about her. It brings back some complicated memories, but I push them down.

Now isn't the time to take a stroll down memory lane.

Thankfully the window in the bathroom is still unlocked. Sage was a fool for unlocking all the windows in a strange house in the first place, and Ryan must not have taken proper inventory of the cabin when he came back. Lake Lure might be a relatively safe area—aside from being home to yours truly—but you never know who's going to visit in the night. In Ryan's case, I'm going to make him regret this.

I'm as quiet as ever as I sneak through the house, careful to stay in the shadows, making my way toward the living room. While I'm in the hallway, I freeze to listen to the situation. Ryan's ranting and raving about something while Sage whimpers quietly to herself.

"You made it all too easy, really." Ryan laughs as he waves his arm around. "You even asked me if I knew him, and I lied. Just a word of advice—in the future, don't be so trusting. Who am I kidding? You don't have a future."

He takes a break from his rant to laugh at his own bad joke while Sage whispers the word *please* over and over again.

"Why would I spare you when he didn't spare Amelia?" My blood runs cold. Ryan's voice is emotional, like he's teetering on the edge and about to fall.

Amelia? That's who the person following me around was looking into. Does all of this come back to Ryan?

"Do you know how hard it is for a guy like me to land a girl like that?" There's a moment of silence, and I imagine Sage shaking her head. "It might look like I have it all, but I don't. Not anymore, anyway. When he killed her, he took everything from me. She was beautiful. Young, with strawberry-blond hair, and the most beautiful blue eyes you've ever seen. I was taken with her immediately, but unfortunately for all of us, so was your fucking boyfriend."

My eyebrows draw together in confusion. Amelia wasn't with anyone before I killed her.

I inch closer to get eyes on him just in time to see his fist slam into the wall. Sage is shivering in front of him and holding an arm over her breasts and covering her groin with her hand as much as she can. Neither of them sees me, and that's for the best.

A part of me wants to take advantage of the situation and lunge at Ryan right now, but I need him to continue. I need to know how he found out I'm the one who killed Amelia.

"They never found the body, you know. No body, no crime. After searching for two years, the police gave up entirely. Amelia's parents are dead and gone. She didn't have any siblings, and all her friends have long since forgotten about her. But I haven't." He steps closer to Sage and grabs her arm to push it away from her breasts. "The police told me she ran away. Got cold feet before the wedding. But I found her journal where she talked about Travis. He pretended to be her friend until she let her guard down, and he killed her."

Shit. How did I miss a fucking journal?

"Please, just let me go," Sage pleads with tears streaking down her face. "I don't have anything to do with that. Travis means nothing—"

Ryan interrupts her with a condescending laugh. He points to the fireplace mantel and some trinkets resting on top. "I have cameras. I've seen just how much he means to you. I rented out my cabin and sent you to his address, hoping he would kill you and I would catch him in the act. Instead, you did something even better. You gave me a more fitting chance of revenge. You did that for me. I suppose I should thank you."

Ryan slowly moves closer to Sage as she backs away, and I know I can't wait any longer. If he lays another hand on her, I'm going to blow up. I move toward him as quietly as I can out of the hallway, tiptoeing around broken glass to ensure I don't make a sound.

My eyes are glued to Ryan like a hawk hovering above a field mouse. Sage's eyes flicker to me, and Ryan notices. Unfortunately for him, it's too late. I'm already behind him with my hands on either side of his head. He tries to flail against me, his finger pulling the trigger, and the gun goes off, shattering a window.

I break his neck, and he goes limp before I let him collapse to the ground. I stare at him for only a moment to make sure he's dead before my eyes search for Sage to make sure she's okay. She runs into my arms, and her entire body shakes as she sobs against me.

Not exactly how I pictured our reunion. Less violins and heartfelt confessions, more corpse on the floor and broken window draft blowing directly up my ass.

My muscles go stiff, as I'm still not used to comforting someone this way. I came here angry at Sage, with every intention of letting her know that. But right now all I can do is try to comfort her, however difficult that may be.

I wrap my arms around her and hold her close. "It's going to be okay," I whisper in her ear, not knowing how true that is.

Chapter Thirty-Four

Travis immediately gets to work when I stop crying. He killed Ryan, and now he has to dispose of the body. I feel like I'm on autopilot, wandering around the cabin aimlessly. I spent ten minutes holding a mug of coffee I didn't remember pouring, talking to a dead houseplant like it owed me rent. At some point I think I tried to microwave a spoon. It doesn't even occur to me that this could potentially be linked to me until I'm watching Travis load Ryan's body into his SUV.

The weight of everything Ryan told me is still on my shoulders, and I don't know how to shake it off. Even though Ryan was an absolute creep who deserved to die, a part of me feels bad for him. Travis hasn't admitted to killing Amelia. Other than instructions about things to do to help him, he hasn't said anything. But I know it's true.

Travis probably killed her and disposed of her at the crematorium he bought or one of the abandoned factories he used in the past. Her ashes are probably scattered somewhere already, taken away with the wind and gone forever.

The idea of him killing Nicole was already bad enough. She's innocent and doesn't deserve to be targeted by someone like him. But seeing the direct repercussions of someone losing a loved one makes it even more complicated. Then there is the fact that Travis saved my life yet again. I didn't think it could be more complicated, but alas.

Neither of us says anything during the drive to the crematorium. Travis gave me his sweater to stave off the evening chill, and even with the heat blasting on me in the car, I can hardly feel anything. My entire body is numb after what just happened.

Travis does everything himself when we get to the crematorium, and I just sit idly and watch. It might not be very helpful, but Travis has done this by himself for a long time. He is about to press the button to start the oven when a spark of anger has me stand up and stop him. Ryan meant to kill *me*. I should be the one to send him off.

"Let me do it." I walk across the room and push his hand aside. "I want to watch him burn."

Travis doesn't say anything, but he lets me take over. I press the button to turn the ovens on and watch as flames rise. It won't take long before it's hot enough to completely disintegrate Ryan's body to ash. I stand beside it the entire time, waiting. Travis lingers over my shoulder but doesn't stop me.

I'm the one who opens the oven door, and I watch as Travis pushes him inside. I close it and keep my eyes glued to Ryan's body the entire time he's in there. Travis stands beside me, doing the same thing. There's a quiet reverence in the room, as if we are silently worshipping the flames. I half expect Gregorian chants to start playing or for someone to hand me a hymnal titled *Hotter than Hell: A Cremation Companion*.

Flames rise from the bottom of the oven, licking against Ryan's cold flesh as they swallow him whole. I watch his body turn to ash feeling like a weight has been lifted off me. The memory of everything he could have done to me, things I saw in his eyes from the moment I met him, seems to burn with him.

"What happens next?" I ask Travis without looking at him. My voice is calm and emotionless, and I keep my eyes trained on the fire. "I can't handle the thought of you killing innocent people. So what happens next?"

He doesn't answer right away. I don't need to look at him to know he's thinking about that himself. I'm sure it's not the first time the thought has crossed his mind either.

"I can't kill you. But I can't stop doing what I do either," he says with a hint of disappointment in his voice. I can't tell if it's because he can't kill me or because he can't stop. Either way, it's unsettling. "Maybe it's best if I just let you go."

That finally takes my attention away from the fire, and I look at him, putting a stony expression on my face. After everything he's told me—after everything I've seen—can he really just let me go?

"I trust you not to turn me in. You could have done that a long time ago, and you haven't." He offers me a strained smile, but I don't smile back. "Besides, you'll be implicated enough."

How is he so casual about this? I'm more irritated now than I was when he told me about Nicole to begin with.

He and I have been through a lot together in a very short time. Certainly that would mean we've bonded, right? To most normal people, saying goodbye would be difficult. But then again, Travis isn't a normal person.

It's just that easy for him to let me go.

"Why didn't you just let Ryan kill me if I mean so little to you? That would have made both of our lives so much easier." The words are out of my mouth before I can take them back, and Travis can see how emotional I am now. Farewell, my stoic exterior.

For the first time all day, I see a reaction on his face. He looks offended, like I reached over and slapped him across the face for absolutely no reason. Trust me, if anyone deserves to get slapped, it's Travis.

"How could you say that?" he asks, his voice pitched an octave higher as he backs away from me. "Just because I can't kill you doesn't mean I want someone else to. I can't imagine a world without you in it, Sage."

Tears well in my eyes and fall down my face before I can even try to blink them away. While it may not be the heartfelt declaration I'm looking for, I know this is as close as it gets for Travis. I step closer and open my arms wide, prepared to wrap them around him for a hug. Maybe we can get through this after all, because he does care about me.

But instead of accepting my embrace, he moves out of the way and doesn't look at me. My mouth opens, and my breath hitches in my throat with words I can't fully say. Instead, I just drop my arms by my sides and turn to the oven once again.

Silence fills in the room. It feels simultaneously full and empty, the weight of everything in our past and all the unspoken things hanging between us. It's almost unbearably heavy.

My eyes burn, and I feel my throat bobbing up and down as cries threaten to break out. I can't let Travis see me like this—not right now. I choke them back and bite the insides of my cheeks, hard, to focus on anything but my breaking heart.

When Ryan's body is nothing but gray ash scooped into a cardboard box, we leave. There's no souvenir vial this time. Travis drives all the way to his house in silence. I don't have to ask him to go to Ryan's house to gather the few items I still have there; he does that all on his own.

While he's gone, I pack up everything else I have at his house. I grab my camera, my laptop, the rest of my filming equipment, and the clothes I didn't intend to take when I was leaving on foot. Travis comes back with my hastily thrown-together backpack before I'm finished.

"Do you have everything?" he asks. I don't know if there's a part of me that wants him to beg me to stay, but his willingness to let me go is earth-shatteringly heartbreaking.

"Yes." I grab all my bags and set them down by the front door.

"I've called you an Uber. They'll be here soon."

"Thanks."

I can barely bring myself to look at him while I wait for some stranger to come pick me up. It's awkward. Neither of us says anything, but both of us want to.

The entire future I had planned out in my head is slipping through my fingers, and no matter what I do, I can't bring it back. I just can't accept that Travis is going to kill whoever he wants, regardless of their innocence. Knowing that I'm sleeping in bed next to a monster—a *predator*—every single night would be the death of me. I wanted to think that I could change him, but I was wrong.

God, I hate having to admit that.

The sound of tires riding up the driveway catches our attention, and we look out the window to see blinding headlights pulling up. Travis's phone beeps a moment later, and he looks at it to see a notification from the driver letting him know they're here.

"I guess this is goodbye." My voice is as emotionless as I can make it. I busy myself by grabbing bags to avoid looking at him.

"For what it's worth, things are going to be different with you gone," Travis says, forcing a half smile on his face. Is this his way of telling me he's going to miss me? That my presence here has actually been something he's come to enjoy? It's too little, too late for him, unfortunately.

"Make sure you put Ryan's ashes in the trash when you take it to the dump." I take a deep breath and drop the strap to my duffel bag on my shoulder before looking at him. I clench my jaw and force myself to stare him deep in the eyes. "Travis, if you hurt Nicole, I will never forgive you."

He doesn't say anything, and if he wants to, I don't stick around to hear it. I leave immediately and walk over to the Uber. Thankfully, the driver is a woman. But knowing what I do about Travis, I can't help thinking how dangerous it was for her to come here alone. She could have been walking into a trap. God knows the person who ordered her Uber is dangerous enough.

"All set?" the driver asks in a surprisingly chipper voice. I nod and buckle my seat belt, forcing my eyes to remain glued to my hands in my lap as we back out of Travis's driveway. From my peripheral vision, I can barely see his silhouette standing on the porch, watching me go.

I ask my driver to stop at the spot where Nicole usually hangs around so I can try talking her into leaving this area, but when we get there, she isn't anywhere to be found. *Crap.*

"Anywhere else you want me to stop?" My driver's chipper voice turns a tad annoyed.

"We're good to go. Thanks," I murmur before sinking back into my seat.

As soon as we're out of town, the dam breaks, and tears stream down my face like a waterfall. My breath is ragged, and it feels like I'm going to hyperventilate. I don't even care that I'm in a public place with a stranger sitting a foot away from me. She doesn't say anything, and I don't even acknowledge her.

It's about an hour-long drive to Asheville, and I cry the entire way. The only time I stop is when I lean my head against the back of the seat and close my eyes, inhaling deeply to try to calm myself down. The Uber smells like goat cheese, and the thought of it makes me laugh to myself before I immediately break out in tears once again. I silently apologize to the driver for potentially trauma-bonding her with the world's worst Hallmark breakup movie. If she pulls out tissues and a chocolate bar, I might just propose.

I never thought I would have to say goodbye to Travis. I guess that's just another thing I was wrong about.

Chapter Thirty-Five

Travis

Sage left three days ago. Actually, if we're being specific, it has been sixty-eight hours and forty-six minutes since I last saw her. It feels like months have passed within each minute. No matter what I do, I can't get her out of my mind. She lingers in my house like a ghost. Just this morning, I threw my laundry basket across the room because I swore she was hiding behind it. Turns out it was my hoodie—pink, of course, because she washed it with red. That woman left with my peace and my dignity.

Wherever I go, I see, out of the corner of my eye, her nest of pink hair piled on her head in the messy bun she always wore. I have to do double takes to make sure it's not actually her. It would be on brand for her to show up out of nowhere, anyway. Weirdly, I find myself wishing she would.

My house is quiet. Just the way I like it.

You would think that would give me plenty of time to take care of everything I need to do. But instead, I sit in the silence and analyze every aspect of it—everything it's missing. I don't hear the faint sound of music playing through her too-loud headphones. I don't hear her softly reading under her breath as she prepares to film for her latest video. I don't hear her giggling at stupid TikTok videos. I don't hear her in the kitchen making some elaborate dish, the sound of a kitchen knife scraping across the counter.

It's amazing how loud this silence is.

I try to go about my days and forget about her. My routine, which I have missed dearly, will bring me out of this funk. I get back to my schedule. I just can't focus. No matter what I do, Sage worms her way to the front of my mind, and I have to contend with the fact that I may never see her again.

That morbid thought is interrupted by the ringing of my phone. As always, my first thought is Sage. Hope blooms in my chest until I see Peter's name flashing across the screen. Of course she isn't going to call me. Before I answer, I curse myself for even thinking that she would.

"Yes," I almost grunt.

"Travis, I dug up something on the Ryan and Amelia connection." Peter gets straight to the point, as always. "At first, I really couldn't find anything. Officially, Amelia didn't have a boyfriend, let alone one serious enough to almost be her fiancé. However, I talked to one of her former girlfriends, who told me that Amelia did go out with a Ryan once. Apparently she wasn't interested in him, but he told people around town that they were dating and even talking about marriage."

"So the whole thing was one-sided," I conclude.

"It seems that way, yes," Peter confirms. "Do you want me to keep digging?"

"No." I hang up the phone, having no patience for pleasantries right now . . . or ever, really.

I feel slightly satisfied knowing the whole picture now, but that doesn't erase the anger and disappointment in myself for missing that she'd had some psycho obsessed with her in the first place. Anyone keeping that close an eye on her should have come up, regardless of the circumstances. I spent the rest of the afternoon scolding myself for that mistake.

My watch alarm goes off at 5:00 p.m., alerting me to dinnertime. I go to the kitchen and throw together everything I need for a veggie lasagna. Of course, it brings back memories of Sage, something I'm quickly realizing I might never be able to escape from. I do my best to force them aside as I prepare my food and wait for it to cook.

When it's done, I let it cool and bite into it. Like every morsel of food I've had since she left, it's bland. I even tried adding hot sauce. Five drops later, I was crying—not from the spice, but from the deep emotional betrayal of discovering I can't even make sad veggie lasagna properly. I don't know if it's because my taste buds have somehow decided to stop working or if the food Sage was making was just that much better than what I cook. Either way, it's not satisfying.

I eat it regardless, knowing I need to keep my body nourished. Everything I'm experiencing right now is nothing more than a blip in an otherwise well-oiled system. Maintaining my precise body mass and health is integral, considering what I do. If I don't have the strength to overpower my victims, that leaves too much room for mistakes to be made.

After dinner, I sit down at my desk and crack my knuckles before logging on to the computer. This is what I live for. It's my favorite part of what I do, the surveilling and stalking of my victims.

But instead of opening up all the software I use to stalk people, I idly stare at the blue desktop screen for a few moments. Sage's words echo in my mind: *"If you hurt Nicole, I'll never forgive you."*

For some reason, it's stopping me. It shouldn't matter. Sage is gone, and she's not coming back. Besides, she's not going to know what I do anyway. Nicole is going to vanish without a trace, and Sage won't be able to do anything to keep tabs on her.

"I wonder if she made it to Asheville okay," I whisper to myself, tapping my finger on my desk. I go to the web browser and type in the URL for Instagram, but I stop myself. It's not time to look into her. It's time to focus on Nicole. Now that Sage is gone, I shouldn't have any distractions. I can get back to doing what I love.

I close out of the browser and open up my surveillance software to try to get tabs on Nicole. It's late in the evening, and Nicole is exactly where I expect her to be. She's in the alley she showed me the first time I met her, sitting on a blanket with a bottle of cheap wine. Her hands are shaking, and there's a sheen of sweat over her face. This is probably the first drink she's had in a couple of days.

While I stare at her, I find myself wondering about her past. Is she really as innocent as Sage says she is? How am I supposed to know anything about that? Sure, her face looks young and sweet. Underneath all the grime and filth she's covered in is the visage of a young girl who's had a difficult time in her life.

"Stop that!" I shout in my office. I slam my hands on the desk and close out of the software. It's like Sage has somehow infiltrated my mind and is constantly reminding me about her. I don't care about my victims' lives. The only thing I do care about is that I'm targeting someone who won't get me caught. Why the fuck am I thinking about Nicole's past now?

I furrow my eyebrows and stare at my blank desktop screen for a few moments before I give in and type in Sage's Instagram handle. Maybe if I can just see her, know that she's okay, I can forget all about her.

My heart skips a beat as the page loads, and I see all the selfies she has taken and posted. They're all virtually identical pictures of her smiling in the exact same pose, almost making her grid look like the Andy Warhol print of Marilyn Monroe.

There's only one new post, and it's a picture of her smiling in the backyard of the Airbnb she checked in to after leaving. Lush green grass surrounds her, and she's clearly poolside. The caption reads Goodbye, Lake Lure. Hello, Asheville! Exciting new content coming soon! My latest vlog will be a little delayed, so bear with me lol. Taking some time away from the screen to focus on myself, but I'll update you all soon!

I study her face for a while. She's smiling, but the happiness she's projecting to the camera doesn't reach her eyes. I can see right through it, just like I can see through her. She's sad. I don't have to wonder for long to know why.

What confuses me most is that the more I stare at her, the more the ache in my chest grows. I don't understand why I feel this way. While she was here, we had some good times, as well as some bad. Yet she was nothing but a hindrance to me. With the exception of Eli, she threw a wrench in every plan that I had. She treated my routine as if it was a joke, and she tried to manipulate me into doing what she wanted me to.

I had to let her go. If I didn't, both of us would have been at risk. I couldn't let her interfere with my life, and she couldn't change me into who she wanted. It was a recipe for disaster.

I don't understand why my body is betraying me. I shouldn't feel upset that she's gone. I should be happy, and I should be relieved. I didn't make myself this way—I was born this way, and I'm only giving myself what I need again. That's why she's gone. And I should have peace, but I don't.

My alarm on my watch beeps again, and I jump in my chair. I've completely lost track of time staring at the picture of Sage, and now it's time for my workout for the day.

She's not even here and she's fucking up my schedule. I don't know if I'll ever be able to go back to how things were.

Regardless, I try to gain control, and change into some athletic shorts. I hop on the treadmill and start running. Exercising has always been an incredible way for me to forget about all my struggles. Running is like a form of physical meditation, and the endorphins help reduce cortisol levels and, therefore, relieve stress.

Normally I can focus on my movements to ensure I'm maintaining a proper posture. My strides are strong and powerful, and I focus on the sensations in my body with every step I take. But right now all I'm thinking about is her.

Getting her to exercise with me was like getting a cat to go for a swim. She hated exercising. The last time she was in here with me, I ended up fucking her on the weight bench. The memory of that is at the forefront of my mind, and I feel the blood rushing from my head to my cock.

I force that aside and take a few deep breaths to refocus my attention on the run. I focus on my arms as they move back and forth with each stride, my breathing as I try to level it, and my legs as I maintain the proper pace I need to effectively raise my heart rate.

For a couple of minutes, it feels good. The endorphins flooding my system as my heart starts to beat faster, just like I want it to. Then, out of the corner of my eye, I swear I see Sage in the mirror. I look, holding my breath as I keep moving on the treadmill, and realize she's not actually there.

And just like that, all the work I've done to get her out of my mind during the workout was for nothing. She's back in the forefront of my mind, walking around the treadmill and admiring my body as I move. The last time she watched me run, she threw popcorn at me like I was a zoo exhibit. Said she was "encouraging performance through live audience engagement." I nearly tripped trying to dodge a kernel.

I can almost hear her voice as if she is actually around me. *"I don't like working out, but I do enjoy the show."*

No matter what I do to try to refocus, it doesn't work. All I can think about is her, and the sex we had right here in the gym. My cock strains against my shorts, and I'm thankful they're breathable— otherwise I'd possibly be in pain right now.

To try to forget about it, I push myself harder. I run faster at a steep incline and try to focus on my burning limbs and my ragged breaths. I push myself harder than I normally do in an exercise, but it doesn't help.

"Fuck!" I shout as I slam my hands against the rail of the treadmill. It rattles before I grab hold of it and press the off switch.

I need to be able to focus, so I do what I have to and go back to my desk.

I pull up Sage's Instagram account once again and stare at pictures of her in her bikinis, with the real smiles on her face. I pull my cock from my shorts and start slowly rubbing it while I look at her. I'm hard and throbbing just at the thought of her in the same room with me.

Images of her in my office with me flood my mind, and I picture her getting on her knees in front of me to take my cock in her mouth. I remember the way she would moan when I held her head against me. How she liked to tease me as much as she could.

When I open my eyes, I can almost see her in front of me, as if she had come all the way back here just to suck my cock. I can perfectly remember the way her mouth wraps around me, the warmth that envelops me when she takes me deep into her throat.

My cock throbs and stiffens as I think about her tongue tracing its way down my shaft. I wish she were here, so I could run my fingers through her pink hair and hold her down on me. I would give anything to feel her mouth one more time. It doesn't take long for me to come, and the entire time all I think about is Sage swallowing every drop.

When I'm done, I lean back in my chair and close my eyes. Tomorrow is a new day. With any luck, I can forget all about Sage and continue with my plan to kill Nicole.

Chapter Thirty-Six

SAGE

"You can stop here," I say as my Uber pulls up to the dirt road leading to Sunroot Commune—my childhood home. I spent the past few days in Asheville, but I still felt too close to Lake Lure. I had to get away far enough so that I wouldn't get the stupid idea to drive to see a certain someone. There isn't a lot of parking available, so the driver has to just let me off on the side of the road, and I'll walk about a half mile to get to the actual commune nestled in the woods.

I grab my things from the trunk and wave to him to signal that he's good to leave. As I hoist my bag onto my shoulder, the weight jerks me sideways, and I stumble into a patch of prickly brush. I yelp, swat at my shins, and do an awkward dance while trying to yank a burr from my sock without falling face-first into the sand. A squirrel watches with what I can only describe as judgment.

The sun is hot and already burning high in the sky, even though it's not even noon. Of course, that's to be expected on the hottest day of the year in South Florida.

My bags feel ten times heavier as I walk in the heat, and I can't wait to get back to the compound so I can collapse in one of the cool eco cabins.

The compound is mostly off the grid, and because of that, all the cabins are made in harmony with the earth; they're supposed to stay warm in the winter and cool in the summer, but nothing can really fight off the Florida heat, so the cabins have solar-powered fans in them now.

About halfway to the commune, I spot a golf cart kicking up dust and dirt as it drives directly toward me. I squint and feel a small jolt of excitement in my chest when I spot my parents. They're waving vigorously, with wide smiles on their faces. I stand where I am and wave back, thankful they took the initiative to pick me up. Walking the rest of the way would have been torture.

"I can't believe you're actually here!" Mom shouts as she jumps out of the golf cart and wraps her arms around me. She holds me a little tighter than she normally would, and I know it's because she thinks I'm still mourning the loss of my relationship with Travis.

When I called them and told them I was coming, they asked if he would be joining, and I had to tell them he wouldn't. They wanted to ask questions, but they saw the heartbroken look on my face, and that was all the answer they needed.

"You look well," Dad says as he kisses me on the cheek and holds me in his arms.

They grab my bags for me and toss them in the back of the golf cart. I can't help but smile and laugh as I look at my dad wearing his Sunroot Solstice Festival shirt from last year. It's a pale-orange shirt with a graphic of the sun hugging a person with sweat beading down their face and the word *Sol-Mate* written below.

"What have you guys been up to?" I ask.

"I led morning yoga. We did some sun salutations," Dad says, looking over his shoulder at me with a grin. "The sun waved back. We're just tight like that now."

I roll my eyes, forcing a fake laugh at his terrible joke. Normally I would love his ridiculous dad jokes, but I can't bring myself to let out a genuine laugh. Mom is clearly tickled by it, as she laughs and nudges him on the shoulder. Watching the two of them together only reminds me of me and Travis, and I have to look away to force the memory aside.

Even though I try to hide my heartbreak, they notice. I can see the pity on their faces when they look at me. I wish I could forget about it and move on, but it's not that simple.

When we get to the commune, I see loads of familiar faces. People wave at me, and some even approach to chat, but I tell them all I'm too exhausted from traveling. I just need time to unwind and take a break from the heat before I can socialize. A group of kids playing tag dart by, and one of them stops dead in front of me, eyeing my travel-weary appearance. "You look like a melted candle," she says with zero malice, just pure child honesty.

I blink at her, then nod. "Fair."

She shrugs and sprints off, leaving me questioning all my life choices.

Everyone here is always mindful about respecting other people's privacy. Of course, gossip runs through the commune like a plague, but I know they won't bother me right now if I don't want them to.

We get to the cabin, and I'm thankful for the semi-cool air around us before plopping down on the sofa. My parents sit on either side of me and look at each other before looking back at me.

"I was thinking I would make something fun for dinner tonight," Mom says with a soft smile. "I got some chicken from Carl, and I was thinking I'd make the Marry Me Chicken you love so much."

I bite my cheek and blink away the immediate tears that start to form. Of course, of all the dishes she knows how to make, that's the one she mentions now.

"You know what? I'm actually not feeling that great. Why don't we save that for another night?" I force a smile, and she nods.

"There's a bonfire tonight, too, if you want to come. The whole compound is going to be there." My dad smiles at me with eagerness in his eyes.

Honestly, the last thing I want to do is be surrounded by a bunch of people, having to pretend like everything is normal for me. It's not, and

I don't know how I'm going to fake it. But looking at the excitement in his eyes, I find it hard to say no.

"That sounds fun. I feel like I should just get some sleep before, though." I fake a yawn and stretch before standing up. "There was a screaming baby on the plane, and it was a nightmare. I really am beat."

I don't listen to any protests even if they plan on giving them, because I walk directly to my old bedroom. It's been a while since I spent a night here, and I'm flooded with nostalgia. I remember staying up late here with friends and giggling about boys we had crushes on. Once, I even sneaked my first boyfriend, Paul, into the room in the middle of the night to make out.

Even now, when I think about it, Paul's face is replaced by Travis's, and I groan while I force the thought aside. I fall back on the bed and hold a pillow over my face as I try to get my thoughts straight. Eventually I close my eyes and fall asleep.

I wake up a few hours later with the sun still shining through the window and some laughter ringing through the cabin. I change into fresh, non-sweaty clothes and make my way out to see what's going on.

My parents are sitting at the kitchen table with board games sprawled out in front of them.

"You're up! I was just about to go get you to see if you wanted to play Life with us," Mom says. Both of them look at me with wide smiles. Even through the smiles, I can see the concern in their eyes.

I nod and join them. Maybe this is good for me. I can get invested in the game, and through a little bit of friendly competition, I'll have a few minutes where I'm not constantly thinking about Travis.

Unfortunately, it's not so easy. We play the game, and at first things are going well. I've got a good job, and I live in a nice house that I can barely afford. Then I have to decide if I'm going to get married. For some reason, this pretend decision for a small pink peg in an orange car is a big one.

I'm not thinking about the game anymore. I'm thinking about the future I lost with Travis. The two of us could have been together, and now we're several states apart and I have no idea what's going on with him.

My stomach twists at the idea of everything he could be up to while I'm not there. I remember Nicole and the excited look on his face when he found his next victim.

"I'm sorry," I say with a shaky voice as I excuse myself from the table and go back to my room.

My parents try to distract me with other things for the rest of the day. They ask me to watch a new movie with them. They want to ask me about books I've read and tell me to show them footage from my travels. I just can't do it. I ignore them and close my eyes to try to stop thinking about Travis.

A few hours pass, and my dad knocks on the door; pushing it open, he comes in to sit down on the side of the bed. He smiles softly and brushes my hair behind my ear.

"I know you're in pain, sweetie. I wish I could take it away from you, but I can't. The best thing we can do is get you out of here." He taps on my temple, and I can't help but smile back. "Are you still up for the bonfire?"

My instinct is to say no, but I sit up and toss my legs over the side of the bed and nod. "Let's do it."

I follow him out of the cabin, and we walk toward the beach, where a dozen other people are all sitting around a roaring fire with marshmallows and chocolate bars all around them. The smell of roasting marshmallows is like a balm for my soul, and I just know that a perfectly gooey, burned s'more is going to cure me—at least that's the hope.

I sit down and make small talk with some of the elders in the commune, telling them all about my travels. For a while I forget about more-recent events. I'm focusing on the logistics of my Instagram and YouTube, and everything I'm going to be filming for the solstice festival. It feels good. It gives me hope that I can actually move on from this.

"If it isn't Juniper Sage Featherstone," a familiar voice says behind me. I turn around to see Steve. His full name is Steve Sunshine, yet another victim of the atrocious flower-child names, but he just goes by Steve. "It's been a while."

I stand up and walk away from the bonfire to talk to him. "It sure has."

Steve was a former boyfriend of mine. Well, I thought he was my boyfriend. He happened to think he was a free spirit who could roam between partners freely without telling any of us.

Despite the fact that he's a sleazy guy using free love as an excuse to fuck around, he's exceptional in bed. At least, he was when I was with him. By the way he's looking at me now, there's no doubt in my mind he thinks this is a prime opportunity to hook up with me again.

"How have you been? I've heard you're some hotshot celebrity now," Steve says with a smile.

"Hardly. I make YouTube travel videos." I laugh and look him up and down, wondering what it would be like to sleep with him now. It would certainly help me take my mind off Travis, at least temporarily.

Almost as soon as the thought comes, it goes away. That wouldn't help anything. I know all I would be thinking about is Travis. No other guy has had my attention the way he does. I don't know if I'll ever be able to be with another guy, but I sure as hell can't be with Steve.

"You know what, I actually have to go," I tell him, backing away and shrugging casually. "I'll see you around, though."

I head back to the cabin and ignore the stares of everyone watching me as I go. Mom and Dad are still at the bonfire, so I take this opportunity to fall back in bed to have a little bit of peace.

I grab my phone and pull up the camera roll, looking at a few of the pictures I have of Travis. He didn't let me take pictures of him, but I sneaked a few. They're mostly candids of him in the kitchen, walking around the house, and even some of him in the gym working out.

My mind immediately goes to the thought of him being here with me, burying his face between my legs and slowly teasing my clit. My pussy dampens, and I grab my bullet vibe from my bag. I stare at the picture of him in the gym while I massage my clit with it.

Electric jolts of pleasure burst through my body as my eyes trace the muscles on his chest. I remember what it felt like to run my fingers along them, and I close my eyes to think about that now. I think about the way his body seemed to completely envelop mine when he was on top of me.

I pull the vibrator away from my clit and slide it inside, imagining it is Travis's cock. It doesn't feel as real, but I force those thoughts aside and let my imagination take hold.

I lose control of myself, thinking about him bending me over the couch the first night we made love and just taking me. My moans are loud, and there's nothing I can do to stop them. I think about Travis, throbbing and twitching inside me as he's ready to come, and just the thought of it sends me over the edge.

I cry out, my body convulsing on the mattress as my hand moves quickly between my legs.

My bedroom door suddenly opens, and I scream, pulling my hand away and looking to see my mom standing there with a worried look on her face. Her eyes widen as she takes in the scene before her, and she immediately covers her eyes with her hands.

"Why don't you knock!" I shout, grabbing a blanket to cover myself.

"I heard screaming!" Mom shouts, turning away from the room to run off.

"Close the door!" I shout, falling back on the bed and covering my face with a pillow. I hear the door slam shut, and I wish I could disappear.

Well, that was mortifying. But I guess that's what I should have expected, being back home.

From down the hall, I hear my dad's voice. "Everything okay in there?"

"Don't go in!" my mom shouts back. "She's . . . communing with her inner goddess!"

I bury my face in the pillow again. *Yep. Totally back home.*

Chapter Thirty-Seven

Travis

Today's the day.

Of course, by "the day," I mean the one where I try not to look like a serial killer in a Baptist church sweater while baiting an alcoholic through town. Everyone has hobbies.

Planning Nicole's kill has been more difficult than any I've ever done. Sage has been at the forefront of my mind, and it's been hard to focus. But I just know that after I'm done with this, everything will be right. I'll be back to normal. I just have to get through this.

The plan for Nicole is to lure her away. I've been watching her, and I think I can get her to trust me. Today, I tracked her through the Ingles supermarket security cameras. Right now she is hanging out behind the store, looking through their trash; she's desperate. She hasn't had a drink in a few days, and her nerves are frayed.

Before I leave, I replace the live feed with a prerecorded loop so I won't be showing up on any security footage.

I gather everything I need into the trunk of my SUV and change my clothes. As much as I like wearing my all-black kill suit to lure someone away, I can't dress like that. I have to look innocuous. I put on a pair of dark-brown khakis, some dress shoes that have the brand name and trademarks on the bottom burned off, and a dark-green sweater.

I look like I could be handing out flyers on a Sunday morning. That's exactly what I want her to think.

I've been focused all day, and I'm perfectly on schedule. I'm dressed, and the car is loaded right on time to head into town and find Nicole. I check the surveillance videos one last time to see that she's exactly where I want her to be. Right now, on the other side of the lake, a half marathon is catching a lot of attention. People are dressed in silly costumes, and almost everyone in town is gathered around to cheer them on as they run.

That means someone like Nicole is all by herself, with few people around to witness what happens to her.

But as I'm standing in front of my car and thinking about what I'm getting ready to do, something doesn't feel right. Something's off, and I can't put my finger on it. I normally feel excited before a kill. Right now something feels wrong.

The thought of killing Nicole doesn't even feel good anymore. It's not doing what it usually does to relieve my homicidal urges.

But maybe that's because I'm out of practice. My last kill was interfered with by Sage. I didn't get to live it out the way I wanted to. I need this kill to reset everything. I know that when I'm done with Nicole and her body is burning, I can put the past behind me once and for all.

That thought alone carries me into town. I take the winding roads down the mountain as I go over the plan countless times in my mind. When I get to the grocery store, I park my car and head inside.

I don't grab a lot. Mostly just the stuff to fill a canvas tote bag and make it look like I was here already. The last thing I need is for Nicole to get in my car and think she's the only reason I was in town. That's bound to set off a lot of red flags.

I grab some fruits and vegetables, and a few heavily processed deli meats and cheeses that I'll probably end up throwing out. I also throw in a random vegan yogurt for good measure. You never know—maybe Nicole's a picky dumpster connoisseur. I imagine her turning down the ride over a lack of probiotics. Then I check out. I go back to my car and put the bags in the front passenger seat, fluffing them up to make them look fuller.

I take a few deep breaths and walk to the back of the building, where the dumpsters are.

"Hello?" I call out as I slowly walk down to where I know she is.

My eyes land on her as she backs against the brick wall and clutches her hand close to her chest. I look around just to make sure she's alone, and she is.

"Sorry, I don't mean to scare you," I say with the warmest smile I can conjure. "I've met you before, haven't I? Your name is . . . Nancy, right?"

She looks me up and down, and I watch as she relaxes ever so slightly. She straightens and takes a cautious step toward me with her hands balled in front of her.

"Nicole, but Nancy is close, I guess." She laughs under her breath and waits for me to explain why I'm here.

"I work at Lake Lure Baptist Church, and we're having our annual Lakeside Lunch," I begin, taking a few slow steps toward her. "It's for the less fortunate in the area. There are clothes and sanitary products for giving away as well. I was just grabbing a few things at the store to cook, and I know this alley can sometimes have . . ."

I trail off to make it seem like I'm nervous about calling her homeless. She nods, and I see her thinking. I know she must be hungry—starving, even. Plus, the clothes she has are tattered and filthy. She needs to eat, and she needs new clothes, but she is calculating the risks internally.

"I don't know if I have a way to get to the lake," Nicole says, shaking her head slowly. "Thank you for the offer."

I nod and nervously stuff my hands in my pockets. I feel the syringe loaded with drugs. I turn around and start walking back to my car, as if I'm going to give up on bringing her.

I stop mid-stride and turn back to her. "I completely understand if you want to say no, but I'm heading up that way now. I wouldn't mind bringing you back either," I say with a gentle shrug. "I promise, it wouldn't be any trouble."

She gulps and looks down at the little nest she's made for herself here before taking a deep breath and looking back at me. "Are you sure?"

I force a smile on my face again. "I'm positive."

She walks over to me with a nervous smile, and I lead her around the building to my car. I open the front door and exaggerate as I roll my eyes.

"I'm a dummy—the passenger seat is filled with my crap. Would you mind sitting in the back seat?"

Her eyes fall on the overstuffed grocery bag, and she laughs. "Of course not."

We get in the car, and I realize I have her exactly where I want her. It was almost too easy. I reach my hands in my pockets as if I'm fishing for my car keys, but I wrap my fingers around the syringe. All I have to do is pull it out, sink the needle into her thigh, and she'll be out in seconds.

But as my thumb touches the plastic, Sage comes back to the forefront of my mind. *"If you hurt Nicole, I'll never forgive you."*

Ever since she left, I have been repeating that to myself over and over. The idea of losing her forever has been there, but it's tangible now. This is the moment that will potentially affect everything between us. Right now there is a chance that things can change. If I go through with this, she'll be gone for good.

In that instant, an entire lifetime of moments with Sage lingers before me. I'll never see her smile again. I'll never get to walk into the kitchen and smell whatever delicious food she's cooking again. I'll never get to kiss her and hold her body against mine. I'll never get to see her basking in the sunshine as I stare at the constellations of freckles on her face. I'll never get to stare at her eyes, admiring the brown specks there as she squints them and laughs.

The dull ache in my heart is stronger than it's ever been. I can't ignore it this time, and I don't want to. I have to fix this.

"I—I can't find my keys," I stammer, pulling my hands out of my pockets. I pretend to search in the bag, looking around everywhere I can for the keys while Nicole sits in the back seat, confused. "I'm so sorry. I'm going to have to call AAA. I think we're going to miss lunch."

"Oh," Nicole says with disappointment. I look at the bag, and I hand it to her.

"This was for the lunch. Why don't you take this instead?" She hesitates. I push it closer to encourage her to take more, and she finally does.

"Thank you," she says as she hops out of the car. In my rearview mirror, I watch her head back toward the store with a spring in her step. She has no idea how close she came to never walking again. And here I thought today would end with a bonfire and a body count. Instead, I'm handing out grocery bags like a demented DoorDash. Five stars for not murdering anyone—progress?

When she's out of view, I grab my phone and immediately search for Sage on Instagram. I don't want to waste another moment away from her. I just have to figure out where she is.

She's posted something new, and I almost want to be angry with her about it. It's a photo of her on a beach in front of a tall wooden effigy, like something from *The Wicker Man*. The caption is all about the solstice festival coming up tomorrow, with an address to the commune.

Putting her address online is foolish, but especially with everything she's been through. There'll be time to reprimand her for that later. I put the car in drive and type the address into my GPS. Ten hours is a long time to drive, but she's worth every moment of it.

I just hope she can forgive me.

Chapter Thirty-Eight

SAGE

Preparations for the festival begin at sunrise. The actual festival is set to begin at 10:00 a.m., but there is a lot of work that goes into setting up beforehand. I didn't even have to set an alarm this morning because my parents were running around the cabins shouting about everything related to the festival before the birds were even singing outside.

As I roll out of bed, I trip over my own tangled charging cable and nearly face-plant into a pile of handmade tie-dye T-shirts I forgot I left on the floor. Classic commune booby trap. My mother's voice floats in through the window, yelling about "aesthetic harmony"—whatever that means before 6:00 a.m.

Even though I'm not looking forward to the insane amount of preparation ahead, I am looking forward to a busy day. I'm going to have a lot to film. Plus, helping my parents with everything they need before the festival begins is going to put my mind far from Travis Blacksburg. It'll be a much-needed reprieve.

Not only am I going to be filming the actual festival for my vlog, but I'm also going to have an entire video series about the commune. When I've mentioned it to people in the past, they've all been very curious about where I grew up, and now is the perfect time to give them that information.

"What's up, travelers!" I excitedly say into the camera. Filming today, I don't have any fancy lighting or microphones, just a lavalier on top of my camcorder and the beautiful sunlight shining down. "Today I'm filming in the commune I grew up in. Sunroot has been around for decades, and one of its most exciting features is the annual summer solstice festival."

I point the camera at my father, who is standing in the center of the commune with a clipboard, frantically flipping through papers as he directs people where to go.

"Say hi, Dad!" I say, waving in front of the camera. He is momentarily distracted from all the work he has to do as he starts talking to the camera and introducing himself. I can't help but laugh, thinking about all the comments I'm going to get about how funny my dad is.

After a minute, my mom walks up and slaps him on the butt. "There's no time for funny business right now. Get back to work." She smiles at the camera and waves. Just as she's about to strike a pose, someone from the crystal meditation tent sprints over in a panic because the rose quartz has been mixed with the smoky quartz, which apparently "messes with the vibrational frequencies." Mom sighs, muttering something about how the only frequency she wants is coffee.

I walk around and introduce a lot of the other people in the commune, giving little bits of background about each of them. When the festival finally starts, I stand by the gate and film all the people who were lined up to come in when the gates opened. Some of them wave at the camera and smile excitedly as they're ushered into the heart of the commune.

The central hub is now decorated with celestial charms that make it look like we worship the sun year-round. An artisan market is set up with just about every person from the commune running some kind of stall to show off their role in the community. Live music is being played from a stage, showcasing a whole lineup of bands from both the commune and the surrounding area. People are gathered around and clapping their hands as they sway their hips to the gentle rock music.

The festival is absolutely bustling. My parents are still running around with their clipboards and helping to direct all the festival workers on what they're supposed to be doing. Despite the stressed looks on their faces, I know that they live for this. They've been high-priority volunteers before, and they love the fast-paced environment.

Unfortunately for me, it's almost impossible to get a moment with them to interview. Instead, I focus on B-roll shots of the festival itself. I walk around with my camera in hand and film the various artisan booths, some of the performances, and I even go on one of the sunshine hikes through the woods.

I feel like I'm on autopilot for the most part. But even though I'm trying to focus on filming alone, Travis still creeps his way into my mind.

I get caught up wondering if he would like this or if he would hate everything about it. Part of me thinks he'd like it because everything is homemade and organic, things I'm sure he loves because it wouldn't throw his precious body out of whack. But then again, it's loud and crowded, and a lot of the people here are just being performative sun children, only here for their Instagram feeds.

I'm filming the entrance from afar, trying to show just how vast the crowd this year really is. I zoom in on it and freeze as Travis's face pops up. I lower the camera and squint to look out at the market, but I can't see any clearer.

I must be dreaming. There's no way in hell Travis, of all people, is here.

I lift the camera up again and zoom in, shifting the lens around slightly to try to get a closer look at whoever I thought was Travis. I just know that I can figure out who they really are and rule out the possibility of him being here altogether.

But as I do, the camera lens lands on a face I know without a shadow of a doubt is his. Travis is here. My heart skips a beat in my chest, and I feel like I'm not breathing. I don't know why he's here, but I know what I want him to be here for.

He's searching the crowd for something, and I keep the camera on him the entire time. Eventually his eyes land on me, and he pushes through the crowd, getting closer with each step. I zoom the camera out and watch until he's close enough that I can see him perfectly clear without the optical zoom.

Up close, I can see how exhausted he is. His eyes are heavy with bags under them, like he hasn't slept in a while. His hair is normally perfectly put together, but it's unkempt and disheveled today. He barely even looks like himself.

"You're here" is all I manage to say when he's standing right in front of me.

"I drove all night to get here in time," Travis says. He seems more alert than he did before. His eyes widen, and the exhausted look on his face is replaced by what I might interpret as peace.

"I don't understand. Why come all this way after everything?" I bite my lip while I wait for his answer. I drop the camcorder and stare at him, saying a silent prayer in my mind that this is what I think it is.

"Because I love you, Sage."

My breath hitches in my throat, and he takes a step forward to put his hands on my arms.

"I started thinking about losing you, all the things that we could be doing together that we weren't. The idea of living my life without you by my side is unbearable. I would rather not live at all."

I'm far enough away from the crowd that no one can hear us. I look over his shoulder, nervously double-checking that we're alone before continuing anything else. There's a lot between us that nobody else can know about, and I have to be completely certain.

"What about Nicole?" I clench my fist beside me, digging my fingernails into the palm of my hand as I wait for his answer. This is the make-or-break moment for me. I can't be with someone who will hurt innocent people.

"I didn't hurt her. I let her go." He takes a deep breath and runs his fingers through his hair. "It's going to be difficult to change, but I'm willing to try. I'll only kill from an approved list, if that makes you happy. No more targeting people without your permission."

"Really?" I can't help the smile that grows on my face. This is all I wanted when I found out who he really is. Knowing that he's going to give up this part of his life and let me in is a gesture from him that I can hardly comprehend. "You would do that for me?"

"Sage, I would do anything for you," he replies with a genuine smile on his face. "I love you."

"I love you so much." I don't waste another moment not kissing him. I toss my arms around his neck and pull him down and press my lips against his. His tongue slides in my mouth, and I grab hold of his shirt and crumple it in my fist.

It's been too long since he was beside me, and I don't want this moment to end.

"Oh!" someone says beside us. We both pull away, my arms still wrapped around his neck, to see my mom standing beside us with her hands clutched to her heart. "Travis, you're here."

My dad walks up behind her with his face still turned toward his clipboard, only looking up briefly. He does a double take when he sees me embracing a man, and the clipboard drops to his side.

"Travis, I know you met on FaceTime, but now, officially, these are my parents. Guys, this is Travis," I say, finally backing away from him and nervously letting my parents step closer.

My mom looks between us and immediately pulls Travis in for a hug. His entire body goes rigid, and he slowly moves his arm around her to reciprocate. I can't help but laugh, seeing how robotic he looks. Getting him to hug me was already difficult enough. Hugging my mom, who is a stranger to him, must be torture.

They start peppering him with questions, completely ignoring all their festival responsibilities. I see how anxious Travis is and step between them.

"If you guys don't get back out there, a nonsanctioned orgy is bound to break out," I jokingly warn.

My father immediately grabs the clipboard and waves goodbye before running off toward the artisan market.

"Won't you stay till the end of the festival?" Mom asks Travis with a pleading look on her face. "It would mean so much to us."

Travis looks back at me, and I raise my eyebrows to mimic a sad puppy dog, hoping he'll say yes. Not only is it important to my parents, but I also want him to see this part of me.

"I'd be happy to." He smiles and wraps an arm around my shoulders.

Mom runs off to finish doing everything she needs to do, and I grab Travis's hand to lead him through the festival. I've gotten enough B-roll footage that I don't have to worry about it as much. I just need to make sure I film some of the solstice offering ceremony tonight.

I show Travis around the commune, telling him all kinds of stories about growing up here. Even though he's tired, and I'm sure this is well out of his comfort zone, he listens with a smile on his face. He hardly ever lets go of my hand the entire time.

As we're walking, Steve sees me again and waves us over.

"Okay, this is Steve. He and I used to date."

Travis clenches his jaw as Steve introduces himself to us.

"Sage, you've got to come by the cabin while you're still here. You and I really need to catch up," Steve urges, completely disregarding the fact that I'm holding another man's hand in front of him.

"I don't know if we'll be here that long," Travis says as he pulls me closer to him.

Steve looks us up and down and nods, seemingly understanding what's happening. "Well, the offer always stands for you, Sage." He bounds off after a few moments, and I turn to Travis with an awkward laugh.

"Any chance he could be put on the list?" he asks, and I shake my head.

"He might be a douchebag, but that's hardly criminal." I laugh, standing on my tiptoes to kiss him again. Travis doesn't smile, and I quickly realize he wasn't joking, but that's something we're going to work on.

Steve resurfaces later near the fire with what looks like a homemade pan flute and starts playing a tragically off-key rendition of something that might be "Careless Whisper." Travis narrows his eyes and mutters, "He's definitely top five on the list."

We walk around for the rest of the day, and when the sun begins to set, we head to the beach, where I film the beginning of the offering ceremony as the large wicker effigy is lit on fire. Travis wraps his arms around me and holds me close as we watch it burn together.

It isn't the first time the two of us have watched flames devour something, and I know it's not going to be the last. But right now we can stand together and watch this, knowing everything that's happened between us, and look forward to the future.

Epilogue

Travis

One Year Later

Martin Elliott III has just checked into his hotel room and is currently preparing for a meeting. I watch him from the driver's seat of my car and study his every move. He was on Sage's list.

After she came back to Lake Lure with me, I got her a desktop computer and fully set it up so all her searches would be secure. If she was going to be involved in my process, I had to make sure we were doing everything the right way. I taught her how I operate, from the first step all the way to disposing of the body.

This is the first kill I'm letting Sage take the lead on. Over the past year we've targeted and killed five predators together. Martin is one that Sage wanted to do the heavy lifting on. She even did a practice run in the mirror, rehearsing her fake twelve-year-old voice so much that I caught her singing "Let It Go" like a Disney Channel dropout. When I walked in on her mid-performance, she shrieked, nearly threw her phone at me, and yelled "Privacy, dammit!" in a voice that sounded more middle-aged smoker than child star.

The burner phone we're using to contact Martin chimes in Sage's hand beside me. "He said he'll be ready in about an hour."

"Let's get everything nice and set up for him, then." I put the car in drive and head back to the cabin.

Sage and I make quick work of gathering everything we need while we're there. A little too quick, because at one point she trips over the duct tape roll and almost face-plants into the tackle box. She pops up like a deranged meerkat, waves a knife, and says, "This is part of the plan." I don't ask which plan—ours or a *Looney Tunes* one.

After that little incident, we head toward the lake. That's where we told Martin to meet us.

It's late enough that the lake is completely empty. Nobody else is hanging around swimming for the day. Besides, it's a Tuesday night and people have to work in the morning. Well, not everyone. Martin clearly has time to kill.

"Are you nervous?" I ask Sage before I prepare to leave her.

She shakes her head and takes a deep breath. "Let's kill this fucker," she says with ire in her voice.

After we found Martin in a nearby county, we set up a trap for him. He's a sick fuck who likes young girls. So Sage has been impersonating one. She made a fake Instagram account that she's been posting on semi-regularly using AI images as bait for these creeps. Her online persona is a twelve-year-old named Mary with strict parents who homeschool her, so she doesn't have many friends.

Martin thinks her parents are out of town for a work conference and they're letting her stay by herself for the first time, hoping that she can prove to them she's responsible. Of course Martin had to jump at the opportunity to offer her some company.

Now they're meeting at the lake for the first time. Martin's going to teach her how to swim.

I hide in the tree line and wait, keeping my eyes glued to Sage the entire time. She sits on a picnic table and makes herself look small and frail. She's wearing baggy clothes and a breast binder, so it's less obvious that she's older than she says.

In the distance, I see the silhouette of a man, and I know instantly it's Martin. He waves and calls out for Mary, and Sage stands up to wait for him. He's carrying some food and drinks with him as if it's some kind of friendly, disarming gesture.

"It's so nice to finally meet you!" Sage says in a light, cheery voice. Seeing how she can completely pretend to be a different person is almost bone-chilling. But this is for the greater good.

Martin takes a seat with his back to me, which I'm very thankful for. It makes my job a lot easier if he doesn't fight. He and Sage start making small talk while I sneak out of the tree line and creep my way over to him, syringe in hand.

Before he realizes what's happening, the needle is in his neck and I'm pushing the drugs into his veins. His eyes go wide before they close entirely.

———

"What—where am I?" Martin asks in a terrified voice when his eyes open in the crematorium basement. Sage and I both look at him with smiles on our faces.

"So you have a thing for little girls, huh?" she asks in a dark voice. She grabs a knife from the table and slams it down beside him. His entire body shakes against the metal table, and she laughs.

"Please! I can pay you—name your price, just let me go!" Martin begs.

"Oh, we have no use for your money," I say, tracing my knife up and down his arm. It knicks him, and he gasps from the surprise. I can't help but laugh. "There's much more where that came from."

"How many children have you done this to?" Sage asks him. "We already know about one because she sent you to jail. But how many came before her? How many have you hurt since you were let out on good behavior?"

"I—I don't know what you're—"

Sage slams her hands down on the metal table and stops him from lying. "Did you learn nothing while you were in jail?" Her eyes are like furious beads glaring down at him.

When she first suggested this idea to me, I thought it would be silly. Vigilantes are something for comic books. But I see it now. I see the fury in her veins, and I feel it too. This is what I was meant to do.

Martin refuses to talk, no matter how much she tries to get a confession out of him. So we skip to the next part of our plan.

Sage cuts into his flesh and watches as his blood pools around the knife. Martin screams at the top of his lungs, and I don't do anything to silence him. I know that Sage wants to hear him scream. She wants to hear him beg and plead for his pathetic life.

I work on the other arm, letting the blood slowly drain from him as his breath turns ragged.

"Martin, something tells me you do a lot of thinking with your dick," she says as she stands at hip level. She grabs him by the balls and squeezes, making him squeal more than he has before. "Let's put an end to that."

Even I wince as she cuts his dick off. Don't get me wrong, Martin deserves all this and more for what he's done. It's just a little hard to watch.

The pain makes him pass out, and when it's no longer fun to torture him, Sage plunges the knife into his chest. Before we started doing this together, I was opposed to the idea of letting her help. I thought that I needed to be the one to kill. But getting to watch Sage do it is just as intoxicating as doing it myself.

"How do you feel?" I ask as we turn on the oven. This is the first person she's actually killed by her own hand.

"Powerful. Like I'm in control of something for the first time in my life," she says, almost looking like she's in shock herself.

We wait for the oven to heat up before putting Martin's body inside. I clean off the table, wiping up his blood and sanitizing it. Sage watches the fire for a few minutes, then walks over to me and pulls my face close to hers for a kiss.

She's hungry, like my kiss is water in a desert, and my mind is immediately pulled from cleaning. I lift her up and set her down on the table.

"Fuck me," she whispers in my ear. I kiss her neck, nibbling on the flesh delicately as I fumble with the button on her jeans. She lifts her hips so I can slide them off and toss them to the ground.

I massage her through her panties before ripping them off and unbuttoning my pants. My cock is already hard, and Sage wraps her hands around it to feel for herself. She smiles and kisses me, teasing me more.

I pull away and lower my mouth to her pussy, immediately finding her clit with my tongue. Sage leans back with her eyes closed as she raises her hips ever so slightly.

"You feel so fucking good," Sage moans as I slide a finger inside her.

"And you taste delicious," I reply before burying my face in her pussy.

With every moment that passes, my cock throbs more and more. My hands climb up her shirt and fiddle with her nipples while she holds them against her. Just when she's on the verge of coming, I pull my mouth away from her and plunge my cock inside.

Sage jolts upright and moans uncontrollably as I sink my entire shaft inside her. I start off slow, savoring the feeling of her around my cock, but I get more frenzied as I move. I quicken my pace, and eventually the metal table is moving an inch every time I thrust into her.

"You're so fucking naughty," I whisper in her ear as I feel her pussy clenching tighter around me.

How did I get so lucky? Most women would run for the hills if they even suspected a man could be dangerous. But Sage stuck around—even when I didn't want her to. Now I'm here with the love of my life, both of us high off a kill and screwing each other's brains out.

Her legs wrap around me to draw me in more with each movement, and I do my best to fuck her exactly how she wants. I can feel just how turned on she is with every thrust, and it only makes my desire for her grow.

"Oh my god, Travis!" Sage cries out as her body spasms and shakes on the table. I can't take it any longer, and I completely lose control, filling her with every drop of my cum.

When both of us are finished and catching our breath, I stare at her and can't help but think about how lucky I am to have her. The two of us meeting by happenstance. Sure, Ryan might have orchestrated some of it to get revenge on me. But Sage knocking on my door instead of his was fate intervening. She and I were supposed to find each other.

I know now that Sage is my soulmate. Not only that, but I believe the two of us were meant to be partners in crime, literally. Looking back at my life, I can't even comprehend how I managed to get through everything without her. I know now I want her by my side for as long as I'm breathing.

"Marry me," I say, leaning down and giving her a kiss on the lips. She backs up and looks at me with a wrinkle in her eyebrows.

She sits up straight and tries to decipher whether or not this is a genuine request. "You're proposing? You don't even have a ring."

"I was going to improvise," I say, digging around in my pocket and pulling out a spare zip tie. "It's adjustable and, technically, a circle."

She rolls her eyes. "Romantic. Next you'll tell me we can use duct tape for wedding bands."

"Don't tempt me," I quip. "We've got a whole drawer labeled 'Rituals and Repairs.'" That makes her snort. "Plus, it's not like anything else about us is conventional." I laugh and raise my eyebrows at her. "Sage, will you marry me?"

She smiles and nods, pulling me close for a passionate kiss. "Yes, of course!"

I wrap my arms tight around her, my future wife. I might not have expected her to come waltzing into my life, but I'm incredibly glad that she did.

ABOUT THE AUTHOR

C. Hallman is a *USA Today* bestselling author who wrote her debut novel in 2018 and has since published over one hundred books in various romance subgenres. Her works have been on numerous bestseller lists and have been translated into eight languages around the world. Born and raised in Germany, Hallman attended business school in her hometown before immigrating to America when she was only eighteen. At nineteen, she married her husband, who was active-duty military at the time. Together, they traveled the country for years before finally settling down. Now they live in the mountains of North Carolina with their three children, two dogs, and one hairless cat. For more information, visit www.authorchallman.com.